Zenobia

Palmyra's Warrior Queen

(Bat-Zabbai)

"Her face was dark with a swarthy hue, her eyes were black
and powerful beyond the usual wont, her spirit divinely
great, and her beauty incredible…"

*Trebellius Pollio,"Scriptores Historiea Augustae,
Vol. III, circa 303 CE*

T.S. Dunn

Zenobia

Palmyra's Warrior Queen

(Bat-Zabbai)

T.S. Dunn

This book is dedicated to my father, for inspiring me to "march to the beat of a different drum."

AND

My mother for reading to her children stories of adventure and inspiration at a young age and ecouraging us to "Dream Big Dreams."

I

MOESIA, 260 C.E. (AD)

The Roman Empire was in turmoil. Famine, plague, invasion, revolt and other natural and man-made calamities decimated the population. A series of short-lived emperors rushed from rebellion to rebellion before they, each in their turn, fell prey to plague, to their enemies, to rival claimants for their throne, or to the treachery of their own soldiers.

It was a gray, gloomy, early spring day in the Roman Province of Moesia *(modern day Bulgaria)*, just south of the river Danube. The skies threatened rain and a light mist hung over a clearing as the sound of marching soldiers and the calling of military cadence grew louder and louder. A Roman column appeared, marching over a knoll and continuing on a road that ran through a clearing.

The clearing was a wet, grassy meadow about two hundred meters wide that was bordered by a thick forest of somber looking spruce trees on either side. The column, consisting of two cohorts of Roman soldiers *(about one thousand men)*, marched along a well-built Roman road that divided the center of the clearing.

Suddenly, a seemingly endless sea of Goths emerged

from the forest on both sides of the road. Screaming and waving their spears and clubs, they charged the Romans. The immediate sight of them struck terror into the Roman forces, especially in the young, untried additions to the unit. For the most part they were much taller than the Romans, with athletic features, blonde hair, blue eyes and light complexions. If not for their scraggly beards and generally unkempt aspect they may have appeared quite comely to their intended Roman overlords.

Marcellinus, a tribune of equestrian rank, was the commander of the two cohorts. He shouted at his men, "Castell formation!" The Roman soldiers on the outside of the column, both the left, right, front and rear sides mechanically turned outward with their shields and spears ready to face the onrushing enemy. Once the maneuver was completed, the Romans formed a seemingly impenetrable human stockade. Four rows of men remained inside the enclosure, ready to step forward and fill the gaps made by fallen men on the perimeter.

When the Goths reached the Romans, men, weapons, and shields clashed.

The formation was difficult to penetrate, but the Romans were outnumbered three to one. Gradually the human wall shrank in size as men fell, leaving holes in the manmade barrier that replacements were no longer available to fill. Marcellinus darted from one opening to another, desperately trying to fill the gaps with ever dwindling success.

Suddenly, over the same incline from which the Roman column had first appeared, their cavalry now emerged, dividing to attack the Goths on both sides of the imperiled Roman column. The cavalry was led by Aurelian, a hard-bitten-looking veteran. He and a dozen of his men separated from the main force and immediately headed toward Marcellinus who was now in grave peril, surrounded on all sides by enemy Goths, virtually alone at his place in the withering column.

After hacking down two Goths from horseback, Aurelian dismounted and his companions followed his lead. He fought like a man possessed, slashing his way toward the younger officer until they reached each other, steadied their outstretched swords, and paused for a moment.

Marcellinus hailed his commander by his nickname. "Old Sword-in-Hand! I was beginning to think you'd forgotten me."

"I didn't want to ruin all of your fun!"

Having cleared the area surrounding Marcellinus, both men removed their headgear. Neither man bore any facial hair. Aurelian *(Lucius Domitius Aurelianus)*, a man in his mid-40s was the older of the two men and was powerfully built. Although he was a full 10 centimeters shorter than Marcellinus, he was still nearly two meters in height, which was much taller than the average Roman soldier. His face was dark and weather worn, with a small crescent shaped scar on his left cheek. He was the commander

(Legatus legionis) of the legion in which Marcellinus belonged.

Aurelian was a man of humble origins. An Illyrian by birth, he ascended to his position - a post that was usually only held by those of senatorial rank - primarily due to his quick, tactical wit and tenacious fighting abilities. In battle, he generally led the cavalry forces, even though that role was normally performed by auxiliaries *(allied, but non-Roman troops)*.

Marcellinus was twelve years younger than Aurelian, and somewhat taller. He was also sturdily built, with a handsome, but rather boyish face. A generous smile normally graced his countenance. He displayed that smile now. Both men had brownish, black hair, but Aurelian's hairline, primarily due to his greater age, had receded somewhat.

They both looked further down the road as the Roman cavalry began to sweep the now panicking Goths down both sides of what remained of the Roman column.

"Should we pursue them?" Marcellinus asked.

"Absolutely! This lot has been harassing our supply columns for some time now. I want them eliminated."

Marcellinus shouted to another officer "Signal full pursuit" and the officer immediately had signal flags hoisted while also shouting the order down the line.

"You know, very few Roman commanders really know how to use cavalry to its best advantage." Aurelian declared.

Marcellinus completed Aurelian's comment, one that he had heard many times before, "But you're going to change all that."

Aurelian continued, "I'm the best …"

Marcellinus joined in, "damn cavalry commander the Romans have ever had."

A wry smile crossed Aurelian's weather worn face as he concluded, "It's true. You'll see."

Those soldiers still alive and lingering inside the remains of their man-made fortress emerged and began to pilfer any items of value from the dead Goths.

Later that day, back at the Roman camp Marcellinus walked toward Aurelian's tent which was easily identified by a white flag just outside the open tent flap. He acknowledged the two legionnaires guarding the opening and entered the well-appointed tent to see Aurelian at a cluttered table to the left of the entrance.

"You wanted to see me?" he asked.

Aurelian rose. "Emperor Valerian has been taken prisoner near Edessa by the Persian king, Sapor. We are informed that when Sapor is about to go riding, he has Valerian kneel and then uses him as a foot stool for mounting his horse. You don't need me to tell you that this is a gross affront to all of Rome. They're screaming for Persian blood. The problem is, at the moment, we don't have the ability - military strength or otherwise - to do anything about it."

He continued, "You've been ordered to report to Gallienus *(Valerian's son and co-emperor)*. I don't know what it's all about, but I assume that, based upon your prior experience in the East, you'll eventually be sent there to assist Odenathus, the King of Palmyra, in his efforts against the Persians."

Marcellinus snorted. "My experience in the East was limited - only two years - but I was lucky enough to participate in some minor successes."

"It's those kinds of things that they take note of when they make a selection," Aurelian pointed out.

The commander stepped out from behind the table and both men exited the tent. They began their walk down the main street of the encampment toward the Left Hand Gate, the northern gate exiting the encampment. "Did you ever meet King Odenathus while in the East?" he inquired.

"Odenathus and his warrior queen? No, I've never met them, but I've heard a good deal."

The older man cautioned, "Well then, if you have also heard of his bride, Zenobia, you must have heard of her legendary chastity, as well as of her beauty. So be careful not to use the same maneuvers on her that you've used on half the maidens in Rome."

Marcellinus grinned. "I think that you exaggerate just a bit."

Aurelian looked sternly at Marcellinus as they continued their walk. It was obvious that the two were ardent friends even though Aurelian was twelve years older and more somber than the younger man. Because of the age difference, Aurelian also had a somewhat fatherly concern for the light-hearted Marcellinus.

Aurelian's legion had headquartered in the same location for almost three months and, as was the custom, a small town consisting of camp followers had arisen in close proximity to the Roman encampment. For the past month, to ease congestion in the Roman camp, many of Aurelian's officers had been billeted in the recently built makeshift homes of the camp followers.

As they exited the Roman encampment, they walked past

a group of soldiers holding a man down and fastening each of his legs to two sapling trees bent over contraptions containing several pulleys. The man continually cried out for mercy, but none was shown. Both trees were then released from the device and their tops sprang upwards, returning to their original positions. As they did so, the soldier was pulled apart, ripping in two.

"What was his offense?" Marcellinus inquired.

"He committed adultery with the wife of a man that had lodged him."

"Don't you think you're being a bit harsh?" Marcellinus asked.

"The man breached the trust of the man that lodged him as well as the Roman government and, by reacting this way to such an offense, I'm ensuring that the remaining troops won't dare to do the same," Aurelian retorted. "Besides, I'm told that Alexander, the great Macedonian King, used the very same punishment."

"Are you trying to tell me something?"

Aurelian cautioned, "Just be careful when you're out East and exercise some self-control. If you do so, you'll avoid trouble."

"Understood," was Marcellinus's only response.

"Good. I don't want to lose one of my best men due to an

ill-advised sexual encounter. Now, what would you say to a good meal and some even better wine before you leave?"

"I accept, with pleasure."

Both men turned and headed back toward Aurelian's tent.

II

LATE SUMMER, 262 C.E.

THE BATTLE OF NISIBIS

More than two years after leaving his commander and friend, Aurelian, Marcellinus rode at the head of a column of two cohorts of Roman soldiers, just outside the city of Nisibis *(modern day Nusaybin in Turkey).* They were accompanied by a small contingent of mounted auxiliaries. Two Roman and two auxiliary soldiers on horseback rapidly approached the column. They reined in their horses before Marcellinus.

One of the Roman cavalrymen spoke: "The Palmyrenes are going to try and retake Nisibis. The Palmyrene troops are just south of the city. Odenathus is waiting for you up ahead. We can take you to him."

Marcellinus turned to Gaius, his next in command and the only other mounted Roman officer. "Keep the column moving in this line until you come to the Palmyrenes, or you get further instructions from me." Gaius nodded and Marcellinus galloped off with the four cavalrymen.

Although Marcellinus and his men had been riding through

semi-arid terrain for several hours, the surroundings had now become more hospitable, with patches of wheat fields interspersed throughout luscious grassy meadows. There was a small rise overlooking the Persian forces to the north. The riders slowed down near the base of the incline. With the exception of the mound before them, the remaining terrain had flattened considerably.

On the hill four men and a woman sat on horseback, all in full armor. The four men were: Odenathus, King of Palmyra; his son Herodes; and Generals Zabdas and Zabbai. The woman was Odenathus' queen, Bat-Zabbai, or, in the Roman and Greek tongues, Zenobia.

Both Odenathus and Zabdas were in their early forties. Odenathus had a beard and bore Caucasian features, but his face was tanned and worn by the desert climate. Zabdas had a rich umber complexion and bore Numidian features. Zabbai was in his mid-thirties. He also bore Numidian features, although his tone had more of a sienna tint. Herodes was in his mid-twenties, barefaced, with a lighter complexion, but tanned and weather-beaten, like that of his father. All four men were powerfully built.

Like Herodes, Zenobia was also in her mid-twenties, but bore Numidian features, with a deep umber color, and was very athletic in build. And, although she was on horseback, she also appeared to Marcellinus to be somewhat tall for a woman. Like her male companions, she wore armor, but as Marcellinus approached, he was awestruck by her beauty. Her short cropped, soft wavy jet-black hair graciously crowned her stunning features. Her rich, deep brown eyes were shaded by long dark lashes. She smiled at Marcellinus. The four cavalrymen accompanying Marcellinus pulled up just short of the group and Marcellinus, continuing on, approached Odenathus. Dismounting, he removed his helmet, genuflected and exclaimed, "Marcellinus of Rome salutes Odenathus, King of Kings".

"You can dispense with the formalities for now, Roman, since we may engage the enemy any minute," King Odenathus retorted. "But, you do seem to know something of eastern manners, unlike most Romans I've met. We will talk later." Then Odenathus's tone grew louder, intending all to hear. "And when we do, you can explain to me why it took over two years to get any reinforcements from Rome. Other than the remnants of Valerian's army, which have joined my own and those two troublemakers, Macrianus and Ballista, your Romans are the first to come from Gallienus since he requested our help."

Marcellinus smiled. "Bureaucracy," was his only response.

However, he was promptly defended from an unexpected quarter. General Zabbai interjected, "Well, you're here now!"

Marcellinus nodded in gratitude. He sensed that this was

a man that would become a good friend.

Before Marcellinus's arrival, the entire group spoke in Syriac, a dialect of Aramaic that was spoken in the Near East. However, upon his appearance, they all switched to Koine, a Greek dialect[1] that was the lingua franca of much of the Mediterranean region and especially the Roman Middle East.

Marcellinus rose, put his helmet back on and mounted his horse.

Odenathus entreated apologetically, "Forgive me, Roman. I have forgotten my manners. This is my son and co-ruler, Herodes, my generals Zabdas and Zabbai and my lovely Queen, Zenobia." Each nodded as they were introduced and Marcellinus acknowledged them in return. They then all turned to watch the Persian force assembling before them. The Persian leader, Sapor, on a rise just behind his forces, spoke to various aides. Two servants on either side of him held a small awning shading him. He appeared bored.

As the Palmyrene leaders watched the Persians assemble, they grew uneasy. Herodes was the first to speak. "Their cavalry is more heavily armed. Even the horses are larger and better armored. We don't want to meet them in this open field. Since we lost all of our own heavy cavalry with Valerian when he was defeated, we have none to match theirs. Anyway, they must return home now.

They have no provisions and there are none for them in Nisibis. We've already taken most of them when we took Carrhae. I think that we'll just have to do what we've done so successfully for the past two years. We'll harass them and what's left of their supply train as they return to Ctesiphon.[2] Hit and run. That's all we can do for now."

"They don't appear to be too worried by our presence, do they?" Odenathus observed.

"Let their overconfidence be their doom!" Zenobia suddenly exclaimed.

The Persian cavalrymen and their horses assembled a thousand meters in front of the Palmyrenes. They were evenly divided on either side of the infantry - half on the right and half on the left. Herodes then observed, "It's got to be hot under all that armor in this blazing sun - even just standing there."

Zenobia's eyes grew wide. "You are right! So, what if they chased us?"

"They would destroy us, if they caught us," Herodes responded.

"But they will not catch us because they are carrying a lot of weight that we are not." Her enthusiasm began to grow. "If they chase us for two or three kilometers[3], they'll be a bit tired, won't they?"

"They will be exhausted! - And their horses too!" Zabbai replied, beginning to glean Zenobia's intentions with a growing enthusiasm.

"They will barely be able to raise a sword or spear. Easy targets for our arrows – lots of arrows!" Looking at Odenathus, she suggested, "Remember that marshy ground a few kilometers back? How well do you think they could maneuver on that ground, especially if they had just chased us for two or three kilometers?"

Odenathus merely smiled and nodded. He was also starting to garner what she was about to propose.

Zenobia offered her plan *Revealed as the battle unfolds.*

After she related all the details of her scheme, Odenathus said but one word, "Done."

Marcellinus was stunned. "I must admit that the plan shows merit, but…"

Odenathus smiled. "Why does my queen dictate our battle plans?"

"Well I…" Marcellinus stammered.

"Roman, I think that you will find that Queen Zenobia has quite a head for battle strategy."

Unbeknownst to Marcellinus, the Palmyrene forces had recently taken the city of Carrhae, and their success was primarily due to the battle strategy provided by Queen Zenobia. "Very well," Marcellinus uttered resignedly. But then, attempting some ill-conceived flattery, "Perhaps Queen Zenobia's wisdom matches her incredible beauty."

Zenobia scowled, "You will ride with me, Roman. We'll see if your sword is as sharp as your tongue."

Odenathus took a sidelong glance at his wife and then spoke. "Let's collect the men about 1,500 meters from the Persian's right flank." The group dispersed and started moving the men into formation.

Marcellinus walked his horse over to the four riders that accompanied him. To one of the Roman riders he said, "Go and tell Gaius to stay where he is. We will not need any infantry for this work, at least not for now. However, we may need the cavalry auxiliaries later. So tell him to let the men rest, but stay alert."

The man saluted, "Right away, sir." He turned and rode off.

Then, to the others, "You three, come with me." Marcellinus and the three men rode toward Zenobia's cavalry group, which was already in position, facing the Persians. When he arrived, he maneuvered his horse beside Zenobia's and turned to face the Persians. She did not acknowledge his presence.

Still facing the Persians, he sat in silence for a moment, but then, in a whisper, "I must say that I have never before had such a desire for one of my fellow commanders. And to get the chance to fight beside that soldier is such a thrill."

Zenobia scowled. "Perhaps I should inform King Odenathus of your desire? If you keep wagging that tongue of yours in such a manner the only desire you'll fulfill is to meet the gods of the underworld this day," she threatened. Then continuing, "Need I remind you that we are Roman citizens just as you are and not one of your subject peoples. Although he has never been to Rome, Odenathus was made a member of its Senate long ago and, not long before Valerian's capture, Odenathus received from him honorary consular status. But even if we weren't Roman citizens, for all intents and purposes we Palmyrenes have complete and undisputed control of this portion of the East that was once controlled by Rome. So don't think that you can treat me like some royal wench from one of the puppet ruling families that Rome has placed at the head of one of its provinces."

During a long and uncomfortable pause Marcellinus recalled Aurelian's warning of almost two years ago. "Don't listen to my speech, Your Highness. It's just the nervous rambling of a soldier about to enter battle."

Zenobia remonstrated, "For that reason and for that reason only I will not report your lack of respect. If my husband or Herodes heard that comment you'd be off your horse and flat on your back by now."

"Duly noted Your Highness." Marcellinus now anxiously waited for the battle to begin and end the uncomfortable silence that prevailed. And that wait seemed endless.

Zenobia scowled once more and turned her attention toward the Persians.

✦

Zenobia's plan began to unfold:

> *"Let us sit until they get impatient enough to attack. If they send just a small force, we'll surround and destroy it."* ...

Sapor's son Hormizd, growing impatient, rode toward his father. Hormizd was in his mid-thirties, overweight, but eager to show his martial skills to his father. He had two servants on either side of him shielding him from the sun. "Shall I send a detachment to disperse them?" he implored.

"Such a small force to engage them?" Sapor questioned.

"They'll probably turn and flee the moment we attack.

And if they don't, our men's superior armor will protect them. Besides, what is the loss of a mere hundred men to us?" Hormizd countered.

Sapor sighed, "Do as you will, my son."

Hormizd anxiously issued commands to a messenger who rode to the Persian cavalry commander on the right flank. A skeptical commander looked at Sapor for confirmation. Sapor nodded his head in approval. The commander reluctantly barked an order. One hundred cavalrymen broke out of position and headed for the Palmyrenes.

Upon reaching their objective, the Palmyrenes divided and encircled them. The small Persian force was now attacked from all sides. Although they were much more heavily armed and equipped, they were soon overcome.

Zenobia's plan continued to unfold as the battle progressed:

> *"But sooner or later they'll commit*
> *a larger force and then we'll flee."* ...

The Persian cavalry commander watched his men being destroyed. He looked anxiously to Sapor.

Sapor advised, "I think you'd better send those men some help soon, my son. Perhaps the remaining cavalry on our right flank will do?"

An exasperated, as well as agitated,, Hormizd replied, "Why not send both flanks and rid ourselves of these nomadic dogs once and for all?"

"You would leave our infantry unprotected?" Sapor questioned.

"They won't need protection. We'll destroy the Palmyrenes within minutes."

Sapor, growing annoyed, responded, "As you wish."

Hormizd promptly sent an order to the cavalry commanders on his right and left. This time the commander on the right did not question the order. He was eager to join the fight. Within moments, the cavalry on both the right and left flanks tore away from their positions, heading toward the Palmyrene force. Having finished off the smaller Persian force sent against them and seeing the larger force in route, Herodes received a nod from Odenathus and signaled the men to dismount. After they did so, he shouted, "Draw arrows!"

Each man drew an arrow from the quiver attached to the saddle on his horse and attached it to the bowstring.

"READYYYYY!"

The men raised their bows to a forty-five degree angle.

"REL<u>EEEE</u>ASE!"

Hundreds of arrows flew at the Persians. Some bore fruit, striking both men and horses. Nevertheless, although some Persians fell, the hail of arrows only further annoyed the others, and they increased their speed. All the while the Palmyrenes continued sending a barrage of arrows.

As they charged, more and more of their number succumbed to the seemingly endless hail of missiles. Yet, still onward they charged. When they were within 100 meters, Herodes signaled his force to mount and retreat. They turned and bolted.

The Persians eagerly chased the Palmyrenes, but after a kilometer their horses began to feel all the weight they bore and started to slow down.

> *Half the distance to the marshy area, we'll split. I'll go to the right, Zabdas and Zabbai to the left. And you, my king, will continue straight ahead...*

Zenobia signaled to Zabdas and Zabbai. Both men nodded. Zenobia, Marcellinus and their forces turned to the right. Zabdas and Zabbai's forces turned left. Odenathus and the main force continued forward.

If they split up to follow each group, we'll just ride until we lose them, but... if I guess correctly, they'll follow the King...

The ranking Persian cavalry commander saw the Palmyrene groups going left and right. Then he looked forward to see Odenathus straight ahead of him. He pointed his sword forward and his entire force followed Odenathus's group.

Zenobia pointed toward a cluster of trees and made a circular motion with her finger for Marcellinus. He nodded.

Zabdas, Zabbai and I will each circle about behind them at a safe distance

Once they reached the trees, they circled around the cluster and returned in the direction from which they came. However, they now were heading toward the right side of the rear of the Persian force. Zabdas and Zabbai, mimicking Zenobia's maneuver, had also circled about and soon arrived on the left side of the Persian's rear.

The Persians, still focused on Odenathus' group, doggedly followed the main Palmyrene force, failing to heed the potential danger in their rear. Exhausted riders and their horses continued to fall to the ground. Herodes pointed to the marsh and a patch of trees beyond it. Odenathus nodded and they prepared to slacken their pace. More horses and men collapsed around the Persian commanders. Other horses and their riders were panting and sweating.

Then Odenathus's and Herodes's force slackened their pace and gingerly crossed the marsh with their much lighter load bearing horses. The gap between them and the Persians narrowed.

The lead Persian commander, debating whether to call off the chase, saw that the Palmyrenes had relaxed their speed and a smile crossed his face. Encouraged, he screamed and pointed forward with his sword. However, more Persians and their horses continued to collapse in fatigue.

The main Palmyrene force made it through the marsh as the Persians entered it. The soft ground was much more difficult for the heavier load bearing horses to ride through. More men and horses fell.

> *After you pass through the marsh, you'll stop, turn and face them. They'll just have entered it. The soft ground will limit their movements and they'll be exhausted...*

Once out of the marsh Herodes held up his hand and

shouted, "HAA<u>ALLLL</u>T!" The Palmyrenes stopped.

"Turn AB<u>OUUUUU</u>T!"

The men turned on their horses. Then… "Dismount!"

They all dismounted.

"Draw arrows!"

Each man drew an arrow from his quiver and attached it to the bowstring.

"READ<u>YYYY</u>!"

The men again raised their bows.

"REL<u>EEEE</u>ASE!"

Once again, a seemingly endless barrage of arrows flew at the Persians. Many hit their mark, downing the ever-dwindling number of Persians that, because they were closer and moving much slower, had become easier targets.

The plan entered its final stages:

> *We'll stop sixty meters behind them. We'll finish most of them with our arrows…*

Zenobia and Marcellinus's group and Zabdas and Zabbai's group were still separated by a hundred meters, but now both groups were only sixty meters from the marsh and the Persians' rear. Zenobia, Zabdas and Zabbai each held up their hands and shouted simultaneously, "HAAALLLLT!"

Both groups, although still separated by a hundred meters, cried virtually in unison…

"Dismount!" Then…

"Draw arrows!" Then…

"READYYYY!" Then…

"RELEEEEASE!"

The Persians were now being hit by arrows from both front and rear. They turned about in confusion. They held their shields above their heads for protection. Odenathus and Herodes, with their men lined up, fired volley after volley of arrows at the totally confused Persians who now tried to maneuver in the marsh. They were sitting ducks being felled by both arrows and sheer exhaustion. Their commander, in desperation, ordered them to halt and take out their own bows and arrows. Knee deep in mud, they began to shoot at Odenathus' main force with some effect, but they still couldn't match the sheer volume of arrows that were hitting them from all directions.

Zenobia, having just finished releasing an arrow, saw Marcellinus sitting on his horse watching the spectacle. "Feeling useless? Perhaps you Romans should learn to shoot a bow?"

Marcellinus, hearing her, began to steer his horse in a relaxed trot toward the marsh.

"And where exactly are you going?"

"To do what I do best: fight up close, hand to hand."

Zenobia shrugged her shoulders and continued firing arrows.

Marcellinus began to ride around the perimeter of the marsh, intending to circle it until he arrived at Odenathus' forces on the other side. Across the marsh, Odenathus glanced to his left. One of his captains had been hit by a Persian arrow. Signaling Herodes, he rode to his left and joined the men there.

Meanwhile, the lead Persian commander was under a shower of arrows. From beneath his shield he saw Odenathus's movement. With his own bow, he concentrated his shooting in Odenathus's direction, directing his men to do the same. The Persian arrows, limited as they were, still had some effect at thinning out that portion of the Palmyrene line. Then, in an act of desperation, the commander drew his sword once more and shouted a command. He and some ten men began to slowly struggle in the muck toward Odenathus.

One of the Persians, still shooting his bow, hit Odenathus in the shoulder. The blow knocked Odenathus off his horse. Seeing the king fall, the Persian commander and his men frantically headed toward the fallen king, hacking down, or at least moving, every Palmyrene in their way.

Marcellinus, seeing the king fall, increased his pace.

The Persians reached the spot where Odenathus lay. All the Palmyrenes in the area protectively surrounded their wounded king, but the heavily armored Persians prevailed against the lighter armor of the Palmyrenes and the protective circle surrounding the king slowly disintegrated. Finally, the last Palmyrene fell. The Persian commander jumped off his horse and raced to the fallen king. When he arrived, he smiled and raised his sword to strike the final blow. But, as he started to slash downward, Marcellinus' sword appeared, rapidly decapitating the Persian leader.

Marcellinus then began to hack away at the remainder of the Persians. They either fell or fled. In a few moments, no enemy remained. He jumped off his horse, picked up Odenathus by the shoulders and, with much difficulty; laid him over his horse and led the horse away from the battle.

Across the marsh, Zenobia saw Marcellinus leading the king's horse and recognized the king's form draped over the saddle. She signaled to the rest of her company to continue their barrage of arrows while she and three men mounted their horses and rode toward Marcellinus. Marcellinus stopped a short distance from the fighting and laid the king on the ground. Zenobia arrived a few moments later, jumped off her horse and fell before her husband.

"My king! My dear king, are you all right?"

Odenathus winced in pain, "I'm fine, my dear. It's only a flesh wound."

Seeing that the wound was not mortal, Zenobia switched her tone to one of anger. "Why didn't you stay with Herodes?! What were you thinking? You could have been killed!"

The king smiled, "I'm fine now, thanks to my Roman protector."

Marcellinus lowered his head humbly. Zenobia turned to him and spoke haltingly. "I thank you, Roman, for your courageous act. All of Palmyra thanks you."

They looked at each other for a long moment. Then Marcellinus proclaimed, "All of Rome is thankful to Odenathus, King of Palmyra."

The king interjected, "You two may flatter and scold me later. We still have a battle to win."

Zenobia nodded, got up and turned to the three men with her.

"Stay here with the king." She walked over to her horse as Marcellinus mounted his.

"Stay here, My Lady and tend to your king. We can handle the rest."

Zenobia, now subdued, "Thank you Roman."

Both smiled before they parted. Marcellinus looked at Zenobia a bit longer than he should have, making her slightly uncomfortable. She turned to tend to her wounded spouse as Marcellinus galloped off.

By this time Zenobia's original group had converged with that of Zabdas and Zabbai. Marcellinus approached the two generals. In a loud, hoarse whisper he spoke to both men and nodding, they both shouted in unison, "Store your bows and draw your swords!" Then, holding up their swords, "Let's finish them, men. CHARRRGE!"

The Palmyrenes in the Persian rear, with Marcellinus, Zabdas and Zabbai in the lead, charged into the muck to attack the surviving Persians. Herodes, seeing the trio charging the Persians from the other side of the marsh, lowered his bow and shouted. "It's time to finish them with our swords, men." He put away his bow and drew his sword and his men did likewise. Then, raising his sword and pointing it toward the Persians, "CHARRRRGE!"

> *After we thin them out, we'll finish the rest up close, hand to hand.*

The main Palmyrene force, with Herodes in the lead, entered the muck and charged the Persians from their side of the marsh. In minutes, the remaining Persians were killed, wounded, or taken prisoner.

Herodes then rode in the midst of his men, stabbing the air with his sword.

"Hail Palmyra! Hail King Odenathus!"

The Palmyrene soldiers followed his lead, stabbing the air with their swords and crying out in unison, "Hail Palmyra! Hail King Odenathus!" Then the men added, "Hail King Herodes!"

Herodes turned to Marcellinus. "My father?"

"He's fine. He wants us to finish them."

Herodes turned to his men, as well as Zabdas and Zabbai's men who were now all in the muck. "Men! Our work is not yet complete. We still have their infantry to finish."

He turned to a Palmyrene officer. "Keep your men here and clean things up."

As an officer and some of his men were removing the armor from the dead Persians and their horses, he exclaimed, "We now have the makings of our own heavy cavalry unit." He then nodded compliance with Herodes's command.

To the others Herodes cried, "Mount your horses, men – and form up." All but 100 soldiers mounted their horses and fell into a loose formation. Herodes pointed his sword toward Nisibis. "Let's finish this!"

Herodes, followed by Marcellinus, Zabdas and Zabbai led the mounted Palmyrenes back toward Nisibis.

✦

Just outside Nisibis, the Persian infantry was beginning to stir and grumble after standing for so long in their armor under the hot sun. Still mounted, Sapor and Hormizd looked bored. They stared in the direction in which their cavalry had departed. Suddenly Sapor sat up on his horse straining his eyes toward the horizon.

Soon everyone was straining to see through the haze as a small cloud of dust moved toward them. The eyes of one officer widened in surprise. The man rode quietly, but excitedly toward Sapor. A second officer followed him. The first man whispered, "It's…It's the Palmyrenes!"

"The Palmyrenes?!" Sapor was incredulous.

In a subdued tone, the second officer confirmed the other's statement. "The Palmyrenes! It's the Palmyrenes!"

Sapor, now furious, glared at Hormizd. Then he instructed both officers.

"Prince Hormizd and I are leaving. Delay the enemy as long as you can." Both the men and other officers that had recently gathered around him nodded.

Hormizd was stunned. "We are not going to stay and engage them?!"

Sapor responded with venom, "Not without a cavalry we're not! They'll annihilate us! You do remember that you dispatched all of our cavalry after them?"

Hormizd lowered his head and turned his horse. Sapor, Hormizd, their servants, some high ranking officers, and Sapor's personal guard fled the field, leaving behind their entire infantry.

Many infantrymen grew anxious watching Sapor leave. The remaining Persian officers, realizing their peril, halfheartedly commanded their men. "Prepare to engage the enemy!" The men ignored the order. Other commanders began to shout and beat the men, but none moved. Soon the remaining Persian officers were impaled with spears by their own men or pulled off their horses and pummeled. As the Palmyrene cavalry arrived, the remaining Persian infantrymen surrendered to the Palmyrenes.

Herodes then directed Zabdas, "Stay here with your men and move them and the other prisoners into Nisibis. We'll chase Sapor."

Zabdas nodded and Herodes raised his sword once again. "Form up, men! We're going to give Sapor a chase he won't soon forget!"

The Palmyrenes, led by Herodes and including Marcellinus and Zabbai, formed up quickly and set off in the direction of the fleeing Sapor while Zabdas' men began to search and strip their Persian prisoners.

Several weeks later, the victorious Palmyrene army, led by Odenathus, entered the Western Gate of the city of Palmyra. Citizens crowded both sides of the Grand Colonnade cheering their returning heroes.

"Odenathus! Odenathus! King of Kings!"

The procession stopped at the Agora[4] where two men stood on a recently constructed platform. The older one was in his early forties, lightly complected, with a dark beard streaked with gray. His name was Verodes. The younger man was clean-shaven, fair-haired, and in his early twenties. He was Verodes' son, Apsaeus.

Verodes snarled. "The rabble! I stay behind, ardently working to keep things running well. I initiate and supervise all the building projects that make us the rival of Rome. Our streets are full of trade. And who do they love?" As Verodes ranted, the crowd could still be heard chanting in the background. "Odenathus! Odenathus! King of Kings!"

Apsaeus interjected, "I've heard they chased Sapor all the way to the Euphrates - that they took all of his treasure and twelve of his concubines."

Verodes wore a smile on his face that concealed his disgust. "Well, how can I compete with that?"

"Perhaps you should resign your position and request a cavalry command, Father," Apsaeus suggested.

Verodes, taken aback at Apsaeus' suggestion, regained his composure. He spoke haltingly. "Then who would run the city during the king's frequent absences? Let Odenathus have his day. For us, there will be others."

Odenathus, Zenobia, Herodes and Marcellinus reached the platform. All but Marcellinus dismounted and climbed the platform steps. Both Verodes and his son continued to smile, masking their true emotions. Odenathus warmly greeted Verodes, his argapet[5], "Hail Verodes! - my strong right arm. I'm forever grateful for your service."

With an ingratiating smile, Verodes responded, "It is your victories that keep Palmyra strong and prosperous, My King."

Odenathus then commented, "I noticed three new statues when riding down the Colonnade - and two of them are of you, Verodes. It will be you and not Odenathus, Herodes, or Zenobia that the future will remember."

Verodes became anxious and answered defensively. "The Senate ordered the statues built. They said that people should know their argapet."

Odenathus continued. "Those two make a total of eight in your likeness. You'll have the best-known face in Palmyra."

The argapet stammered, "Your Excellency…"

Laughing, Odenathus interrupted, "I'm just having fun with you, my good man. Without your valuable efforts, we'd be lost."

Verodes bowed slightly, "Your recognition of my meager efforts is greatly appreciated, Most Noble Excellency."

On a more serious note, Odenathus declared, "Please divide up the spoils of the campaign."

"I will attend to it at once, My King." And then to his son, "Come, Apsaeus." Verodes and Apsaeus bowed to Odenathus and the two departed. The crowd began to congregate in front of the platform.

Turning to Zenobia, the king requested, "My love, would you please go check on our true treasure."

Zenobia's face lit up with enthusiasm. "With the greatest pleasure, my king." She kissed him on the cheek and descended the platform.

Then, almost as an afterthought, Odenathus called down, "Why don't you take Marcellinus with you? I'm sure he wants to clean up."

Zenobia, although slightly annoyed at this last request, politely answered, "Yes, My King." She mounted, then after a few paces, glanced back at Marcellinus. "Well …, are you coming?"

Not having heard the king's request, Marcellinus awoke from his reverie and began to follow Zenobia.

✦

At the Royal Palace, a few moments later, Zenobia and Marcellinus dismounted and entered The Great Hall. Unlike most other palace main lobbies of the area and period, The Great Hall of the Palmyrene palace was devoid of any furnishings. No mosaics graced its walls, but numerous tapestries were suspended between window openings throughout the oversized and cavernous foyer. And, in lieu of any formal seating or other accommodations for waiting visitors, various semi-tropical plants were spaced sparingly throughout the room - each plant grouping paired with a pew-like wooden seat. In contrast to the spartan accoutrements throughout the room, the floor was a polished white marble. There were at least twelve hallways that exited this main chamber and made the entire structure closely akin to a later day railroad roundhouse.

Numerous servants genuflected and scattered as the pair entered. Attempting to quickly be rid of Marcellinus, Zenobia pointed, "You can use the east chambers to freshen up. Hadwan will take you there." One of the male servants following them nodded in compliance.

But immediately, before the two men had time to depart, three children charged Zenobia: Vaballathus (her son, age seven); Faustula (her daughter, age six); and Timolaus (a younger son, age four).

In chorus, the excited children screamed, "Mother!"

Marcellinus stepped back to avoid the impact as the children nearly knocked Zenobia over. She struggled to maintain her balance as they hugged her legs and waist. She bent over to hug each of them, smothering them with kisses.

The two oldest children, Vaballathus and Faustula had complexions of light ochre with hair a rich russet color, each somewhat favoring their father's features. But Timolaus was graced with the same deep umber colored skin and the same soft wavy black hair as his mother. All three children had inherited Zenobia's rich deep brown eyes.

Vaballathus, the oldest of the group and second in line to the throne after his older brother, Herodes, was tall for his age and exceptionally lean. Faustula, although not quite as tall, was also extremely lean. Timolaus was short and squat, but perhaps only due to his tender age.

"Ohhh! I missed you all soooo much!"

As they embraced their mother, one by one, the children began to gaze at the stranger in the hall. Timolaus left his mother's embrace and began to circle Marcellinus, looking at him in fascination. Zenobia had hoped that Marcellinus would be in his quarters when she greeted the children, but adjusted to the situation. Taking notice of the children's fascination, she explained, "Children, this is Marcellinus. He is a Roman soldier and a friend of ours."

Marcellinus bowed. "It is an honor to meet you all.

Then to Marcellinus, Zenobia introduced each of them. "This is *(pointing to each one in turn)* Vaballathus, Faustula, and Timolaus.

The children continued to stare at Marcellinus and Timolaus persisted in circling him. Then, pausing momentarily, the young prince uttered, "You can't be Roman. Romans are three meters tall!"

"I was, but the desert shrank me somehow." The children snickered.

Then the Roman tribune inquired facetiously, "Why do you all have Roman coins behind your ears?" Each of them grabbed their ears and felt all around them, wearing confused facial expressions.

Faustula was the first to respond, "There aren't any coins behind our ears!"

Marcellinus bent over and reached behind her ear. "Then what is this?" He pulled a coin out from behind her ear. The children stared in awe. He repeated the process with the two boys. "And this? ... And this?" The children were speechless. Zenobia laughed as Marcellinus handed each of them a Roman coin.

"Do you know magic?" Vaballathus inquired.

Faustula pleaded, "Teach us! Teach us!"

The children began to jump and plead, but Marcellinus was unmoved. "Sorry! A magician never reveals his secrets."

The children groaned as Julia, the children's tutor, entered the hall. She bowed to the queen and nodded her head politely at Marcellinus, who returned the nod.

"There you are! I thought pirates took you!" she exclaimed.

"We _were_ captured by pirates!" Faustula responded.

"But this Roman saved us. He was much taller when he saved us," Vaballathus added.

"He shrinked!" Timolaus interjected.

Zenobia and Marcellinus looked at each other and laughed.

Although she had remained silent during the children's banter, Julia now implored, "Children, you haven't finished your Latin lessons."

Vaballathus was the first to protest. "I hate Latin! Please, can't we stay?"

The children looked entreatingly at their mother. Zenobia demanded reluctantly, "Go finish what you've started. We're not quitters!"

The children were downcast. Attempting to brighten their spirits, Marcellinus suggested, "If you finish your lessons in that most important language…" He paused and smiled at Zenobia. "I may just decide to teach you some magic."

Timolaus looked suspiciously at him. "Promise?"

The soldier responded, "A Roman is always true to his word."

Resignedly, Vaballathus concluded, "Alright, alright. Let's get this over with."

Zenobia now studied Marcellinus in a different light as the children walked off with Julia. Marcellinus's eyes followed the children as they left, then returned to Zenobia. Her eyes met his. Assuming his services were no longer required, Hadwan had left the group several minutes earlier. They were all alone now. After a long moment, Zenobia once again felt uncomfortable. That sensation was becoming more and more common whenever they were together.

She broke the silence. "I'll walk you to your quarters."

"Ah … yes, … thank you."

They entered a long corridor and passed several rooms. Zenobia explained, "Julia is fluent in eight languages, including Latin and Egyptian. But, I must admit, Latin isn't one of my favorites either. It's such an awkward tongue."

"What do you mean? I learned it before I was three years old. How difficult can it be?" Marcellinus said flippantly.

"Are you ever serious?"

"Only in battle, when it's necessary. If not, I avoid being so as much as possible."

"Life is a battle," she countered.

"For some, perhaps, but not for me. It's much too short and uncertain. So it must be enjoyed whenever possible." Then, after a brief pause, he added, "But for now I will be serious. I realize now what a good mother and wife you are, and I intend no disrespect when I say that… [pausing] …you are the most beautiful and interesting woman I've ever met. If he were a beggar and not King, Odenathus would still be a truly fortunate man."

Slightly blushing, Zenobia recovered her composure.

"Odenathus is a good man and deserving of my greatest love and respect. I would never do anything to jeopardize him or my family."

"He certainly is, and I promise never to jeopardize that love. You have my word." They stopped walking and their eyes locked. This time they both broke into a smile.

Zenobia took a few more steps. "This is your room."

"Oh, thank you…I…I was meaning to ask – Where does Herodes fit in?"

Zenobia explained, "He's Odenathus' son from an earlier marriage. His mother died giving birth to him. We grew up together. He is like a brother to me."

"Oh."

Abba, a young male servant, walked by and Zenobia stopped him. "Abba! See to it that our guest, Marcellinus, has everything he needs."

The servant bowed. "Yes, my queen."

Then, turning back to Marcellinus, she inquired, "We will see you at dinner then?"

"Yes, of course…at dinner."

Zenobia smiled and departed while Marcellinus entered his quarters.

✦

Later that evening Odenathus was lounging in the royal dining hall. He presented a much different picture than when dressed in his formal toga or military armor. His sole covering was a tunic that was belted at the waist and unaccompanied by any adornments other than a single purple stripe which ran down the center of the garment. He was drinking a goblet of wine as Zenobia entered.

Zenobia also wore a simple long white tunic that literally brushed her feet. The garment was also belted at the waist and fastened by broaches at the shoulders. Even in such simplistic attire, her beauty radiated pure sunshine.

The dais on which the king's couch rested was raised from the floor by a few stairs. He rose as she ascended the stairs. "There you are. I'm famished! Where's our Roman friend?"

"He should be here soon," she responded. They both sat. Then, after a pause, "But while we wait, I've been meaning to speak with you about something. I'm referring to your earlier comment to Verodes about the number of his likenesses that now grace our city. I'm afraid that his ambition is outgrowing his position."

Odenathus defended his chief administrator. "We all must have a certain amount of ambition and even vanity in order to advance our station in life. I am not entirely without that failing myself. A certain amount of pride is a healthy thing."

Zenobia interjected, "As long as it is kept in the proper check. Again I warn you to tread lightly. Watch him carefully, my dear."

"Duly noted, My Queen," the king responded, indicating that the discussion regarding Verodes was over. "So what do you think of this Roman, my dear?"

"He's starting to grow on me. Somewhere within him are the makings of a very likable and trustworthy friend." After a pause she added, "But that worries me. Do we really want to become friends with him or any other Roman?"

"For now we must. Even though things have not been going smoothly in Rome lately, the entire Mediterranean area has grown accustomed to the order and peace the Romans have provided. People want stability. It's better for trade. It's better for raising crops *and* families. Besides, I like the man. He's growing on me as well. He's saved my life *and* reminded me just how beautiful you really are."

Zenobia countered, "It is I who am fortunate to be wed to

such a wise and kind man and a most capable ruler."

Odenathus stood up and grasped Zenobia's hands. She stood as well, looking into his eyes. "Man tends to become complacent with the beauty he sees and enjoys every day. I had to be reminded by a stranger of just how fortunate I really am…" He continued. "I am grateful to our Roman friend."

"And for what am I owed your gratitude?" They looked to see Marcellinus standing before them on the steps below to their left.

Odenathus quickly responded, "We're grateful that Rome sent such a valiant warrior on its behalf."

Marcellinus rejoined, "Rome is grateful to have such a capable ally."

Still standing on the dais, the king adopted a somewhat more serious tone. "I'm going to be totally honest with you, Roman. It is the duty of a prince to give peace and stability to his people. And, if he is extremely lucky, he may also provide prosperity to them. In the past I have been fortunate enough to provide all three, but these are troubled times. A principality the size of Palmyra may not stand on her own. She must seek the friendship of a larger power, but one that will assist in providing her protection and still leave her as free as possible to manage her own affairs. Once Rome fulfilled that function, but you

Romans have not been so stable yourselves lately. You are plagued with constant rebellion and it appears that you are beginning to split up into fragments. A few years ago I was quite undecided just what course to take. Although I knew that the Persian yoke would be heavier than Rome's, I began to think that it was my only alternative if I wanted to maintain peace and stability for my people. Once, while I awaited some promised assistance from Rome, I traveled to a Persian camp on the Euphrates River. I sent gifts to Sapor and begged an audience from him. He spurned my offer and I am told that he threw my gifts into the river. So, but for the arrogance and shortsightedness of the Persian leader, I might be facing Roman armies on the field instead of those of Persia. Now, Sapor has paid for his haughtiness."

"I and the people of Rome take no offense to your former intentions toward the Persians. You must protect yourselves. Your actions are completely understandable based upon Rome's current state of affairs. What Rome needs is just one good leader to put us back on track. If we could but get that one good, strong leader …"

Odenathus interrupted. "And keep him from getting killed by the same kind of treachery that has destroyed the others. Perhaps you have such a man in mind?"

Marcellinus hesitated momentarily, as if looking into his memories and then continued, "I do, but whether he will eventually succeed to the purple, only the gods know."

Odenathus concluded, "Perhaps this man will one day be Palmyra's savior as well."

"Or possibly her doom!" Zenobia interjected.

"My dear?" With a puzzled countenance, Odenathus looked to his queen.

She looked down. "I don't know why I said that. I just felt some kind of momentary premonition."

Odenathus concluded, "Let's just hope that your premonitions are not as potent as your battle tactics!

Taking their goblets with them, Odenathus and Zenobia walked down the steps to Marcellinus. A servant brought Marcellinus a drink and the three raised their goblets. "Here's to many successful campaigns together!", the king proposed.

"To friendship," Marcellinus added.

"To friendship," Odenathus and Zenobia agreed.

III.

ANOTHER VICTORIOUS RETURN

DECEMBER, 266 C.E.

Odenathus, Zenobia, Herodes, Zabdas, Zabbai and Marcellinus all rode once again through the West Palmyrene gate, leading the victorious Palmyrene forces down the Grand Colonnade, to the cheers of a jubilant crowd.

The scene was similar to the group's return to Palmyra four years earlier. People along the street bellowed, "Odenathus! King of Kings! Odenathus! King of Kings!"

Palmyra's argapet, Verodes, and his son, Apsaeus stood just as before on a hastily built dais in the city's Agora. Verodes's beard had a few more streaks of gray and Apsaeus, still barefaced, had become more sinister looking, like his father.

"You see, my son? People only care for glory on the battlefield! And fortune has given Odenathus continued military success while I work diligently but continue to get less and less credit for my efforts. Who's to say that you and I might not enjoy the same military success, if the gods were willing?"

Apsaeus suggested, "I know I would be a successful general, father, if only given the chance. We'd be a great team, you and me. You could administer Palmyra while I led its armies."

Verodes lowered his voice to a whisper. "Well, circumstances have evolved that may allow us to realize our ambitions."

Apsaeus leaned closer and spoke even lower, " You have my attention, Father."

Verodes continued, "Odenathus and Herodes will attend a birthday celebration at Emesa. They will be lightly armed. With luck, one lone assassin might dispatch the pair during the merriment."

Apsaeus remonstrated, but still in a whisper, "It would be suicide to attack both of them, even if they were not armed at all."

Verodes countered, "But what if the assassin bore a grudge against the King *and* believed that he had supporters in the crowd? What if he believed those supporters would overcome the guards and proclaim him King of Palmyra?"

"You have someone in mind?"

"Odenathus's nephew, Maeonius. He had a falling out with his uncle."

Odenathus and his party arrived at the platform. Verodes straightened. "We cannot talk now. I will explain later."

After Odenathus's group reached the platform, he and Herodes dismounted.

"Come, my son, we must humor the crowd."

Turning to Zenobia he said, "Herodes and I will join you and Marcellinus soon." Then, smiling, he added, "We will know where to find you."

Zenobia beamed and bowed her head slightly. "As always, I obey your commands with the utmost pleasure, My King."

The king and his son began to mount the steps to join Verodes and Apsaeus on the makeshift dais. As they reached the top, the roar from the crowd intensified.

Marcellinus motioned to Zenobia to wait and turned to Zabbai and Zabdas.

In the background they all heard Odenathus and Herodes addressing the crowd.

Zabbai was the first to speak. "You are still dining with us tomorrow night, right?"

"Of course. We have been planning this since we left on campaign. I will be there." Then to Zabdas Marcellinus added, "Have you agreed to join us?

"If Zabbai doesn't get stingy with the wine."

Zabbai scowled, "Stingy with the wine? Last time I served you wine shipped all the way from Campania."

"Yes, all two jugs of it," Zabdas snapped. The banter continued as the pair rode toward the stables.

"So you want quantity instead of quality, huh? Fine! This time I'll drown you in as much of the local poison as you can stomach!"

As they rode away their voices became fainter.

"And what's wrong with the local wine? I drink it all the time. But then, I am not trying to impress anyone."

Zabbai snapped back. "I didn't say wine, I said poison."

Their repartee continued as they rode out of hearing. Marcellinus and Zenobia were still laughing as they rode toward the palace entrance. They dismounted, and servants took their horses. Soon they were through the palace doors.

The Great Hall of the palace was quite the same as before, except this time Zenobia and Marcellinus were attacked by five children. There were Vaballathus (now almost twelve), Faustula (now ten), Timolaus (now eight), and two new additions: Antiochus (age two) and Livia (nine months old).

Vaballathus had filled out his former lean frame, having become somewhat more muscular in appearance. Faustula had also become less lean, but not significantly so, presenting a supple figure that was becoming more pleasing to the eye. It was now Timolaus' turn to affect a lean look, having lost much of his earlier toddler's bulk. The two year old Antiochus had inherited his mother's complexion and other looks, but for Livia, she had not yet adopted any pronounced physical features of note.

Vaballathus stood back from the group, almost aloof, attempting to project a reserved dignity. Faustula carried the infant, Livia, in her arms, but Timolaus and Antiochus ran straight toward Marcellinus and Zenobia who knelt in order to return the smaller children's hugs. Faustula carefully handed Livia to her mother.

The two youngest boys squealed, "Marcellinus!!! Mother!!!"

Zenobia smiled, but feigned annoyance. "Since when is

Marcellinus greeted before your own mother? At least pretend that you care for me as much as you care for him!"

Antiochus reached for Zenobia. "I still wuv you da best mudder!"

Zenobia smiled and then turned to the other children. "What about the rest of you traitors?" Zenobia and Marcellinus slowly stood, Marcellinus with one of the younger boys under each arm. Zenobia cradled her newest addition.

"Don't blame yourself for this. I know magic and you do not. How can you beat that?" Marcellinus lightheartedly vindicated their actions.

Zenobia smiled. Vaballathus continued to stand back as the other children now devoted their hugs toward their mother.

Faustula explained, "You know we love you, Mother, but we must give Marcellinus proper attention. You have father, but Marcellinus has no one but us."

As Zenobia released the other children, Vaballathus stepped forward and gave his mother a more formal hug. "Welcome home, Mother. We've all missed you."

Zenobia kissed his cheek, then addressed the children. "I missed you too ... all of you."

Vaballathus turned and gave Marcellinus a more formal, Roman handshake. "It is good to see you too, Marcellinus." Then, to both Marcellinus and his mother, "Where are Father and Herodes?"

Zenobia sighed. "They will be here soon. They are just taking care of a little politics."

Mere moments later Odenathus and Herodes entered the Great Hall and walked toward the group. Vaballathus and Faustula were the first to see them. Both of their faces lit up.

"Father!" Faustula ran to the king.

Timolaus turned and was the first of the younger two boys to see his father and older brother. He rushed to greet them. "Father! Herodes!" Antiochus followed Timolaus.

Vaballathus walked over slowly. Marcellinus and Zenobia, with Livia still in her arms, followed them. The children warmly greeted their father and half-brother. Zenobia presented her husband with Livia. The baby began to cry.

"With all this campaigning I have become a stranger to my own children." He gazed down at Livia. "You really have not seen too much of your father, have you?" Then, looking up, "Well, I intend to change that! We are not going on any campaign for at least five months…" Looking down once again at Livia, "… and I am not leaving you for even a moment during that time. I promise that you will have had enough of me before I leave again!" He stroked Livia's cheek and leaned over to give her a kiss on the forehead. She stopped crying.

Herodes interjected, "What about Haran's birthday at Emesa in two weeks? We will be gone for at least two or three weeks."

Odenathus grimaced, but quickly rebounded. "We will spend no more than two days at Emesa. We will use dromedaries.[6] So, counting traveling time, we should be gone no more than six or seven days."

Zenobia seconded the king's resolution, "Two days in Emesa it will be then!"

Herodes walked over to where Odenathus held his new sister. Looking down he smiled. "Hello angel." Leaning over further he kissed her cheek.

Suddenly Vaballathus approached Herodes and led him away from Livia. It was quite obvious that he idolized his older brother. "Tell me about your battles and do not leave out one detail! I should be old enough to go with you next year."

Looking at Odenathus and Zenobia anxiously, Herodes responded, 'You must complete your training first."

"I have been training! I practice every day!"

Attempting to mollify him, his older brother offered, "tell you what: you can train with me every day while I am home. I'm not promising anything, but we will see how things work out."

Zenobia, hearing Herodes' promise, gave Odenathus a worried glance. Odenathus took his cue. "Sorry, Vaba, but you still have a few years before you will be able to join us."

"I am almost thirteen! Soon you, Herodes, and Mother will beat the Persians for good and there will not be anyone left to fight!"

Zenobia sighed. "How I wish that were true, Vaba, but I don't think you have anything to worry about on that subject."

To ease his displeasure, Herodes offered, "Well, I think that it is time that you prepare in earnest. Whether you go with us soon or not, it is time for you to begin some serious training." He looked over to Odenathus and Zenobia and they nodded their approval. He continued. "We will start tomorrow."

Julia, the children's tutor, entered.

Seeing her, Zenobia told them, "Children, go with Julia

while we old folks prepare for dinner."

"Awwwwh!!!" was their universal response.

"We will not be long," she said to calm them.

Then, to Odenathus and Herodes, "I'm going to show Marcellinus to his new quarters. We moved him to the west wing."

Seeing all four leaving, Julia entreated, "Come children!" She and the children then entered a corridor while the "older folks" dispersed through various other passageways.

✦

Moments later, in a corridor of the palace's west wing, Marcellinus and Zenobia strolled in silence toward Marcellinus' new chambers.

Zenobia suddenly broke the silence. "Faustula just mentioned something I have been wondering about for quite some time. You have been with us for over four years now and, other than Zabbai and Zabdas, you have no other significant companions. And frankly, I am thinking more about companions of the female type...." She paused and then, "You have told us that you have no wife in Rome and are not otherwise engaged. Yet, you have not courted any of the many beautiful maidens of Palmyra. Is there no woman you've met that you are willing to spend more than one evening with?"

They stopped walking and Zenobia innocently waited for his reply.

"There is one, but she's taken."

Zenobia became uncomfortable, blushed, and lowered her eyes. Still looking toward the floor she responded, "After our first meeting you promised not to make such comments. You know that what you hint at is impossible."

"When we first met I believed you to be exceptionally beautiful, but I was merely acting the way I always do in the company of beautiful women. A greater knowledge of you has only increased your physical beauty to me."

She tried to speak, but Marcellinus held up his hand. "Have no fear. I respect both you *and* Odenathus too much. My father died when I was very young and, in many ways, Odenathus has been like a father to me. Only one other man has ever done as much for me as Odenathus has and that man is a hard-bitten, old Roman general." He smiled, recalling Aurelian and they resumed their walk.

After another awkward moment of silence he explained, "Let's just say that since I've met you, I have become a little more selective."

"You have too much of an idealized opinion of me. I have

many faults and annoying habits."

"But I am sure that Odenathus would agree with me when I say that those faults are insignificant." Then he rationalized, "But, remember that there are benefits to my dilemma that you overlook. I am unattached, not having to deal with the petty jealousies and annoyances of most females. I may see whomever I wish, whenever I wish. In fact, I have grown to like my freedom and would be sorely disappointed if I were to become involved with any *one* woman. So, you have actually helped me, in a way."

"I have a feeling that you'll find someone soon that will make you glad to give up your pretensions to the free life."

Zenobia indicated that they had reached Marcellinus' new quarters by gesturing toward an open door. He shrugged his shoulders and gave a mischievous smile. "Perhaps."

He entered his quarters and Zenobia returned down the corridor.

✦

Later that day, barely an hour after sunset, Verodes and Apsaeus entered the alleyway of a small side street in Palmyra. Just inside to their left, there were wooden boxes and crates, some stacked against the wall of one of the buildings adjoining the alley, some scattered about, appearing to be a set previously stacked against the same wall that had toppled to the ground. They paused and sat on two of the fallen boxes, anticipating a long vigil. But they did not have long to wait as a tall, slender, man with light olive colored skin and jet black hair soon emerged. He looked to be in his mid-thirties. His name was Maeonius. He was Odenathus's nephew.

Maeonius spoke first. "I am told that you want to see me."

Verodes quickly responded, "Yes. And I think that you will find what we have to say to be of great interest to you."

Maeonius glanced to his right and left, then behind him before taking several steps toward the pair. He pulled one of the fallen wooden crates beneath him and sat down directly in front of the father and his son. So this was Odenathus's disgruntled relative. Verodes had heard his name mentioned occasionally, but had never seen him in person.

Maeonius pressed them, "I am all ears. Go on."

Verodes began, "You saw Odenathus and Herodes ride into the city today, did you not?"

"So?"

"You saw the cheering multitudes voicing their

acclamations, did you not?" Not waiting for Maeonius' response, he continued. "To the casual observer it would seem that Odenathus and his son rule a contented populace. Wouldn't you say?"

"Well…" Maeonius began to respond, but again Verodes did not wait for his answer.

"But all is not as it may appear in Palmyra. There are many, many Palmyrenes, many high-placed and influential citizens that are tired of doing Rome's dirty work at our own expense. They see the Roman Empire getting weaker and weaker, yet they also see Palmyra continue to exhaust much of its revenues trying to keep this faltering and decrepit overlord from splintering into a thousand pieces. There are many that seek a change in the direction for Palmyra. They seek a ruler with the courage and determination to throw off the Roman yoke and enable Palmyra to fulfill its destiny. They seek a ruler with vision that will allow Palmyra to take its place among the great ruling cities of the world."

Fire began to appear in Maeonius' eyes and he suddenly stood up and interjected, "I have been saying all along that Palmyra should not be the lackey of Rome. But no one will listen."

Once again, Verodes interrupted, "There are many who will listen - people in high places. You have just been talking to the wrong people."

Maeonius became more excited. "Who are they?"

Verodes sidestepped the question. "For now they wish to remain anonymous. They are worried what might become of them and their positions if their opinions became known. Just as with most mortals, they hesitate. When asked for their opinions by Odenathus or Herodes, they prevaricate. They have doubts. They are uncertain. Even though they are high-born, they are still sheep. They need the right time AND THE RIGHT LEADER to spur them forward."

Then, quite disingenuously, "Maeonius, even though you probably have not even been aware of my existence, I have watched you carefully for quite some time. On several occasions I have seen you have the courage to express your opinions, even when you knew they would not be welcomed by sympathetic ears. And those opinions show GREAT VISION! That is because the same blood that flows through Odenathus' veins also flows through yours. So why should Palmyra not select someone of the same house as Odenathus, but someone much more farsighted to shape its future, the future of Palmyra? We believe, my son Apsaeus and I, that the leader we seek is you!"

Maeonius' passion increased exponentially as Verodes spoke, but after a few moments his enthusiasm suddenly waned and he returned to his seat. "Well there is just one problem with your, so called, "vision". There are a couple of obstacles called Odenathus and Herodes that those of "vision" must contend with. And they will not be so easily done away with. So just how am I to pull off that little trick?"

Verodes attempted to rekindle the flames that would embolden his intended stooge, "Those who eye the prize must have the fortitude and courage to seize an opportunity and take it. The faint-hearted never achieve greatness."

"Fortitude and courage are one thing. Sheer lunacy is another," Maeonius retorted. "Due to my prior difficulties with them, I never see them privately any more. And when they are in public, they are covered in protective mail and heavily armed. Not to mention the fact that they are surrounded by their personal guard."

Apsaeus interjected, "But opportunities do present themselves. And if one is watchful, one might be present at the right time and place to profit from the occasion."

Some of Maeonius's initial enthusiasm returned, "You know of an upcoming "opportunity?"

Verodes retook the lead from his son. "In two weeks' time, both Odenathus and Herodes travel to Emesa to attend a birthday celebration for a former comrade-in-arms. He is now a wealthy merchant and his name is Haran. Neither father nor son will wear any protective mail or be armed at the feast, since it would be considered an insult if they were. Only their personal guards will accompany them to the event. The rest of their escort will probably hit the nearest brothel as soon as they pass through the city's gates. The wine will flow freely and so, even their personal guards will grow careless. Some of the guards support our cause. If a lone assassin were to wait for the right time, if he were to move quickly, if he did not hesitate or waiver, he would be able to plunge his blade into the hearts of both father and son before there was time for any remaining loyal guards to react."

Maeonius interjected, "What then? I assume you have me in mind when you say "assassin". After I kill them, am I to fight off their guards that remain loyal single-handedly, or with the help of the few guards that are with us?"

"Certainly not! That's where we come in. We are also invited to the celebration. Apsaeus and I will enter with an entourage of thirty carefully picked men. Since I am argapet of Palmyra we will not be searched for concealed weapons. As soon as you dispatch the pair, we'll subdue his loyal guards, his friend Haran and any other sympathizers to his cause. Since we won't be in Palmyra, the total, including their personal guards, cannot number more than fifteen men. We will then proclaim you, Maeonius, King of Palmyra." To fan the growing flame within Maeonius, both Verodes and Apsaeus smiled and proclaimed in unison *(but in subdued tones)*, "Hail Maeonius, King of Kings!"

Maeonius still had his doubts. "What if I am only able to

kill one of them and not both?"

Verodes responded emphatically, "You must kill both! They rule jointly. Their line must be totally eradicated so that you are the only alternative. When we return to Palmyra we'll take care of the remainder of his seed. Any future contenders must be eliminated."

Maeonius's skepticism continued, "What if an opportunity never presents itself? What if ...?"

Verodes interrupted him, "I do not suggest that there are no risks. There are. But how long will it be necessary to wait for a more favorable opportunity than the one that will present itself at Emesa? The faint-hearted will waiver, but those that will rule will seize the moment."

After some reluctance Maeonius muttered in a low tone, "Well..."

Apsaeus did not let him finish. "Come on Father. He lacks the courage. We're wasting our time." Both father and son turned to leave.

"Wait!" Maeonius called out, with some reluctance, but then, with increased enthusiasm, he exclaimed, "I will do it."

"You will not waiver? You will not falter? You will show leadership and courage? Your movements will be deliberate and sure?" Verodes prompted his patsy.

Maeonius stood up straight and attempted to speak with conviction. "I will not waiver. I will fulfill my destiny."

Verodes and Apsaeus looked at one another and the former spoke. "We will contact you in ten days' time. If you are still of the same mind we will fill you in on the details. In the meantime you will need to select a weapon that is sure to do the work, but no longer than a cubit in length so that it may be concealed."

"Perhaps two weapons of the same size will be better?" Maeonius suggested. "I may catch them together and kill both with one thrust."

"Perhaps." Verodes said hesitantly.

Then Maeonius continued, still trying to convince them - as well as himself - of his resolve, "You can be sure that I will do my part."

Verodes then concluded, "I know that my estimate of your ability will prove itself. Until we meet in ten days…"

They clasped arms and Maeonius walked away, turning back momentarily and saying, "Until then."

As the father and son watched him walk away out of the alley and, more importantly, out of earshot, Apsaeus asked, "What if he changes his mind and decides to inform on us?"

A smiling Verodes responded, "What? Do you think Odenathus would believe the word of a trouble-making nephew over that of his trusted argapet? If he does change his mind at any time we will need to dispose of him."

His son now posed a second question. "I realize that they may choose not to search you or me, but do you really think that the guards will not search a group of thirty men accompanying us?"

With a wry smile Verodes responded, "Of course they would be searched. But that's only if there are thirty men to search."

Apsaeus first appeared puzzled, but then saw clearly his father's intentions. "You mean that there will not be thirty men with us, right?"

"If and when that stooge is fortunate enough to kill one or, better still, both of them, you will personally dispatch him to revenge his bloody and monstrous crime. You, in effect, will be the hero of the day. And if we play our cards well, we may - you and I - become the next co-rulers of Palmyra."

Apsaeus continued, "Then none of the imperial guards are in the conspiracy either, correct?"

"Correct," Verodes replied.

"But what about Zenobia and those five brats of hers?"

Verodes countered scornfully, "She is a woman; a non-factor. She may appear in military dress and go on campaign with him, but how much of a threat can she be? However, Odenathus' other progeny, especially the boys, do present a problem. I have made arrangements to have all five eliminated while we are in Emesa. By the time we return from the feast, the House of Odenathus will exist no more. And then, who better to select as his successor than the one who has actually been running things all along? The one who is seen by the citizens of Palmyra every day and not merely during brief interludes between military campaigns. Naturally I will need to select a much younger and stronger man as co-ruler. One who'll learn the art of administration and be able to step into that function when I am no longer around. But also one who'll provide for the city's defenses and, if the opportunity presents itself, be able to enlarge Palmyra's dominions as Rome's power diminishes and her empire splinters into small petty territories – just as it is doing now."

The two exited the alley and walked down the narrow street. Apsaeus remarked, "I will show the people of Palmyra what a real military genius can do."

Verodes smiled. "For that we must have patience my son. First things first."

They walked silently away for several minutes when, suddenly, Apsaeus asked, "How do you plan to eliminate the remaining children anyway?"

"I have others well placed in the palace – an insider very close to the family - as well as some trusted guards. I'll fill you in with the details later."

✦

Several days later Herodes, Marcellinus and Vaballathus were training with several other soldiers in the palace military training courtyard. There were hanging mannequins, racks of assorted weaponry, targets, and many other martial tools at the perimeters of the compound.

Herodes was instructing Vaballathus in a sword fighting drill when Odenathus and Zenobia entered the courtyard. All of the soldiers training in the courtyard, with the exception of Herodes, Vaballathus and Marcellinus bowed and then backed away to the perimeters of the training area. The latter three removed their helmets.

Zenobia announced, "We'll be leaving within the hour."

Herodes and Vaballathus stopped their training.

"I'm ready to go. I just came down to the yard for a final workout with Vaba."

"Please don't call me that anymore! I'm too old for that name."

Herodes immediately smiled and corrected himself, "I'll see you in a few days, *Vaballathus*."

Meanwhile, Marcellinus will practice with you. Just don't take any of his archery suggestions!"

Overhearing Herodes, Marcellinus turned to face him directly, smiling, but in a confrontational mode, "I heard that. And I want you to know that it was funny the first ten times you said it. I know that I couldn't handle a bow when I got here, but that was five years ago. I'm not such a bad archer these days and you're going to find out! I hereby challenge you to an archery contest when you return."

"Naturally there'll be a wager on the outcome," Herodes added, but the statement was more in the form of an inquiry.

After a brief hesitation, Marcellinus replied, "Of Course."

Herodes settled the matter, but spoke facetiously, "That's good, because I could use the extra money. I'm a little short this month." Herodes winked at his younger brother.

Vaballathus spoke up. "Don't worry Marcellinus, I'll practice the bow with you while Herodes is gone."

Marcellinus looked patronizingly at Vaballathus. "Thanks, I could use the help."

Herodes placed his hands over his heart to feign heartbreak. "Betrayed by my own brother!"

"I just want to help him get better" Vaballathus apologized.

"Don't worry, I'm just kidding, Vab…", he stammered, but then corrected himself, "Vaballathus. I'll see you in a few days."

The youth nodded his head and Herodes ruffled his hair.

Zenobia then turned to Marcellinus. "Are you sure you won't join us?"

"No. A Roman is the last thing Haran will want at his birthday celebration."

A smiling Herodes shook Marcellinus's hand in the Roman manner.

Zenobia turned to Vaballathus and held out her arms. A somewhat sheepish looking Vaballathus looked at the older men watching from the fringes of the training area before reluctantly hugging his mother.

Then, straightening himself, he shook his father's hand, also in the Roman manner. "Goodbye Father." Suddenly a momentary feeling of anxiety engulfed the boy's entire being. He raised both arms and gave his father a tight hug. A puzzled Odenathus returned the hug.

He then walked rapidly over to Herodes and repeated the process. Herodes looked at the other adults with a puzzled expression, but returned the hug. Vaballathus let go and forced a smile.

"Hurry back - all of you." As they left, Vaballathus raised his hand and waved goodbye to all of them while walking toward Marcellinus.

The king responded over his shoulder, "We certainly will."

IV.

EMESA - A TRAGIC VISIT

At Emesa, in Haran's banquet hall, Haran sat near one end of a very long table. It was dusk and his birthday banquet was ending. His wife Nefa and Zenobia sat at the opposite end of the table. Odenathus was on Haran's right and Herodes and Zabdas on his left. Verodes and Apsaeus sat near the middle of the table.

Many distinguished leaders and nobles also sat at the main table, while others sat at additional tables interspersed throughout the banquet hall. Haran whispered something to Odenathus and then stood and raised his goblet.

Looking at Odenathus, Haran proffered a toast, "Honored guests, I toast your health once again!" He then turned from Odenathus toward the others and took a drink. Standing, everyone joined in the toast. "And now, since the gods have provided us with such a beautiful evening, let us go outside to enjoy it! I have arranged several spectacles for your amusement! He pointed at the door to his right. Sluggishly, but deliberately, everyone stood and slowly made their way toward the door. Zabdas and a few others continued eating and talking a while longer.

Verodes and Apsaeus were the first to leave. As they departed, the Royal Palmyrene Guards just outside the door set their goblets down, stood and adjusted their armor and weaponry. Other guests slowly exited the hall and began their journey down the wide meandering walkway that led to the center of town. A crowd lined both sides of the walkway to see the famous King and his warrior Queen.

Odenathus, Herodes, and Haran gradually strode through the doorway. Soon Zenobia and Nefa walked out. Each group was surrounded by four of the Royal Guards as they exited.

It was truly a beautiful December evening. A balmy desert breeze cooled the unusually warm night air. The sky was clear, but a full moon illuminated the night sky, rendering the torches that were placed at two meter intervals somewhat superfluous.

Verodes and Apsaeus searched the crowd. Apsaeus was the first to see the tall and slender Maeonius.

His eyes looked wild, like those of a madman. Apsaeus wondered whether the king's nephew had fortified himself with some strong spirits to bolster his courage. "So much the better," he thought. He nodded to his father to look in the same direction. Maeonius's eyes met theirs. Verodes gave him a slight nod.

Although the encroaching crowd had breached the

borders of the walkway, they parted for the royal guests as the latter made their way toward Emesa's agora. Maeonius maneuvered to stay close to his targets. Odenathus, Herodes and Haran stepped lively, talking as they walked. They looked up occasionally, smiled and waved to the crowd. Zenobia and Nefa then entered the walkway.

Verodes vaguely pointed in Maeonius' general direction. Suddenly he shouted, "Look out!"

At the sound of Verodes warning, the two guards that covered the rear of the protective enclosure guarding the leaders stopped instantly and turned about, assuming a defensive position. The pair at the front of the enclosure took another two paces before heeding the warning. Their delay created a gap between those guards in the front and those in the rear – a gap wide enough for Maeonius to breach and make his move.

As soon as Maeonius penetrated the enclosure he drew a blade from beneath his tunic, raised it and, just as Herodes turned, slashed him straight across the throat. Blood sprayed the side of Maeonius' face as Herodes collapsed to the ground. The assassin then quickly lowered his blade, stepped toward Odenathus and pierced the king's abdomen just as the king turned about. He ripped upward with the blade and Odenathus, a dumbfounded look on his face, slowly fell to the ground.

The stunned guards quickly recovered. All four surrounded

the assassin. With a crazed look, Maeonius looked about the crowd. "Arise Palmyrenes! Arise for your new king!"

Verodes glanced apprehensively at Apsaeus. In a low, urgent tone he spoke to his son. "Hurry! Finish him quickly!"

Apsaeus rushed forward and nimbly slipped into the guards' small circle. Maeonius smiled, thinking he was about to receive the promised assistance. Verodes, intending to sound like just another voice in the crowd, shouted, "Death to the murderer!!! Kill him!!! Avenge the house of Odenathus!!!"

As Maeonius stepped toward Apsaeus, the latter drew a dagger and thrust it into Maeonius's abdomen, ripping upward. A puzzled-looking Maeonius grabbed Apsaeus and staggered a few steps forward, driving Apsaeus back on his heels. But, to the relief of both father and son, the assassin fell to the ground, without uttering a word.

The crowd was stunned. Zenobia rushed to Odenathus's side. She put his head on her lap and cradled it as tears streamed down her cheeks. Odenathus tried to speak, but Zenobia put her hand over his mouth and shook her head. Sobbing, she pleaded, "Shhh. Please, do not speak. I know…"

In a gurgling voice, Odenathus inquired, "Herodes?"

Still trying to calm him, she responded, "I don't know."

Odenathus, sputtering some blood, summoned all his strength. "Our sons…" he paused and summoned more of his remaining strength. "They must keep Palmyra's throne!" He paused once again and then, "Promise me that you will help them."

Zenobia hesitated. Odenathus grabbed her garment just below the collar and pulled her face downward, close to his. "Promise me! Swear it!"

Zenobia hesitated, but then with resolve, vowed, "I … I swear it."

With difficulty, he smiled and released his grip. Opening his hand, he placed his palm on her cheek. He struggled, but smiling he said, "Beautiful queen…" Then with his last breath he uttered, "… good wife…"

Tears streaming down her cheeks, Zenobia held his hand to her face. She lowered her head and kissed his lips as blood trickled from the corners of his mouth. She raised her head and lowered his head to the ground.

A tardy Zabdas arrived on the scene. Seeing Zenobia with Odenathus, he went directly to Herodes. After only a few seconds he stood up, took off his cloak and covered the body. He walked back to Zenobia and helped her to her feet. The trembling Zenobia looked up and, seeing Zabdas's last act over Herodes's body, stammered, afraid to hear the response she knew that she would,

"He is gone?"

Zabdas affirmed by sadly nodding his head.

Not only had she just lost her husband and the father of her children, she also lost his oldest son. She had grown up with Herodes. They were as brother and sister. She fought back her tears and wiped her face as she tried to compose herself.

Verodes, with great difficulty, concealed his pleasure. As Apsaeus walked to his side, his father, in a low muffled whisper sputtered, "I never thought he'd succeed in killing both of them! The gods surely favor our cause!"

However, the older man quickly adopted a somber look, stepped forward, cleared his throat, and raised his arms to address the crowd. "Citizens! Citizens and subjects of the Great Kings, Odenathus and Herodes! It is a sad and unfortunate day for the people of our lands." Verodes's words quieted the ever-escalating hum of the stunned spectators, but before he could continue, Zenobia interrupted.

"Citizens of Emesa and Palmyra! Our great and noble king, Odenathus ..." She hesitated to suppress some tears and then resumed, "... and his equally noble and courageous son, Herodes, have been murdered!" She cleared her throat and then, composing herself, continued, but now with vigor and conviction, "but his sons Vaballathus, Timolaus, and Antiochus yet live. And the same royal blood of Odenathus flows in their veins. I return to Palmyra to convene its Senate. We will inform you soon of their decision."

She turned to Zabdas. "Will you …?"

Anticipating her request, Zabdas interjected, "I will see to their remains." Then, turning to the four guards, almost in a whisper, he said, "Make the bodies ready for transport."

The guards began to wrap the bodies of their fallen rulers as Zenobia turned to face Verodes. Both Verodes and Apsaeus looked stunned, but they quickly recovered and assumed somber expressions as Zenobia faced them, her eyes still filled with tears. "Come, Verodes!" She headed toward the dromedaries.

The older furtive conspirator fell in behind the queen but at a safe distance, not offering a reply. His son, Apsaeus, fell in right behind him. Although Verodes's disappointment appeared to have been mollified, Apsaeus's mood had worsened. As he spoke in a whispering rage, he actually spit out the words, "And we still have those sniveling brats to deal with!"

Verodes generated a sly smile. "Remember what I told you about our plans for them. They are being attended to as we speak. Remember that we have help inside the palace, including someone very close to the family." He paused. "Soon the royal family will experience another dreadful calamity." Recalling an earlier conversation with his father, Apsaeus began to smile.

"The first round is hers, but when she discovers that her remaining family members are also no longer in this world, she'll fall apart. Then we'll make our move."

The two villains masked their smiles as they reached the dromedaries. Zenobia mounted one made ready by an attendant and departed immediately. Her startled guards rushed to follow her, mounting quickly as the animals became ready.

Verodes and Apsaeus were the last in the group to leave, waiting for Zabdas to gather the remains of the fallen leaders and ready them for their final return to Palmyra.

In Palmyra, on the evening following the assassinations, Marcellinus and Vaballathus had just finished their training session, which had lasted somewhat later into the evening than usual. The pair walked down a corridor leading to the great hall of the palace. In addition to their swords, a bow and a quiver of arrows hung loosely at the back of their tunics.

Marcellinus praised the youth, "You still need work with the sword, but your archery is excellent. You're a true

Palmyrene."

"I think that archery is in our blood," the prince responded, but after a pause, "You know, I'm getting hungry again."

"Well good luck getting some food now, unless you're willing to wake someone."

"I'm not helpless. I think I can scrounge up some food for myself."

"You know, I'm a bit hungry too," the older man added. "I think I'll join you."

Just as they entered the Great Hall of the palace, they saw a woman entering another corridor. Vaballathus was puzzled, "Isn't that...?"

Marcellinus covered the lad's mouth and then put a finger up to his own lips, signaling the lad to *"Be quiet!"* Their conversation turned to whispers. Marcellinus, no stranger to intrigues in his younger days in Rome, whispered, "I don't know *who* that was, but why is she headed toward the princess's bedchamber at this hour?" Then, after a long moment, "And where are the guards at the entrance to that corridor?"

Vaballathus, glancing around, whispered, "Where are _any_ of the guards?"

Marcellinus looked directly into the boy's eyes. "Zabbai is dining with Mael, the Numidian, tonight. He should still be there. Do you know where the Numidian lives?"

The young prince nodded.

Marcellinus, solemnly instructed the lad, "Go there as fast as you can. Tell him to send for more men, but that he should come at once."

"But I want to stay with you!" the youth protested.

"If you stay here, we may not have enough men to stop what I think is about to happen. You must go! The lives of your brothers and sisters depend on your speed!" Vaballathus turned to leave, but Marcellinus stopped him. "Wait!"

Still speaking in a somewhat hoarse whisper, "When you return with Zabbai, go directly to Timolaus and Antiochus' bedchamber." Then, almost shoving the lad, "Now go!" Marcellinus watched as Vaballathus walked quickly toward the main door of the hall. Then, in a loud whisper, he urged, "Run!"

The prince ran out of the door. As Marcellinus moved across the Great Hall, still holding the bow in his left hand, he placed his right hand instinctively on the hilt of the sword that was fastened to the belt strapped about his waist. He quietly entered the princess' foyer, but the guards normally present there were also missing. He peered into the room. On the left side of the bed, he saw a hooded woman crying. She stood over the sleeping Faustula, stroking the princess' hair. He drew an arrow and set it. Still crying, the woman reached into her cloak, pulled out a dagger and raised it into the air to strike. Marcellinus took aim. "Stop! Don't move!"

Realizing she had been discovered, the assassin thrust the blade downward toward the sleeping child. But before the blade reached its destination, Marcellinus released his arrow impaling the woman to the headboard of the bed. At the arrow's impact, she emitted a terrifying scream and Faustula woke with a start. In the crib to the left of Faustula's bed, Livia also woke up, screaming. Still affixed to the headboard by the arrow, the intended assassin slumped over, but the arrow still pinned her to the headboard, preventing her from collapsing to the ground.

Marcellinus rushed to her side. It was Julia, the children's tutor. "Julia? Why?"

She struggled to speak, "They'll kill my brother! I didn't want to do it! They'll kill my brother!"

"Who? Who is going to kill your brother?"

Attempting to lift her hand to point toward the princes' room, but failing miserably, she uttered her final words "The boys! Help the boys! There's still time."

The centurion pleaded, "How long do I have?" but Julia, still in an upright, but slouched position, was dead.

In tears, a confused Faustula looked from Julia to Marcellinus. Livia, still crying, kicked and punched the air. Faustula, after a long moment, left her bed and picked up the wailing infant. Holding the whimpering child, "Why did you hurt Julia? Why?"

"Because she was trying to hurt you."

"But why?"

Marcellinus was just as puzzled as Faustula. "I don't know." Then he remembered what Julia said about the boys. "There's no time to explain. You're still in danger and your brothers are too. I'm going to help them now. Where's a safe place for the two of you?"

Faustula quickly composed herself and, speaking calmly and deliberately, "My mother's chamber. They won't go there because she's gone." She pointed to another corridor leading from the room. "That hallway goes directly there. All our rooms have corridors leading to Mother's."

"Perfect! Go there, but hide when you get there. I don't want to take any chances." Then, looking at the weeping infant, he pleaded, "Can you get her back to sleep?"

"I think so," the princess replied.

"Good. Wait in your mother's chamber until Vaballathus or I come for you."

Faustula nodded her head and helped Marcellinus wrap a blanket around herself and Livia. She entered the corridor to her mother's chamber, calming the sobbing infant as she moved. "There, there, Livia. It'll be all right."

Noting how quickly she adapted to the situation and steadied her nerves, Marcellinus commented, "You know, you are a lot like your mother."

Faustula turned and smiled before she disappeared into the corridor. Marcellinus removed the arrow that held Julia's body in place, lowered her and then gently push her lifeless body under the bed.

Soon he emerged into the princes' foyer. He could have followed Faustula and Livia into Zenobia's bedchamber and then entered the young princes' chamber from that corridor, but he didn't want to lead any remaining assassins in that direction should he fail to stop them. He crossed the foyer and peered inside the room. They were both sleeping together in an unusually large bed.

Walking to Timolaus' side of the bed, he put one hand over the boy's mouth and shook him gently with the other hand. Timolaus's eyes opened wide when he saw Marcellinus. The Roman put his finger to his lips to signal the prince to be quiet. The boy nodded and Marcellinus uncovered the boy's mouth. Walking around the enormous bed, he repeated the process with Antiochus. The boys both sat up and, speaking in a whisper, Marcellinus pointed to a corridor. "Does that corridor go to your mother's room?"

Timolaus nodded his head in confirmation.

"We're all in danger. I want you to be very brave and go to your mother's room. Your sisters are hiding there. I want you to hide with them and wait until Vaballathus or I come to get you. Do you understand?"

"I want to stay and fight with you! I'm almost ten. I can fight like a man!" Timolaus pleaded.

Marcellinus countered, "I need you to protect your sisters. You're the only other man here. If they get by Vaba and me, it will be up to you. Can I count on you?"

Timolaus straightened, "You sure can!"

Marcellinus gave a blanket to Timolaus for the two boys and one of his small daggers. "Use this dagger only if you must."

Timolaus looked at the weapon with awe. Then, attempting to assume a soldier's attitude, "You can count on me." Turning, he led Antiochus to his mother's room, speaking to his younger brother as they entered the corridor. "Come, Antiochus. We must protect the princesses."

The pair was soon out of sight. Marcellinus arranged the blankets to make it look as if the boys were still sleeping. Then, as he stood behind the bedchamber's partially open door, he heard footsteps and muffled voices in the foyer. He quietly drew his sword. A man in the uniform of a palace guard entered, then another. Marcellinus saw still another man in the foyer through the slits between the door hinges. The first two to enter divided and crept to each side of the bed.

Stepping from behind the door, Marcellinus raised his sword to shoulder level and swung it at the third assassin entering the room, decapitating him instantly. The other two, initially startled, looked at him, but it was too late for one. Swinging his extended sword in reverse, Marcellinus stepped forward and also decapitated the man on the side of the bed closest to him.

The remaining assassin, still looking at Marcellinus, slashed down at the forms under the blanket on the bed. Then, realizing that he'd been deceived, he stepped back from the bed and prepared to fight. Going to the foot of the bed, he approached Marcellinus. Initially they circled each other with their swords outstretched, but after a long moment, Marcellinus lunged at what he believed to be the final assassin, continually slashing and hacking at the man. Before long his fury and skill overcame the man and he too fell, joining his companions in death.

But there was no time to rest. Marcellinus turned to see

four more men entering the foyer of the prince's chamber.

"Damn!"

He rushed to close the bedroom door as the four new intruders raced forward to stop him. Just as it is about to close, one of the assassins was able to get his right shoulder, arm and sword through the opening and all four men began to push against the partially closed door. Trying to hold the door shut with most of his weight, Marcellinus mustered as much strength as he could and slashed down at the man's arm that had protruded through the door opening.

The man howled as his arm was severed from his body. He pulled back and slowly slumped to the floor of the foyer. Two of the assailants increased their force against the door and the third began to hurl his body against it at intervals.

The opening began to widen as the third man continued his body blows against the door. Realizing the futility of his efforts, Marcellinus timed the thrusts and, just as the final lunge made contact with the door, he abruptly stepped back, allowing the door to swing wide open. Two of the three assassins fell forward. He slew the man falling closest to him instantly, but his fatal thrust brought him virtually to a kneeling position. As he pulled his sword back to strike again, he looked up to see another looming over him, his sword about to bear downward upon him.

However, before the man was able to strike, an arrow pierced his neck. The man gave out a gurgling noise and fell on top of Marcellinus. Quickly pushing the corpse off of his body, Marcellinus looked to see Zabbai, bow in hand, having shot the arrow that saved his life. Zabbai and Vaballathus rushed into the room and joined Marcellinus in surrounding the last intruder.

"I want him alive!" the centurion exclaimed.

Suddenly the man drew a dagger and slashed his own throat. Blood spattered on all three men.

A frustrated Marcellinus bellowed, "Damn him to Hades! We needed him alive!"

Zabbai looked into the foyer at the one-armed man lying on the ground, bleeding to death. "The one in the hallway is still breathing!"

They all surrounded the wounded assassin in the foyer. "He must get help as quickly as possible. Our men should be here shortly. They can take him to the healer."

In a few moments, four Palmyrene soldiers came running in. Zabbai instructed them, "We want this one alive. Take him to the healer. And be careful with him."

Two of the men nodded, picked up the wounded man and carried him away. Zabbai, Marcellinus and Vaballathus reentered the bedchamber and examined the body of the man killed by Zabbai's arrow. Vaballathus puzzled, "Barub?"

"The captain of the guards," Zabbai added.

Marcellinus thought out loud, "That explains the absence of the guards."

"Were there others?" Zabbai queried.

"I think we have them all." Then, pointing to Vaballathus, the Roman added, "They were probably sent to kill you and your brothers while Julia killed your sisters."

Vaballathus was incredulous. "Julia? But why?"

"She said something about them killing her brother, but before she died she warned me about the threat to your brothers."

Vaballathus looked sullen.

"I think that we have everyone but the man who sent them," Zabbai reflected.

"Perhaps our one-armed survivor may help us." Marcellinus paused and then, "We need to insure that he's well-guarded!"

"Of course! And we'll also need to keep the children guarded until Odenathus returns," Zabbai added.

"I'll take care of the children. Just make sure that the guards on that prisoner are trustworthy. Then get some sleep." Then, after further reflection he added, "And thanks for saving my life!"

Leaving the foyer and, with his back to Marcellinus, Zabbai held up his right hand to acknowledge the comment and kept walking.

Marcellinus put his arm over Vaballathus's shoulder as they entered the corridor leading to Zenobia's bedchamber. "Because of your speed, your brothers, sisters, and I are still alive. Thank you too, my friend, for saving all of our lives."

✦

Early the following evening, Zenobia entered the gates of Palmyra. All along her return route she had vacillated between sudden torrents of tears and then a stiffening, almost eerie calm. She was accompanied by ten Royal Palmyrene Guards and the two messengers that had been sent by Zabbai late the evening before. She now appeared tired, sullen, but apprehensive. Several hours earlier, Zabbai's messengers had informed her regarding the attempt on her children's lives.

Just inside the gates, a bowing Zabbai greeted her. "Where are Kings Odenathus and Herodes, My Queen?"

Appearing distracted, she responded, her voice trembling, "Both he and Herodes have been murdered."

Zabbai lowered his head, saying nothing. There were soldiers everywhere.

"Where are the children?" she inquired.

"They are in your bedchamber, My Lady. Marcellinus is with them also. He has not left their side since the attacks."

In Zenobia's bedchamber Marcellinus paced the room. All the corridors but the main one had been barricaded. Four guards stood in the foyer. Faustula sat, fast asleep on her mother's bed. Timolaus and Antiochus slept on either side of her with their heads on her lap. Vaballathus slept in a large cushioned chair. Livia was peacefully asleep in her cradle.

A soldier approached, said something to the guards and entered Zenobia's bedchamber where Marcellinus waited. "Well?"

"The man is dead, Sir."

"Damn!" Marcellinus put his hand to his forehead in frustration. Then... "Thank you."

Zenobia entered the foyer and rushed to Marcellinus. They embraced; she buried her head into his chest and began to weep.

"They're fine. They've just fallen asleep."

"You don't understand. Odenathus and Herodes…they're both dead!" She tightened her embrace.

Marcellinus was stunned. "How? Who?"

"Maeonius - because of an old grudge. I think that he actually thought that he would be made king after committing the murders."

Marcellinus reflected, "I don't know. I can't believe what took place here was all because of an old grudge."

Zenobia, after a thoughtful pause, looked up into his eyes, "Thank you so much for saving the children!"

"I had help from Vaballathus and Zabbai." There was a quiet pause as their eyes met. Marcellinus stepped away from the embrace and held both of her hands. "Odenathus was a good man and a great king."

Zenobia straightened up. "The finest."

Wiping her tears, she glanced at the sleeping children. "My mother told me never to wake a sleeping child. But just this once, I'm not going to heed her advice." She approached the children, speaking softly. "Children! Children! Wake up! Wake up!"

V.

ZENOBIA'S ORIGINS

The woman that Zenobia referred to as her mother was not her biological mother. Her natural mother, Nefira, died giving birth in the house of Hairan, Odenathus' father.

When Nefira was 6 years old, she was captured in a raid just outside the North African Roman province of Numidia[7] and sold as a slave to a Roman merchant that was based in the town of Maxula, just south of the once prosperous and powerful city of Karthago *(Carthage)*.

The merchant, appreciating her beauty, even at such a tender age, kept her as a household servant for several years. However, even before she reached the age of ten, he began to note Nefira's quick wit and proficiency with numbers. Little by little, Nefira began to accompany the merchant on business trips, assisting him in keeping track of his inventory, as well as his profits. And, since the merchant's wife always remained at home at their villa in Maxula during his often-lengthy-and-sometimes-arduous business trips, before Nefira's thirteenth birthday, the merchant began to satisfy his sexual lust on the now blossoming beauty.

At 14, Nefira became pregnant. The merchant, aware of her situation, was determined to sell her while on a business trip to Aegyptus *(Egypt)*. Since Nefira was only 4 months into her pregnancy at the time, the merchant determined that he would be able to fetch a better price for her before she began to prominently display her condition. In Alexandria, he sold her to an emissary of Hairan, Odenathus' father, a prominent member of an aristocratic Palmyrene family. Hairan had sent his emissary, Habob, to Alexandria, the famous center of knowledge and learning, to acquire copies of certain manuscripts. Habob, not being told that Nefira was with child, intended to keep the flourishing beauty for himself. However, upon his return, Hairan, also noting the girl's great beauty, assumed that Habob had acquired Nefira on his behalf. Habob, not wishing to incur the displeasure of Hairan, agreed that he had indeed acquired the girl for his employer, but told him that he had paid double what he had actually paid for the girl. Hairan readily paid the inflated price.

Nefira was added to Hairan's household. However, soon after her arrival, he was informed by his wife that the girl was pregnant. And, under his wife's now-watchful eyes, Nefira remained untouched for the remainder of her pregnancy.

Nefira died soon after giving birth to her daughter due to some complications that were never quite known. The newborn was promptly named Bat-Zabbai, which in native Palmyrene (Syriac) means "daughter of Zabbai", but how it was determined that the father's name was Zabbai, was never explained. It was later conjectured that Zabbai, *(Not to be confused with General Zabbai),* a servant in Hairan's household, was designated by all in the household to be the conceiver of Nefira's daughter. In the common Greek dialect, Koine, her name was translated as Zenobia. Hairan's wife, having no real interest in the newborn, put her under the care of Sara, a tutor employed by several of Palmyra's elite families to educate their young. Sara was provided a small monthly allowance for the child's support. Thereafter, Zenobia was seldom visited by either Hairan or his wife. Sara, a gentle and loving woman, became Zenobia's surrogate mother.

Odenathus was seventeen at the time of Zenobia's birth. Sara had tutored the lad in his youth, but had not done so since his marriage at age fifteen. The objective of Odenathus's marriage to his first wife, Surah, was to consolidate power with that of another aristocratic Palmyrene family. However, with the passing of time, although the marriage had been an arranged one, Odenathus and Surah soon fell deeply in love with one another – an unexpected and unusual outcome of the marriage pact. In the second year of their marriage, Surah bore Odenathus a son, Herodes, but she died shortly after giving him birth. Odenathus was devastated. He found his only solace in his newborn son. Initially, he would spend hours playing with the boy, often ignoring other pressing duties.

After what Hairan considered a sufficient time of mourning had elapsed, he spoke to his son and convinced him to allow Sara to care for the boy during the daytime hours, allowing Odenathus to take care of his obligations as a leading member - and potential future leader - of Palmyra. Odenathus was fond of his former tutor, the gentle, soft-spoken Sara, and, also realizing the benefit of her tutoring skills, reluctantly, but wisely agreed to the arrangement. In addition, when in the field on military service, Herodes would stay with Sara until Odenathus's return.

When not on military service, every morning, after a modest meal, Odenathus would walk the boy to Sara's simple dwelling about half a mile from the palace. When he did so, he would see the angelic looking young toddler that Sara claimed to be her daughter. Odenathus knew that Bat-Zabbai (Zenobia) was born in the palace within months of Herodes's own birth and that his mother had placed her with Sara, but never raised the issue of Zenobia's maternity with Sara.

✦

Sara had been born and raised in a family of scholars in Alexandria, Aegyptus *(Egypt)*. Even though it was not common practice to educate women at that time, she received an excellent education in the sciences and the arts from both of her parents. She was also schooled in the Greek (koine), Latin and Syriac languages, as well as several Coptic (Egyptian) and Persian dialects.

At the tender age of sixteen, she had fallen in love with a visiting Roman soldier, ten years her senior. He was enroute to join a Roman force headed for the Persian border, but promised to take her to Rome at the end of his service if she would come with him to the East. Against strong opposition from both parents, she slipped away with him in the early morning hours one day. He had lodged her in Palmyra, leaving some funds for her support, vowing to return at the end of the military campaign and take her to Rome. He never returned. She never discovered whether he was killed in action or just lost interest in her. She waited in vain for almost a year. Then, with her funds exhausted, and too humiliated to return home, she began to tutor some children of Palmyra's elite. With the excellent training that had been supplied by her parents, she soon had enough pupils to provide for her support.

Sara had modest ambitions, at least from a monetary point of view. With the small monthly stipend she received for Zenobia's care and the more-than-ample fee she received for Herodes, she soon felt she had no need to further supplement her income. Therefore, she dismissed all of her other students and was able to concentrate all of her love and skills on the pair. Sara now felt complete. And soon Herodes and Zenobia became as brother and sister.

✦

Odenathus was quite unusual for a noble male of that time. He loved children. And since his son, Herodes and Zenobia were so close, he would often take the pair on walks, or to events that were being staged near the marketplace by Palmyrene artists to entertain the children of the city.

As Zenobia grew into her teens, increasing in both beauty and wisdom, Odenathus became ever more enamored with her, in ways considerably distinct from those he originally felt for her as just the companion of his son. Shortly after Odenathus's elevation as king, Sara died peacefully in her sleep. After a period of profound mourning, Zenobia was eventually convinced to move into the palace. And, even though he was almost two decades her senior, it wasn't long before Odenathus asked for her hand in marriage. Herodes, although initially taken aback at his father's proposal, soon warmed to the idea that Zenobia would be part of the household.

VI.

ZENOBIA AS REGENT

Two days after the assassinations and attempts on the royal children, Zenobia and Vaballathus sat in the throne room. Babai, a Palmyrene senator, entered. He walked to within three meters of the royal pair and bowed.

"Your Excellencies, the Senate has confirmed Prince Vaballathus as King of Palmyra and all its dominions, with his most valiant and noble mother, Queen Zenobia, as his regent until he reaches his eighteenth year."

"Eighteen?!" Vaballathus objected.

Zenobia smiled and placed her hand quickly, but gently on Vaballathus' hand, which rested on the arm of his throne. "Thank you, Babai. We will do our best to deserve the confidence of the Senate and the people of Palmyra. Please send word to Emperor Gallienus of the Senate's decision."

"It will be done, My Queen." The senator bowed, turned and departed.

Vaballathus remained incredulous. "Eighteen? That's six

whole years from now! Herodes became joint king with father when he was sixteen!"

"Your father was alive then. People weren't really acknowledging Herodes as ruler, but more as your father's successor." Then, after a pause, she pleaded, "Please be patient, my son. You have many glorious years as king ahead of you and you will prove your valor and skill when you join us in our next offensive against Sapor."

This last line appeared to appease Vaballathus.

A herald appeared. "Lord Verodes requests an audience, My Queen."

"Most certainly."

As the herald left, Verodes entered, bowing low.

"Most Noble Rulers, it appears that Barub was the chief author of the assassination plot."

Zenobia reflected, "Barub? He was a capable officer, but did he have the means to plan such a thing?" Then, pausing, "Yet, if I could only believe that he was, it would make me feel much safer that the instigator of all this heinous mischief is no longer with us."

"Written evidence, in Barub's hand, was found in the homes of all of the conspirators." Verodes held out the papyrus documents. A guard stepped forward, took the documents, and handed them to Zenobia. She briefly examined them as Verodes continued. "It appears that Barub was a descendant of a former ruler of Palmyra. Odenathus's grandfather, Vaballathus Nasor, was responsible for his removal from the throne.

Zenobia handed the documents to Vaballathus.

"Both Barub and his father had sworn an oath to regain the title and Barub finally acted on that oath. Barub was often seen in the company of Maeonius, according to witnesses."

For the first time in days, Zenobia appeared relieved. "Well, that explains much. I am thankful for your diligence, Verodes." Vaballathus returned the documents to Verodes.

"My sole desire is to assist the Queen Mother and the son of the most noble Odenathus!" He bowed at the waist and walked backwards out of the room.

Verodes emerged from the throne room into a corridor just outside, where a waiting Apsaeus joined him. They didn't speak until the door closed behind them.

"Did she believe it?" whispered Apsaeus.

"Of course. I'm her faithful argapet. She only glanced at the documents. Her trust in me may perhaps be her only flaw. But it will be a fatal one, I assure you."

"So we've stopped any inquiry that may lead to us, but how do we gain control now?"

"The guard on the Royal Family will surely be much more diligent in their tasks for quite some time. We must once again be patient and await another opportunity." After a pause, Verodes continued, "Besides, she's only a woman. How long can she rule this city?"

"What about Julia's brother? Where is he?"

"He was killed as soon as we took him. I didn't want to tie up a man guarding him." Verodes affected a sinister smile as he began to walk down the corridor toward the exit.

Apsaeus now strode beside him. "So everyone that could have implicated us to the assassinations is dead?"

"Precisely, my son."

They both exited the hallway.

VII.

NORTHERN ITALY - GALLIENUS' COURT MARCH, 267 C.E.

Several months later, Valerian's son and co-emperor, Gallienus, sat on a marble throne at one of his many far-flung palaces. Since Valerian's demise at the hands of the Persian King, Sapor, Gallienus had become sole emperor of Rome.

Although in his late 40s, Gallienus was still powerfully built, displaying a soldier's appearance in every sense of the word. His elevation as sole emperor had not softened his lifestyle or his demeanor. With auburn hair that was beginning to gray at its extremities, he was barefaced, but with the trace of a beard under his jaws and chin, which was somewhat the fashion at the time.

Numerous senators, other nobility and courtiers were seated around the room. While speaking to General Heraclianus and a few advisors, Gallienus was interrupted as a young herald entered the hall. Stopping just before the steps leading up to the dais, the herald announced, "Most August Gallienus, a messenger has arrived from

Palmyra." Gallienus looked up and, speaking loud enough for all to hear, "Certainly! King Odenathus of Palmyra is our most valiant ally."

The herald modified the emperor's remark, "My Emperor, the messenger is from Vaballathus, King of Palmyra and Zenobia, Queen Mother and Regent."

Everyone in the room exchanged puzzled glances. A buzz of murmuring voices filled the room. The messenger from Palmyra entered and genuflected. "Most noble Gallienus, I bear news of the murder of Kings Odenathus and Herodes, his son and heir."

Gallienus appeared genuinely distraught. "This is dreadful news. Dreadful news for all of Rome. Kings Odenathus and Herodes were our most trusted comrades. How did this happen?"

"A captain of the palace guards initiated the plot. Odenathus and Herodes were its victims. However, the lives of the remaining members of the Royal Family were saved by the Roman officer, Marcellinus."

"Ah! Marcellinus. How fortunate for the citizens of Palmyra that Rome sent such a capable emissary to assist them," Gallienus crowed.

The messenger continued, "Odenathus's titles have now been conferred on his heir, Vaballathus, to be guided by his mother, Queen Zenobia, as regent." Gallienus, puzzled, turned to his attendants and advisors, "A *woman* as regent in such a volatile area?"

"Queen Zenobia, the Palmyrene Senate and the citizens of Palmyra, therefore, announce the accession of Vaballathus, King of Kings." As the messenger continued, Gallienus's face reddened. "Senator of Rome, Honorary Consul, Roman Duke, Vice-Regent of the East."

The last title stirred Gallienus into action. He spoke slowly at first, but his speech gathered momentum. "Please convey to the people of Palmyra and the widow Zenobia our condolences for the deaths of the most noble and valiant Kings, Odenathus and Herodes." He paused, and then, "Also inform them that we recognize the boy Vaballathus as King of Palmyra and will monitor, with some apprehension, the regency of that youth under his mother's guidance." Then after another pause, "But also tell your new king and his regent mother that Odenathus's and Herodes's Roman titles died with them. It is not for the citizens of Palmyra, their senate, or their queen to confer them upon anyone. They were given to Rome's loyal and *proven* allies."

"But these titles have been justly earned by Odenathus, Palmyra's former king. Is it not right to bequeath them to his son and heir?"

Gallienus stood up, furious. "SILENCE! Go and tell your

King and Queen Regent the words that I have spoken and keep your insolent opinions to yourself!"

Then, pausing, in a more controlled voice, "Tell Queen Regent, Zenobia, and King Vaballathus that all Rome grieves to hear the news of King Odenathus's and King Herodes's deaths. Give them our best wishes for success and tell them that their continued assistance on our Eastern Borders will be greatly appreciated. Regarding the boy's Roman titles, we will defer rendering any decision for now."

The Palmyrene messenger bowed, and somewhat uneasily, replied "As you wish, Emperor Gallienus." Gallienus nodded and the messenger straightened, turned and left the hall. Another buzz of chatter escalated as he departed.

Gallienus turned to General Heraclianus and, in a low voice, whispered "We may have left these Palmyrenes on their own for too long. They may need the benefit of Rome's enlightened supervision."

Now assuming a more moderate tone, "You are to accompany me at once. I go east to meet the Heruli. I'm going to give you as large a force as I can spare to take to Palmyra. We'll say that your mission is to campaign against Sapor, but I really want you to make sure that this woman and her...child...realize just who *is* in control. Tell them that they may join your expedition under *your* authority. If they give you any trouble you may need to give them a reminder to let them know who's in charge."

General Heraclianus wavered, "My Emperor, they say this woman is a great strategist and an equally great warrior. Marcellinus's dispatches confirm this."

Gallienus retorted, "He also says that she is very beautiful. Perhaps his judgment is somewhat clouded."

Then he looked firmly at the general. "My good Heraclianus, in all of your experience, have you ever met a woman that was capable of doing what they say about this Zenobia? Do you actually believe that a *woman* may be a better general than a *man*?"

Haltingly Heraclianus replied, "Of course not."

"Very well then…For the time being *you* will be in charge in the East. We will see how the boy measures up to his father. If he does, we'll leave him in control of the area *after* he comes of age. But under no circumstances are you to leave this woman in control. Now go and prepare for departure. We leave in two days."

Heraclianus had achieved his position as general by political and family ties, and not through success in any major military engagements. The few martial actions that involved him would be better classified as skirmishes than battles, and the actual fighting in those skirmishes had been conducted by two capable subordinates that were both now fighting in the western provinces of the empire.

Heraclianus was in his early fifties, roughly three years older than Gallienus. However, while there was little difference in their age, in many ways Heraclianus was the exact antithesis of Gallienus. He generally avoided any sudden outbursts or threats, except when they might place him in a more favorable light with those of his superiors. He was about three centimeters taller than Gallienus and slightly more muscular. However, his broadening midsection displayed some of the ill effects of the self-indulgences and decadence found rampant in Roman nightlife at that time. He was balding on the crown of his head and his blackish hair was rapidly turning gray. He was now, and had been for several years, beardless, due to its swift transformation to gray.

"Should we inform Marcellinus of our intentions?"

Gallienus was quick to respond. "No! It is obvious from his dispatches that he has become too close to the Royal Family. You can inform him later, in person."

"As you wish, My Emperor." Heraclianus, a better courtier than a general, was still uneasy with his instructions. He bowed, turned, and departed.

✦

The next afternoon, as Heraclianus prepared for his departure with Gallienus, Marcellinus, Zenobia and all her children but Livia were in the palace garden.

The garden was Zenobia's favorite place to relax and, after Odenathus' death also became her favorite location to spend time with her children. It was accessed by a corridor exiting the Great Hall and was centered by a long portico which had been extended as a colonnade that traveled more than thirty meters to an exterior gate. Various flowering vines scrambled up each column in the colonnade, crossing the overhead beam until they joined their sister vines that had scurried up the column's partner on the other side of the walkway. Benches were situated along the walkway, between each column.

Two uncluttered spaces, each containing an open flowery meadow, punctuated only by an occasional citrus tree, extended twenty meters on either side of the colonnade. The entire garden was bordered by two stone fences that began at the palace walls on either side of the colonnade, bordered each meadow, turned and met at the exterior gate at the end of the colonnade.

That afternoon, Timolaus, with great difficulty, was attempting to perform one of Marcellinus's magic tricks. After his third unsuccessful attempt resulted in failure, the boy's embarrassment increased as his small audience snickered and attempted to stifle their laughter.

Attempting to console the prince, Marcellinus recalled, "The first time I tried that trick I was dining with some of the chief priests of Jupiter. I was so bad that I almost injured one of them. So they said they would offer sacrifices to the god on my behalf if I'd agree never to show them any more magic."

"Really?" Faustula innocently inquired.

"Would I lie?"

Laughing and in unison, Zenobia and all the children replied, "Yes!"

As Marcellinus joined in their laughter, Zenobia looked thoughtfully and smiled at him. She was falling in love, or perhaps her long-suppressed love for him was finally surfacing. Marcellinus was unaware of her gaze. She awakened from her reverie as a page entered.

"Most Royal Majesties … A messenger has arrived from the eastern frontier."

Zenobia stood, "Please let him enter."

The page bowed and left the room. Zenobia turned to the children. "Children, please go and prepare for dinner."

Timolaus pouted. "Why does Vaballathus get to stay?"

"Because he's King now, and he's also older than you. The time will come for you to risk your life for Palmyra."

The younger prince turned and gloomily joined the other children as they left the garden.

The messenger entered and bowed low. "My King and Queen Mother, Sapor has crossed the Euphrates with a large force."

Marcellinus and Zenobia exchanged anxious glances.

Zenobia was puzzled. "At this time of the year?"

"He has sent word that he wishes to parley."

Marcellinus interjected, "Then why has he brought his army with him?"

"Because he's no fool," Zenobia whispered to Marcellinus.

"If we intend to parley with him, we're going with our own forces as well" Marcellinus countered.

Zenobia sighed, "I hate to leave the children so soon."

"Well we must go and meet him, whether we choose to parley or not," was the centurion's only response.

"You stay here. Marcellinus and I will go," Vaballathus

offered.

The Queen Mother pined. "The day will come when I'll be able to accept that offer, but not quite yet." Then, turning to the messenger, "Thank you for bringing us this information."

"I'd like to speak with this man regarding the size and composition of Sapor's forces."

"That is an excellent idea, My King." Zenobia said, attempting to placate the youth.

Vaballathus turned to leave with the messenger, but abruptly turned and rushed back to his mother. Whispering in Zenobia's ear, he asked, "What exactly is a parley?"

Maintaining a solemn demeanor behind suppressed laughter, she whispered, "It's where enemies meet to talk."

Without uttering a word, he turned back to the messenger, "I need details regarding Sapor's forces. How much cavalry and infantry does he have? Be as specific as possible."

The young king left with the messenger and Zenobia and Marcellinus were now alone. "It may be because I'm getting older, but now my fondest wish would be to rid myself of my duties and enjoy more time with my family."

She paused. "I long to find a place where I could raise and educate my children and not worry about training them to be warriors, kings or queens."

Marcellinus smiled. "Maybe someday that won't be such an impossible dream after all." They looked at each other, and, for a moment, it appeared that they might embrace, but he restrained the urge and added, "Let's go to dinner. The children are waiting."

In the five years since Marcellinus had met Zenobia, very little had changed in her physical features. Her soft, wavy, jet-black hair even now crowned her stunning features. However, it was now longer, to the extent that it frequently rested on her right shoulder. Her rich, deep brown eyes were still shaded by long dark lashes. And even though she was now approaching her thirtieth year and had borne a total of 5 children, she had only increased in beauty, at least in Marcellinus' eyes.

Marcellinus had also aged. He was now approaching forty, but, with the exception of a few gray hairs on his temples, little had changed in his appearance either. A few years earlier he had attempted a beard, but, noticing that all of his developing facial hair was gray, he aborted the effort and his face resumed the same bare appearance as it had when Zenobia first met him.

✦

Zenobia, Marcellinus, and Vaballathus prepared to leave the following morning. Vaballathus unsuccessfully tried to conceal his pleasure that he was going, while Timolaus was equally unsuccessful at concealing his displeasure that he was not.

A page approached and bowed. "Cassius Longinus has arrived, Queen Mother."

Zenobia enthusiastically replied, "Please direct him here at once."

The page bowed again and left. Antiochus mumbled something and Marcellinus laughed as Zenobia tried to calm Timolaus. As they spoke, a cherub-faced man with a long, white beard in his late fifties and of middling height approached. He bowed slightly, but reverently. "Alas, to finally meet the most noble King Vaballathus and his famous mother, Queen Zenobia."

"You have quite a reputation yourself among the learned, Cassius Longinus. It is also *our* honor to meet *you*." the Queen Mother replied. Then, she directed her right hand at each individual as she introduced them. "This is our Roman friend, Marcellinus, my sons, King Vaballathus and his brothers, Timolaus and Antiochus. And these are my daughters: Faustula and Livia." Each child bowed as they were introduced. "Children, this is Cassius Longinus. He's a Syrian, but he has taught at the Academy in Athens for quite some time. Hopefully, some of you will attend the Academy one day."

Longinus bowed to the entire party, "I'm honored to meet you all."

"Vaballathus must depart with Marcellinus and me just now, but the other children eagerly await your enlightened instruction." She gave a sidelong glance at Timolaus as she said "eagerly". "So will I when we return."

Noticing the regret on Timolaus' s face, the sage spoke, "Prince Timolaus, one day, when you join your older brother in battle, will you advise him to use the battle strategies employed by the Great Alexander, or the Carthaginian, Hannibal Barca, or, perhaps those of the Roman that defeated him, Scipio Africanus?"

A puzzled Timolaus haltingly queried, "Their stra-tuh-geez?"

Longinus explained, "Their battle plans: where they attacked, how they attacked, and why they attacked - how they became great generals."

Timolaus, now picking up speed, stammered, "But I don't know what their stra-tuh-geez were. And, the last two generals, I never even heard of them."

"Well, we'd better get started then…" the tutor countered, "…if you want to become a great general and help your brother conquer Persia someday."

At first the prince paused thoughtfully, almost in a daydream, but then eagerly responded, "Yes, we had better get started! Let's go!"

Longinus smiled, then glanced at Faustula. "Fear not, my child. I'll teach you many other things besides battle tactics."

The princess quickly countered, "I think I'd like to learn their strategies as well. But perhaps you will also teach us the strategies of the great Queen Zenobia?"

Longinus acknowledged his omission. "Yes, I've heard much of your mother's gifts. But I may need your help in that area." Then after a brief pause, "Very well then, shall we get started?"

Under Longinus's spell the children eagerly followed him into the palace.

VIII.

THE MEETING AND PROPOSAL

APRIL, 267 C.E.

Two days later, Zenobia, Marcellinus, Vaballathus, Zabdas, and Zabbai all sat on horseback on a small dune overlooking the Palmyrene and Persian armies. It was the middle of April, but a bit colder than usual and extremely blustery.

In the distance, the Persian army paraded to and fro. A Persian, on horseback, lingered at the bottom of the dune, awaiting a response from the Palmyrene leaders. Zenobia broke the silence. They all continued to stare out at the Persian forces as she spoke. "Do you think we can trust him?"

Marcellinus was quick to respond, "Our forces are almost equal to his and he's not fared so well against us in the past, so if he tries anything, we'll be able to make him pay the consequences."

"I'll go meet with him," Zabbai offered. "There's no reason to risk losing our King or Queen to this treacherous dog and his pig of a son!"

"I am truly touched by your offer, but I do not think that Sapor will be content to meet with you," Zenobia replied. "Either the King or I must go to meet him. So, I will go. Then, if things don't go well, the future of Palmyra will still be secure in Vaballathus."

Vaballathus countered, "Palmyra - and I - would be lost without the wisdom and counsel of its Queen."

"Perhaps, but if one of us must be risked, I am the better choice."

Marcellinus quickly added, "I'll go with you. I'll be no loss to Palmyra."

"The loss of your aid and counsel would be of great consequence to Palmyra, but I accept your offer. You may share my fate." She then called to the Persian soldier below. "Persian! We'll meet your king between our two armies! I agree to his terms."

The soldier rode toward the Persian forces. When he reached Sapor, they saw him speaking to the Persian leader. Sapor then spoke to another guard standing nearby. In a few moments, fifty riders were seen following Sapor and his son, Hormizd.

Zenobia instructed Zabdas and Zabbai, "If you see trouble, attack directly at our meeting place with our whole force." Then to Marcellinus she said, "Let's go."

The two rode down the hill to a small group of men on horseback. Zenobia gave an order and the entire group rode off with her and Marcellinus to meet Sapor.

As they rode, Zenobia turned to Marcellinus and said, almost in a whisper so the others were unable to hear, "It was actually selfish of me to allow you to come, but I just felt that I wanted - or maybe needed - you with me, whatever hand fate may deal to us."

Marcellinus added softly, "Me too."

They arrived at the meeting place between the two armies. Sapor, his son Hormizd, and their escort of fifty Persian cavalrymen were already at the site. Six men from the Persian escort had quickly put up a three-sided tent to keep their leaders out of the cold wind and blinding sun.

Zenobia and Marcellinus dismounted and approached the recently completed shelter. When they reached Sapor there was an awkward silence. After a few moments, Sapor spoke in Persian as his message was translated into Greek Koine by an interpreter standing at his side. "The Supreme Lord of All asks why you do not bow low before him."

"Do we bow before Sapor when we so easily defeat his armies in open battle? Sapor must humble our army before we must bow."

Marcellinus smiled at this remark, but it did not appear to please the interpreter. He translated Zenobia's answer into Persian and Sapor grimaced. He answered in Persian, which was translated once again by the interpreter. "Sapor the Magnificent says that the Great Odenathus led those victories of which you speak. He is told that the Great King of Palmyra is no more. Does a woman now lead the city of Palmyra or does this Roman lead it? Based upon our past experience with Romans, we should find little difficulty overcoming Palmyra in the future."

Marcellinus disputed, "This _woman_ was responsible for your defeat in the plains of Nisibis and at Carrhae several years ago."

As the interpreter translated Marcellinus's comment, Sapor grew visibly enraged. Zenobia put a hand on Marcellinus's shoulder to silence him. When the interpreter finished, she spoke quickly, not allowing Sapor time to respond. "Odenathus was a great and noble warrior, but Palmyra has many great and noble warriors that still live. If you wish to test us in battle once again, we are ready."

The interpreter finished translating. By this time Sapor had calmed himself. He held up his hand and spoke. "Come…This is foolishness…We have also heard much of Zenobia, the great warrior Queen. We did not come here to argue, but to talk. Let us get out of the sun and this cold wind."

Sapor gestured toward the shelter and then turned and entered, followed by Hormizd and the interpreter. Zenobia and Marcellinus cautiously entered the three-sided tent after the three. Inside a carpet had been laid and four large cushions set upon it. The four leaders sat upon them. Sapor spoke. "Sapor extends his condolences on the death of your husband. He was a valiant warrior."

Zenobia nodded in acceptance and Sapor, through the interpreter, continued, "Sapor has come to suggest the union of our two great nations through marriage."

"Palmyra is already an ally of Rome!" Marcellinus interrupted. Even before the interpreter finished translating, Sapor began to laugh scornfully and continued laughing after the interpreter finished. Sapor spoke again and Hormizd began to laugh as soon as his father finished speaking. The interpreter spoke, "Your presence here has been permitted, Roman, as a courtesy to Queen Zenobia. Do not venture to speak any further or we may change our mind."

Zenobia did not appear to be listening, but when the interpreter finished, she placed her hand on Marcellinus's arm to silence him and spoke quickly, "I am interested in your proposal, but my daughter is too young to marry your son."

When the interpreter finished, Sapor gave a light-hearted chuckle. He spoke while gesturing to his son at his side.

The interpreter again translated Sapor's words. "I do not suggest a marriage between my son and your daughter; I suggest a marriage between my son and _you_."

This final statement stunned both Marcellinus and Zenobia. Sapor looked over at his son and then leaned closer to speak to Zenobia. "I will speak to you in the Greek tongue because my son never bothered to learn it. I do not wish to embarrass him. He is a good boy and very eager. He needs a good woman, such as you, to guide him. With you as his wife, he will do well. I do not have many years left in this life."

As soon as he started speaking, Hormizd nervously looked from his father, to Zenobia, to Marcellinus, and then to the interpreter who instinctively knew not to translate his father's words for him.

Zenobia glanced at a confused looking Hormizd. His father called him a boy, but he appeared to be approaching his forties and somewhat obese. He had a short pointed beard, which aimed upward, as it rested on a fold of his enormous double chin.

After Sapor finished his proposal, Marcellinus looked directly at him, using every ounce of will to stay calm. Zenobia, sensing his rage, grasped his arm firmly. She turned and spoke directly to Sapor. "I will consider your proposal, but you must realize that I'm still in mourning and it's yet too soon for me to make any such plans. It would be disrespectful for me to do so."

"Of course." the Persian King quickly replied. "I only suggest this for your future consideration. With you as his wife, Hormizd would finally put an end to the aged and tottering Roman Empire." As he finished, Sapor looked directly at Marcellinus, but his gaze was not returned. Zenobia rose from her cushion and Marcellinus followed her lead.

"Then we may consider you a friend in the future and need not wage war on our borders? Perhaps Hormizd might concentrate his efforts in the East until we meet again?" Zenobia was proving herself to be a master diplomat as well as a battle strategist.

"Certainly!" and, continuing to speak in the Greek dialect, Koine, "May I say that what I've heard of your beauty and wisdom does not do you justice. You far exceed even the most flattering accounts that I've heard. Were I just a little younger, I would ask you to be *my* wife and not my son's."

Zenobia forced a smile. "You are much too kind, Most Noble Sapor."

As Zenobia and Marcellinus turned to exit, Sapor called out, "I wouldn't bring the Roman to our next meeting. It may prove fatal for him."

Marcellinus, exiting the shelter, started to turn, but Zenobia gently stopped him and steered him out of the tent.

They mounted their horses and galloped off, followed by their escort. The ride back to their own forces was in complete silence, save for the sound of the horses' hooves.

Marcellinus and Zenobia dispatched their escort and joined the other leaders. As they turned to face the Persians, Vaballathus maneuvered his horse next to his mother's. They all watched as the Persian leaders left the meeting place.

The Queen Mother turned to Zabbai. "You and Marcellinus stay here and make sure they're headed east. Have a few scouts follow them until they cross the Euphrates. Then join us at the Wiba Oasis."

Zabbai nodded and departed. Marcellinus silently followed him. After watching him briefly, Zenobia turned and departed.

✦

Later that evening, Marcellinus and Zabbai stopped their horses in front of two large tents amid a sea of smaller shelters. One of them was Zenobia's. The other belonged to Vaballathus. Soldiers surrounded both tents. Marcellinus and Zabbai dismounted and entered Zenobia's tent, nodding to the guards as they entered.

Zenobia's tent was furnished as luxuriously as her palace. It was divided into many rooms by elegant tapestries, apparently the same tapestries that adorned the Great Hall of the Palace, demonstrating their utility and the practicality of the Palmyrenes, Marcellinus noted. There were also silk draperies suspended from lines running between the support beams that held up the entire structure. The pair went through two partitions and entered the main compartment.

Zenobia and Vaballathus were at the far end, eating a late evening meal. Three meters to their left, along the wall, was a large bed with a canopy. To their right was a desk for writing with papyrus papers and writing slates strewn about it. Some containers, such as trunks used to carry many of the items and clothing seen in the tent, were placed throughout the room, mainly along the makeshift walls. Zenobia looked up at the late arrivals. "Well?"

General Zabbai spoke. "We watched them leave for over two hours. They're definitely headed east."

"Good. We'll stay here until the scouts return. Zabbai, you must be hungry. A meal awaits you in your tent." Then to her son and the attendants, "Now, I wish to speak to Marcellinus alone." Everyone, including Vaballathus began to leave the tent. Before leaving, the maidservants extinguished all but one of the brightly lit lamps that illuminated Zenobia's chamber.

Vaballathus, yawning as he departed the main compartment said sleepily, "Good night, Marcellinus".

"Good night, My King."

Once all were gone, Zenobia rose and faced Marcellinus. She was wearing the same modest long white tunic that normally graced her appearance in the early evening hours. However, as always since he had met her, even in such simplistic and unpretentious attire, her beauty was incredible to him And now, after their experience earlier that day, almost too much for him to bear.

"During our meeting with Sapor you showed as much self-control as a five year old."

"If he said the same things about Palmyra as he did about Rome, how would you have reacted?" Marcellinus rebutted.

"I would have remained calm if I knew it would benefit my people."

Marcellinus, displaying some ill-concealed jealously, exclaimed, "You're not actually going to marry that overweight, overindulged half-wit, are you?"

"By keeping that possibility open, it won't be necessary to

defend our eastern borders for at least a year. And who's to say that this marriage might not be the best thing for Palmyra?"

"How could marrying that oaf possibly be the best thing for Palmyra? The thought of you with that…"

"You're a Roman! How would you know what's best for Palmyra?"

"Doesn't fighting for Palmyra for the last five years give me an idea of what's best for Palmyra?" He stepped toward her.

"What happens to Palmyra does not affect you!"

"What happens to <u>YOU</u> does!" Marcellinus was too frustrated to speak. He paused, attempted to speak again, but could not. Suddenly, he embraced her and began kissing her passionately.

After a few moments Zenobia halfheartedly pushed him away. She said nothing, gazing at Marcellinus with tearing eyes. Marcellinus stepped toward her again, taking her into his arms.

"I love you … I love your mind, your heart, your big beautiful brown eyes, [He paused to caress her eyes] your lips… [He paused again to kiss her lips]. "I love everything about you. You <u>know</u> this."

Marcellinus suddenly stepped back and away from her.

"But if you don't feel the same for me, I'll understand. Perhaps I should leave."

He looked away with slight embarrassment, breaking Zenobia's stare. Her eyes were now filled with tears. He turned to leave. Without a word, Zenobia stepped back toward Marcellinus wrapped her arms around him and softly kissed him. "You know you really talk too much." She kissed him again. Then she turned and extinguished the last light in the room. Their voices and their forms faded into the darkness.

IX.

ROMANS AT THE FRONTIER

EARLY MAY, 267 C.E.

Still in her night garments, Zenobia leaned against one of the tent's support beams in a dreamlike state, staring into space. A fully dressed Marcellinus walked up behind her and wrapped his arms around her waist. He pressed his cheek against her shoulder as he squeezed her. She reached down, removed his two hands from her waist and turned to face him. They embraced and kissed briefly. She rested her head on his chest.

Zenobia, although gifted with extreme intelligence and an ample supply of martial skills was still very much a woman. Marcellinus was continually amazed how this fierce female warrior would suddenly burst into tears when one of the children would experience some small unpleasant event or mishap, something that was quite trivial in his eyes. However, that was part of her true beauty to him. She was hard when necessary, but suddenly soft when the occasion permitted. Their encounter last night had only reinforced his love for this talented, complex, but extremely gentle woman.

She spoke dreamily. "As a small girl, I was quite unusual."

He snickered. "Oh, really? Who would have guessed?"

She ignored his sarcasm. "I had an unusual amount of athletic ability for a girl. I enjoyed doing what men did and became bored with the tasks normally allotted to women. Herodes encouraged me to train in the martial arts with him. As my skills increased, I also enjoyed beating men in skills they assumed women couldn't do – not entirely displaying superior strength or athletic abilities, but by using my wits as well. Even so, some men, with both sufficient martial skills and enough intellect could overcome my own wits and abilities and defeat me on the practice grounds. Herodes always could and there were some others, but ..."

Marcellinus added, "You are an unusually gifted woman."

She pulled back her head and looked into his eyes. "Am I really? Perhaps more women might also be able to do the same if given the chance."

"They certainly wouldn't be as beautiful."

She rested her head once again on his chest. "I wonder..."

"Wonder what?"

"...if it's possible for someone in my position to live happily with the one she loves."

There was a commotion just outside the entrance to the bedchamber. Marcellinus moved toward the opening.

Almost in a panic, Zenobia exclaimed, "No, wait!"

"I'm just going to see what the problem is."

In a low tone she uttered, "I'll go. Please stay here and out of sight." She moved past a stunned Marcellinus and stepped through the exit to the main chamber. Once outside the opening, but still within the confines of her tent, Zenobia greeted her maidservant, Nalli, accompanied by a messenger. "What is it, Nalli?"

Without waiting for Nalli to respond, the messenger bowed and then spoke in a rushed and excited voice. "My Queen, a Roman force is headed this way."

After a somewhat startled moment, "Thank you for promptly bringing this news to us. You must be tired and hungry." Zenobia turned to Nalli. "Prepare some food and a place to sleep for this man." Both Nalli and the messenger bowed and left the tent. Zenobia stepped beyond the tent entrance and spoke to the two guards stationed just outside. "Wake Generals Zabdas and Zabbai and tell them to come here as soon as possible." The guards nodded and left immediately.

She reentered her bedchamber. Marcellinus had heard everything. He puzzled, "I wasn't informed of any reinforcements."

Zenobia was even more perplexed, "What do you think this means?"

"Maybe they're finally bringing more men as they've promised for years – OR – maybe there's been another change of emperors?"

"Well, I'm not taking any chances. We'll take force to meet force. We'll know their reasons soon enough." Then, after taking a deep breath she spoke, "You'd better go. This is not the time and too soon after Odenathus's death for me to start indulging my passions like some love-struck maiden."

Marcellinus was somewhat stunned. "What do you mean?"

Tenderly, almost on the verge of tears, Zenobia stepped forward and gently embraced him. "I'm a queen and must think of my duty to my sons and my people." Then, after a pause, "I will keep and treasure the last few hours in my heart as long as I breathe. But you and I may not be together, at least not now."

"If not now, when?"

"I don't know, but not now. We must wait. Please don't make this any more difficult." Then, to a sullen Marcellinus she choked, in a whisper, "You were expecting a happy ending? Like that of a child's tale?"

He didn't know what to say. "I…"

"Please make sure no one sees you leave this tent. … Please leave now." Then, after a pause she implored, "Please."

Marcellinus looked up at her, but she only pointed to the exit.

Dejected and sullen, Marcellinus poked his head out of the flaps to her chamber and stepped through to the portion of the tent that functioned as a makeshift foyer. The guards posted just outside the tent remained in place, so Marcellinus pulled a dagger from his belt and slit a hole in the rear of the tent and slipped through the opening he had created.

On a plain about twenty-five kilometers outside Antioch, near the town of Immae (present day Imm, Bab el-Hawa), Marcellinus, Zenobia, Vaballathus, Zabbai, and Zabdas all rode on horseback in front of a large contingent of Palmyrene cavalry. It was early June, 267 C.E. A scout approached and Zabdas raised his hand to stop the entire Palmyrene force.

The scout announced, "They're entering the plain about three kilometers up."

Marcellinus spoke first, "I'll go and meet them."

Zenobia countered, "Zabdas and I are going with you."

"I don't think that's such a good idea. Gallienus may have been assassinated. He paused, "There may have been revolt. This may be a rebel force. Anything can happen these days. You are too important to Palmyra."

"It's not open for discussion. I'm going," she imperiously interjected. Before Marcellinus could continue, Zenobia urged her horse forward and began a brisk trot toward the Roman force. Marcellinus and the two generals looked at each other. Zabdas shrugged his shoulders and followed her. Taking a deep breath, Marcellinus galloped after both of them.

Zabdas and Marcellinus caught up to Zenobia and soon saw the Roman force. There were only four legions (about 18,000 men) of Roman infantry. They marched along the road, flanked on both sides by cavalry. The cavalry were foreign auxiliaries. Numidian cavalry guarded the Roman right flank (side) and a mixed group of Arab and Persian refugees guarded the Roman left. The wide plain accommodated both cavalry units as they expanded at least fifteen meters on either side of the road.

When the Romans saw the Palmyrene leaders, word was sent to Heraclianus at the center of the column. He rode forward with his personal guard through the ranks and ordered his army to halt. Marcellinus, in the uniform and armor of a Roman soldier, was easy to distinguish among the approaching Palmyrenes.

"I see Marcellinus. Let the men rest here" he declared. Then to his staff and personal guard, "Let's go." Heraclianus and his group rode to within thirty meters of the three approaching riders and stopped. Marcellinus, Zenobia and Zabdas slackened their horses' pace to a walk.

Marcellinus spoke first. "Greetings, Heraclianus. Hopefully your unexpected visit does not bode ill tidings."

"The only ill news I possess is from Palmyra." He looked directly at Zenobia. "Queen Zenobia, I wish to convey my condolences regarding the loss of King Odenathus, and the equally noble Herodes. All of Rome mourns your loss."

"I thank you, but did Emperor Gallienus send an army to convey his condolences?"

"Most certainly not, Queen Zenobia, but Rome has been ably assisted by the efforts of Odenathus and Herodes for so long, that Rome has graciously decided to provide you with the military leadership that you require until the young king is old enough to rule."

"The Palmyrene people are most grateful to the Emperor for his offer, but we are in no need of such assistance. However, if you've brought troops to supplement ours, we are grateful."

"We have been ordered to the Euphrates River to fight our mutual enemies, the Persians. We will use *your* forces to supplement *ours.*"

"I have recently concluded an informal truce with Sapor that should last for at least the next twelve months. *And* if there is any supplementing to be done, it will be *your* forces supplementing ours." She reminded him, "*Our* forces, under *our* leadership, have succeeded against the Persians, not those of Rome."

With ill-concealed condescension, Heraclianus appeared to be goading the queen into a confrontation. "Most Noble Queen Zenobia, need I remind you that you are a woman, and the heir to the Kingdom of Palmyra is a mere a child? You need experienced, mature, *male* guidance."

Marcellinus interjected, "Queen Zenobia has been responsible for some of Palmyra's greatest victories against Sapor. She is a brilliant tactician. I have witnessed many of her successes."

Heraclianus challenged him. "Need I remind *you,* Marcellinus, that you are a Roman soldier and should submit to the wishes of your emperor?"

"Vaballathus, King of Kings, Roman Senator, Honorary Consul, and Roman Duke and I, his regent, are perfectly capable of defending the Empire against Sapor, thank you," Zenobia interjected.

"Queen Zenobia, your son Vaballathus may be King of Palmyra, but the Roman titles of which you speak were *graciously* bestowed upon Odenathus by Rome. Those titles have died with him." He forced a smile. "They are not to be inherited by a mere boy. They must be earned."

Zenobia became incensed. "King Odenathus earned every one of those Roman titles with his sweat and blood!" She paused momentarily. "He earned these titles for his sons, and I have promised him that they will receive what they deserve. Where was Rome when we stood alone against Sapor? Where would Rome be in the East without the assistance of Palmyra?"

"Queen Zenobia, my orders are to collect your forces, attach them to ours and proceed against the Persians."

"I repeat that I have concluded an informal truce with Sapor. I will not break my promise to him and neither will you. Either have your forces peaceably fall in behind ours or you can return in the direction from which you came. Take some time to reflect on the wisdom of your position." Zenobia turned her horse and raced back toward her forces.

Zabdas and Marcellinus looked at each other for a second and then Zabdas turned and followed her, but Marcellinus lingered. "What are you doing? Is the Emperor willing to risk alienating Rome's greatest ally?"

"These Palmyrenes have been left alone for too long. It appears that they have grown too independent-minded."

Marcellinus was flabbergasted. "Independent? The only reason Rome left them alone for so long is that it had no one else that could successfully defeat the Persians. If not for these *"independent"* minded Palmyrenes, Sapor might be in Rome by now."

Heraclianus was unmoved. "Whatever assistance they have been to Rome in the past, they are still subjects of Rome. If they are unwilling to accept this fact, then we will instruct this _woman_ and her people on their obligations to Rome."

Marcellinus scowled. "I have fought with this *"woman"* and, I assure you that if you try to get physical with her, you'll be the one that will receive the instruction … and it won't be pleasant."

"I have my orders. Have your men fall in behind us!"

"Less than one hundred survive of the three hundred men

the Emperor so *graciously* sent here over five years ago. They have been integrated with the other Palmyrenes which, need *I* remind *you*, are also Roman soldiers." He paused, becoming more agitated. "I will ask those I came with if they wish to leave the men they've fought with, side by side, on behalf of Rome for over five years."

"Whether *they* decide to come or not, I will expect your prompt return."

"I intend to fight with the army that has provided more service to Rome than any other I have known since I joined the military service." He turned his horse and galloped toward the Palmyrene lines.

Upon Marcellinus's return, the Palmyrene forces had now halted about six hundred meters from the Romans.

Zenobia inquired as Marcellinus rode up. "Well?"

"He won't budge. I think he's been ordered by Gallienus to come here and take control."

"After all this time? It doesn't make sense," she puzzled.

"Now that Persia's progress has been halted and Odenathus and Herodes are dead, Gallienus must think that this is his chance to regain control with, what he thinks, will only require a minimal effort by Heraclianus. If he knew how difficult it was actually going to be, he would have sent a better general."

Zenobia was concerned for Marcellinus. "I promised Odenathus that I would protect the rights of our sons. I also led Sapor to believe there would be no conflict between us. I cannot let them advance any further. I know they're your countrymen, but…"

Marcellinus interrupted, "I intend to fight with the men I've fought with for the last five years. But I'll offer those that came with me the chance to return."

Vaballathus interjected, "What about your duty to Emperor Gallienus?"

Marcellinus turned his horse while still facing Vaballathus. "Gallienus is an ass!"

He rode into the middle of the Palmyrene calvary. The remaining Romans that had arrived with him several years ago were now interspersed among the Palmyrene forces. He shouted at the entire group. "Emperor Gallienus has sent this army for the purpose of subjecting Queen Zenobia, King Vaballathus, and all of Palmyra to his will! I do not intend to join them and, if possible, I intend to stop them." He paused. "But I offer to those of you who came here with me several years ago - those of you that have family or lands in Rome; I offer you the chance to join Heraclianus and his forces." He paused once more. "I'll hold no animosity toward those that go with them, but also know that we'll engage in battle with them this very hour! And, if we do so, which force do you think will prevail? Them, or those of us led by Queen Zenobia?"

A Roman soldier who came with Marcellinus many years ago stood in the ranks next to his horse. He looked to a few other Roman soldiers around him and then began to chant. His first words were "Bat Zabbai!" Then he switched to the Greek Koine. "Zenobia!" At first the chant was low in tone, but it soon grew louder with each refrain, "ZENOBIA! ZENOBIA! ZENOBIA! ZENOBIA!"

All of the Romans and some of the Palmyrenes soon joined in as the chant grew loader. "ZENOBIA! ZENOBIA! *ZENOBIA!* **ZENOBIA!**"

Moments later the entire cavalry, both Romans and Palmyrenes all joined in, "ZENOBIA! ZENOBIA! *ZENOBIA!* **ZENOBIA! ZENOBIA! ZENOBIA!**"

The chanting continued as Marcellinus returned to Zenobia's side. "Your army awaits your instructions, My Queen."

A somewhat flushed Zenobia smiled and raised her hand to stop the chanting. Then to Marcellinus, "Do you know anything of Heraclianus?"

"Not a lot. From what I've heard, he's more a politician than a soldier."

After hearing Marcellinus's response, Zenobia, the master strategist, outlined her plan. "Our main objective is to prevent them from going any further east. We've plenty of room behind us so we'll employ the "Hit and Run" maneuver using three groups. The two outside groups will protect us from any attacks from their cavalry and the third will apply the pressure." Then she turned to her generals.

"Zabbai, place your men on our left flank and ..."

"Zabdas, place your men on our right."

"Marcellinus and Vaballathus will stay with me in the center of the road."

"When they start to move forward, we'll let them come within half the distance they are now. Then we'll begin. Now, let's divide."

All five leaders prepared the men. When all was ready, Marcellinus trotted over to Zenobia. "I'll be right back." He turned and galloped off toward the Roman forces.

"Wait!" She was too late. He was already almost halfway to the Roman lines. He stopped within three meters of Heraclianus. "I, and those who came with me, remain with our fellow Roman soldiers and Queen Zenobia."

Heraclianus sighed. "Very well then. Your doom is sealed. Tell your wench to move out of our way or she'll pay the price. We're moving forward."

Marcellinus offered a wry smile. "I'm going to enjoy making you eat those words." He turned and rode back to the Palmyrene lines. When back at Zenobia's side, he turned his horse to face Heraclianus and his forces.

"What did he say?" she inquired.

Marcellinus continued looking grimly forward. "He said he wants to die!"

Heraclianus's army began to move toward the Palmyrenes. Zenobia looked left to Zabbai and right to Zabdas. She issued the first of many commands. Her voice was much shriller than a male voice, but just as audible, if not more so. "Dismount!"

The command passed through the ranks. Since they had been waiting for some time during the parleys, many of the men in the force at the center were already dismounted. But all those still mounted obeyed her command, including those in Zabdas's and Zabbai's groups.

"Ready arrows!"

Every man drew an arrow and attached it to his bowstring. They watched the Romans advance, its cavalry auxiliaries keeping abreast on the infantry's flanks. Zenobia noticed some of the newer, unseasoned men becoming agitated. "Steady men! Steady!"

In a few moments the Romans were within three hundred meters.

"Ready! Aim!"

Bows were drawn and arrows were aimed at a 45-degree angle.

"Steadyyyy! Steadyyyy!" There was a dead silence in the Palmyrene ranks for a long moment.

"RELEASE!!!"

15,000 arrows filled the air. The effect was devastating. The Romans raised their shields against the approaching hailstorm, but the sheer number of the projectiles took their toll. Arrows became embedded in shields, but a full 2,000 of them found their mark in man and beast. The Romans staggered, paused, and then doggedly resumed their advance.

Now Zenobia's commands came in rapid succession.

"Ready arrows!" "Ready, aim!"

Then, "Lower your aim!" The Romans were now closer.

"RELEASE!!!"

Another 15,000 arrows flew. Once again, shields went up, but another 2,000 or so found their marks. The diminished force staggered, but, once again, continued its advance.

Heraclianus' forces were now two hundred fifty meters from the Palmyrenes. After releasing their second hailstorm of arrows, Zabbai and Zabdas' groups mounted, drew their swords and prepared for a cavalry attack. Zenobia's group at the center remained dismounted, firing rapidly two more volleys of arrows at the Romans.

The Romans were within one hundred fifty meters when Zenobia's group mounted and joined Zabdas's and Zabbai's groups in retreat. The bulk of Heraclianus's force was infantry, so they were not quick enough to catch the retreating Palmyrenes. Soon the distance between them was six hundred meters once again. The Palmyrenes turned to face the approaching Romans.

The drill was the same as the last. Zenobia bellowed her commands.

"Dismount!"

"Ready arrows! Steadyyyy! Steadyyyy! Ready aim! Steadyyyy! Steadyyyy!"

"RELEASE!!!"

Again, 15,000 arrows. Again, more casualties. The Roman forces staggered and then continued onward, but by now they were quite frustrated. The Palmyrene archers continued to strike while keeping just beyond their reach. The second volley of arrows brought the Romans ever closer to breaking point.

When they came within one hundred fifty meters of the Palmyrenes, an exasperated Heraclianus shouted, **"Charge!!!!"**

The Roman infantry started to run and the cavalry units on each side did their best to stay on the infantry's flanks.

Noting the charging Roman infantry, she bellowed in her shrill voice, **"Mount and retreat!!!"**

The archers mounted and the entire Palmyrene force turned and rode at top speed away from the Romans. Once 1000 meters separated both forces, they dismounted and turned to face the Romans again.

Long before they reached the evasive Palmyrenes, Heraclianus realized the futility of their charge. He shouted to his staff. '**Infantry, slow to march step!"**

His officers repeated the command. The Roman infantry slowed and resumed their dogged march toward the Palmyrenes. But in his frustration, even though they were outnumbered by six or seven to one, he did not order his cavalry to stop.

The cavalry commanders from both flanks looked to Heraclianus as he shouted his command, "**Cavalry – Charge!!!!**"

Both calvary commanders looked dubious, but then faced the Palmyrenes with grim determination and raised their swords. The commanders from both flanks, virtually in unison, bellowed, "**Charge!!!!**"

The cavalry auxiliaries broke into a full gallop.

Both Zabdas and Zabbai saw the charging cavalry. Together, in rapid succession, they immediately thundered, (Zabdas) "Right flank, mount!" (Zabbai) "Left flank, mount!" Then both commanders bellowed in unison, "**Charge!!!**"

They didn't have far to go. The Roman cavalry reached them in moments and was promptly destroyed by Zabdas's and Zabbai's groups. During the entire calvary engagement, the center faction of the Palmyrene army, still dismounted, continued its barrage of the Roman infantry, pointing their bows at a 45-degree angle and firing their arrows over the heads of both calvary units, but not the more-distant infantry units.

Their task completed, Zabdas's, and Zabbai's forces returned to their original positions beside their dismounted companions in the center of the group, dismounted and joined those in the center by discharging two more volleys of arrows at the Roman infantry.

Without the protection of its cavalry auxiliaries, Zenobia sensed the time was right to attack the Roman infantry. "All groups mount!" The order passed down and across all three groups. Pointing her sword forward she commanded loudly in her shrill voice,

"CHARRRRRRRRGE!!!"

The order was repeated almost simultaneously and unanimously by Marcellinus, Vaballathus, Zabbai and Zabdas,

"CHARRRRRRRRGE!!!"

Zenobia's entire army now bore down on Heraclianus's unprotected infantry. When they had come within fifty meters of the Romans, the latter broke ranks and fled in all directions. That only made circumstances easier for the Palmyrene horseman to ride them down.

Heraclianus and his personal guard of twelve bolted back down the road from which they came. The Palmyrenes, who were <u>all</u> cavalry, divided, intending to follow the small groups of routed men in full flight.

Zenobia, seeing Heraclianus's group and realizing that the remainder of his fleeing infantry were only following his ill-advised orders, shouted at her men:

"LEAVE THEM!!! LEAVE THEM!!! FOLLOW ME!!!!!!"

She pointed her sword in the direction of Heraclianus. Soon her entire force bore down on the routed leader and, owing to their superior horsemanship, were within close proximity of him within minutes. His personal guard, realizing that the Palmyrenes had singled him out for vengeance, scattered left and right.

Zenobia, still focused on Heraclianus, ignored his faint-hearted bodyguards. She and the rest of her men continued onward, focused only on their leader. Marcellinus was in the vanguard, only two meters behind Heraclianus. He jumped from his horse onto Heraclianus and they both tumbled to the ground. Rising quickly to his feet, Marcellinus drew his sword. Heraclianus, still on the ground, looked up.

"Marcellinus, please! Have mercy! Gallienus ordered me to do this! Please have mercy! I beg of you."

Marcellinus, ignoring Heraclianus's pleas, raised his

sword to finish the faint-hearted general.

Zenobia's shrill voice suddenly pierced the air, "STOP!!! I want him alive!!!"

Marcellinus stayed his sword in the air, fighting to control his rage.

Zenobia jumped off her horse. She spoke, softly and calmly trying to sooth the irate centurian. "Marcellinus..."

He answered through gritted teeth. "He...doesn't... deserve...to live!"

Still holding the sword up, his arms began to shake as he fought for control. Zenobia stepped to his side, grasped his arms and pulled them slowly down. "We don't want war with Rome, do we?"

He slowly brought his arms down. He turned and drove the blade of his sword into the ground.

"He will take a message to Gallienus for us," she advised.

"I'll take a message! I'll take a message!" the cowering Heraclianus quickly pleaded.

Marcellinus interjected, "Have you taught this *woman* a lesson yet, or does she need further instruction?"

Trembling, the Roman general exclaimed, "Queen Zenobia is a great warrior!" Then, after a pause, "Queen Zenobia, I salute you."

She responded with scorn, "Get up you pompous fool!"

Heraclianus, still trembling, rose to his feet.

She continued, "I want you to tell Emperor Gallienus that Palmyra is still willing to be Rome's ally in the East, but not its slave! My son Vaballathus will bear all of his father's Roman titles. Do you understand me?"

Although moisture from the sweat of anxiety remained on his face, signs of relief began to appear on his countenance and Heraclianus readily accepted Zenobia's missive. "Yes! Definitely! I'll go tell him at once!"

Heraclianus began to limp toward his horse. Marcellinus and Zabbai looked at each other and then walked over to him. Marcellinus was the first to place his hands on left side of the defeated general. "Here, let us help you."

Zabbai grabbed the general's right side and both men roughly tossed him up on his horse backwards. Marcellinus slapped the backside of Heraclianus's horse and it galloped off, Heraclianus facing the rear.

All the men witnessing the sight laughed uproariously and then resumed their chanting:

"ZENOBIA! ZENOBIA! **ZENOBIA!**

ZENOBIA! ..."

Zenobia mounted her horse and thrust her sword into the air. Soon the entire army had coalesced around their Queen and followed suit. The chant resumed.

"ZENOBIA! ZENOBIA!

ZENOBIA! ZENOBIA! ..."

Their chant was soon followed by prolonged cheering.

She now reminded them, "Let's go see what goodies Heraclianus has in his supply train!"

Once again, the chant resumed:

"ZENOBIA! ZENOBIA!

ZENOBIA! ZENOBIA! ..."

She lowered her arms to calm them and the men all mounted and rode out of sight down the road in the direction from which Heraclianus had come.

Several months after Heraclianus's disastrous defeat

at the hands of Queen Zenobia, he timidly pleaded an audience with Emperor Gallienus. They were in the valley of Nessos, on the border of Macedonia and Thrace. Gallienus had just defeated the Heruli and was holding his temporary court in a substantial tent erected for the purpose.

A herald approached. "General Heraclianus wishes an audience with the Most August Emperor Gallienus."

Gallienus adopted a sour expression. "Show him in."

Heraclianus entered. "Most August Gallienus, I bring bad tidings from the East."

Gallienus interrupted his defeated general. "You bring me no tidings that I haven't heard a week ago from beggars on the street. They say that a woman has humbled the great Roman Empire." He paused. "You have brought shame upon Rome, Heraclianus! What do you have to say for yourself?"

"Most Noble and August Gallienus, we were outnumbered ten to one! They used treachery, just as they did with your father, the Emperor Valerian. These nomads are a treacherous lot!"

"Leave my father out of this! You'll not evade your just censure by comparing your situation to that of my father's!"

"A thousand pardons, Sire, but these nomads use methods

of warfare that are dishonorable. They are a race abhorrent to the gods! Jupiter will surely work his vengeance upon them for their perfidy to Rome, if we only have the patience to wait."

"I don't know what Jupiter will do, but I must go west to meet the treacherous Aureolus and I need you with me. Zenobia and her son will have to wait. Besides, there's no harm in leaving them alone for a while longer. They have kept that region quite stable. But when we finish with Aureolus, I will go myself to rid us of this impudent woman. Now sit and have some wine with me. But keep your excuses to yourself! I want to hear of Marcellinus's traitorous behavior."

Later, in March 268 C.E., Gallienus was murdered at Milan while laying siege to the forces of the traitor, Aureolus. Some said that Heraclianus was involved in the plot. M. Aurelius Claudius, whom Gallienus had made Supreme Commander of Roman cavalry, was made emperor by the conspirators. The new Emperor made Marcellinus's old friend, Lucius Domitius Aurelianus, otherwise known as Aurelian, Commander of the Dalmatian horse and later gave him Claudius's old position as overall commander of the cavalry. During all of the following year, 269 C.E., the new Emperor Claudius and Aurelian were tied up fighting, first the Germanic tribes in Northern Italy, and then the Goths in the Balkans.

✦

An uneasy stalemate had existed between both Rome and Palmyra for over two years after Palmyra's defeat of Heraclianus. However, things had appeared to be quite peaceful and stable during the aftermath.

One evening, Zenobia, Marcellinus, and Longinus were having dinner. They reclined on couches, propping up their upper bodies by leaning on one or sometimes both elbows, while food was placed before them, as was the custom. Initially, the topic of discussion was the fact that many of the Roman administrators in the area had complied with the wishes of Odenathus in the past, but they had proved to be more defiant against Zenobia's requests. Longinus, intending to complement his patroness, spoke. "It's unfortunate that that brain of yours is not in a man's body. It has always been difficult for any woman in power to gain acceptance."

Marcellinus and Zenobia's heads were quite near each other and he leaned even closer to her and whispered, "I, for one, am quite glad that that that brain of yours rests inside that beautiful head. I wouldn't have it any other way."

It was quite impolite of Marcellinus to whisper to Zenobia while in Longinus's company and Marcellinus suddenly realized his error. "I'm sorry for my rudeness."

Longinus had deduced quite some time ago that the relationship between Marcellinus and Zenobia had been more than just professional. And for a man near sixty years old, his hearing was exceptional. However, in his wisdom he decided that it was best to feign ignorance. "For what?" he muttered. "Did you say something?"

Marcellinus, relieved to discover that his blunder had gone undiscovered, or that Longinus had allowed him to believe so, returned to the subject. "I think that Zabdas's little excursion may put them in line. A show of force is the proper thing to do in this case. He should be finished with his march through Roman Arabia by now and beginning his march further south through the Jordan valley."

Both Generals Zabdas and Zabbai had been sent on a southwesterly route with 70,000 men, primarily as a show of strength, to an area that had been the most rebellious of any under Palmyra's assumed jurisdiction.

Longinus now intervened, "Since my arrival here, I have become aware of a Jewish teacher named Jesus that lived in the Jordan valley over two hundred years ago. The man's disciples are continually growing in numbers. Have you heard of the man?"

Marcellinus was totally ignorant of the man and his teachings and immediately responded, "Not I."

Zenobia acknowledged, "I have heard something of the

man. In fact there is a dispute between one of his teachers in Antioch named Paul *[not Paul of Tarsus]* and many of the other church leaders. I have been asked to mediate regarding the dispute."

"That is precisely why I have brought up the subject. It appears that this Jesus attempted to reform the Jewish religion. He told them that they were splitting hairs over too many rules. He preached simplicity. His main contention, from what I can determine, was love of God..." Looking at Zenobia, Longinus interrupted himself with the comment, "As you probably already know, the Jews believe that there is only one god." He continued with his main theme, "Anyway, he preached that all that was necessary to gain eternal life was for man to love God and to love one's fellow man, including one's enemies. He taught that, compared to this one god, man was not intelligent enough to split hairs on fine points of religious faith. His followers are called Christians because he is deemed by them to have been The Anointed One."

Marcellinus interrupted, "Love one's enemies? He wasn't a very practical man, was he?"

Zenobia interjected, "But what if everyone loved their enemies? There would be no enemies to fight. We might all live in peace."

Marcellinus looked directly at Zenobia. "You know as well as I that it's impossible to get "everyone" to do anything.

168 | T.S. Dunn

There will always be some greedy, covetous individual that will want to take advantage of the situation. And when he does, if many of his obstacles were removed because most of the world was trying to "love him" while he was impaling them with his spears, his task would be that much the easier!"

"His solution may be impractical, but just think if everyone believed as this Jesus taught." Zenobia produced a slight smile, while looking off into the distance.

Longinus regained control of the conversation. "I'm afraid that what has occurred since this Jesus's death only confirms something of man's nature to which Marcellinus has alluded. Now, slightly over two hundred years later, numerous factions have developed within his movement. They have developed over disputes regarding fine points of his teachings or what has been purported that he said. His own followers are on the verge of killing their fellow Christians over these semantics. They have also enlisted the aid of local magistrates to settle their disputes, suggesting corporal punishment for those that disagree with them. They are beginning to act directly in contravention to what Jesus primarily tried to accomplish. I think that man may be ready for what this Jesus taught someday, but certainly not at this time."

Just as Longinus finished speaking, a page announced, "Lord Verodes has requested a meeting of Palmyra's Senate for tomorrow morning."

X.

THE PLOT AGAINST ROME

The following morning, just prior to the requested time for the meeting of the Senate, Verodes stationed himself at the entrance to the senate chamber that lay adjacent to the agora. He greeted each senator, the Queen Mother and King Vaballathus as they arrived. Apsaeus was already seated inside at the far left end of the chamber.

Zenobia and Vaballathus stood by the thrones provided for them in the chamber. Marcellinus and Zabdas stood on either side of the royal pair.

After all had entered, Verodes followed the last man through the doors and went to the center of the chamber.

A buzz of barely audible chatter filled the chamber. All were puzzled as to the purpose for this unscheduled meeting. Verodes raised his hands and the murmuring ceased.

He addressed the assembly, "Hail Queen Zenobia, Protector of Palmyra!"

The senators stood and cheered.

He continued. "As I'm sure you all know, Gallienus has been assassinated and now Claudius is the Roman Emperor. And so it goes, one after the other with little long-term continuity among our Roman overlords. There are many among us that feel the spoils and territory of Rome await our Warrior Queen!"

Zenobia, uncomfortable at receiving the praise, interjected, "Please be seated. And remember that I am merely the Queen Regent. Hail Vaballathus, King of Palmyra."

In response, all in the chamber proclaimed in unison, "Hail Vaballathus, King of Palmyra! Hail Vaballathus, King of Kings!"

Verodes remained standing. Everyone but Marcellinus and Zabdas now sat. Marcellinus looked a little uneasy. He was now, after all this time, having some doubts. For one thing, he shouldn't be here. He shouldn't be in the Senate Chamber during this discussion.

Zenobia responded to Verodes's proclamation. "As I have stated many times over the last two years, we do not intend to start a war with Rome! That would be foolish."

Apsaeus now stood and spoke to the entire chamber. "Queen Mother, I apologize for interrupting, but the Roman Empire is falling to pieces. Others will soon step in to gather up the fragments. It would be more foolish to let someone else, someone that might be more threatening to Palmyra, take control."

There were a few whispers of agreement, but most were apprehensive of Apsaeus's words.

Verodes continued for his son, "Worse yet, what if it is not a few, but many? What if the Roman carcass becomes hundreds of small petty kingdoms? Think of the consequences for commerce. Are we not a commercial city?" He paused momentarily, "Our entire system is based upon trade. We must act in *order* to prevent *disorder.*" Again he paused, "We must act now to insure the continued prosperity of the city of Palmyra and its citizens."

A loud hum among the senators rolled throughout the room.

Zenobia hesitated momentarily. "Your words have not fallen upon deaf ears, Verodes. But we mustn't act in haste. After our fortunate defeat of Heraclianus, Rome may have decided that it is wiser to share the empire with a strong ally than to enter into another costly war in the East. And keep in mind that the commerce of this city has done well under Roman rule." Then, after a thoughtful pause, she cautioned them. "And be advised that the army that was sent against us was hardly representative of Rome's might."

Babai, a powerful and respected senator, stood and

addressed his peers, "I'm in agreement with the Queen Mother. We have had no communication from Rome for over two years. Perhaps their reaction to their defeat at our hands will be to continue to ignore the issue."

There was more muttering, but most senators nodded in agreement.

However, Verodes was not to be denied. "My King and Queen Mother, most noble senators of Palmyra, please listen to what a Roman Centurion from Egypt[8] has to say before you render any decision."

Marcellinus, Zenobia, Vaballathus, Zabdas, as well as many senators, exchanged puzzled glances. Verodes looked to a soldier at the door of the senate chamber. "Bring in the Roman."

The soldier opened the chamber doors and called out, "Centurion Timagenes!"

Timagenes, a squat, but athletic-looking Roman soldier, in full military dress, entered the chamber. He walked to within three meters of the royal pair and genuflected. Zenobia and Marcellinus again exchanged glances.

Verodes continued, "I believe the information this Roman brings to be of great importance. My King and Queen, this is Timagenes, a soldier from the Roman garrison at Alexandria."

Timagenes addressed the royal pair, "Your Highnesses, it is my great pleasure and honor to meet the famous Queen Zenobia and the son of the great Odenathus. I am Centurion Timagenes, at your service."

Verodes interjected, "Timagenes has requested an audience with you. He feels that the situation in Alexandria is quite unstable."

The centurion continued, "Most Noble Queen Mother and King, Rome feeds its masses with the wheat of Egypt. But the Roman Empire is crumbling, and most of those in Egypt feel that if they do not break away soon, they may, before long, fall prey to a newer, less tolerant master." He paused, "I have, for the time being, persuaded my fellow soldiers to forestall their revolt, but their anxiety increases daily. Some of us believe that you may prove to be our solution."

There was an uneasy silence in the chamber. Timagenes resumed his proposal. "Palmyra was able to defend the Eastern Borders of the Empire from the Persians when Rome was unable to do so. I have come to seek your aid. We believe Egypt will thrive under Palmyra's protection, and Palmyra will likewise benefit from the wheat of Egypt."

Then, almost as an afterthought, he revealed, "I have taken the liberty to have my men circulate the rumor that you are possibly a descendent of the Ptolemies; perhaps even a direct descendent of Cleopatra. This should add to the legitimacy of your claim in the eyes of the Egyptians."

After Timagenes' last comment, the Queen blushed, affecting a faint smile, but made no comment regarding his final suggestion. Then she stood, "We are honored by your expression of confidence in us, but your request takes us completely by surprise."

Verodes interrupted, "Most Noble Queen Mother, this appears to be an excellent opportunity for Palmyra to gain control of its rightful share of the East. She's served as Rome's watchdog long enough."

Marcellinus now joined the discussion, "Rome has only left us alone because we still protect its Eastern Border and pose no real threat. But they'll never let you take Egypt. It's too important to Rome." He paused, "As Timagenes said, its wheat feeds the Roman masses. By taking Egypt, you'll assure a confrontation with Rome. And the next time, they'll send more than an expeditionary force of a few thousand men and it will be led by a man much more capable than that buffoon, Heraclianus."

Verodes quickly countered, "If we don't go after Egypt, someone else will. And, after they digest Egypt, they may become strong enough to take Palmyra." He then added, "We must decide whether to move forward or fall with Rome. I'm not talking about blind aggression. I am talking about doing what's necessary to keep the prosperity that we've gained over the last two hundred years. Even Marcellinus must admit that if we stay with Rome we may fall with her."

At a loss for words, or a better argument, Marcellinus remained silent.

Zenobia turned to Zabdas, "And Zabdas, what say you?"

The old warrior responded haltingly, "I am a soldier. If you ask, "Are we able to take Egypt?", I say yes. If you ask, "Are we able to defend ourselves against Rome?", I say, it is possible. I only know that I will defend Palmyra with all my strength."

Verodes attempted what appeared to be some sound logic. "My Queen, more than one course of action may be open. If we take Egypt and later decide we don't want to face Rome, we may always give it back and say that we took it only to prevent others from doing so."

After a brief hesitation he continued, "Or, we may come to some sort of accommodation whereby we keep Egypt and continue to provide Rome with wheat…for a price, of course. Rome has often bought its way out of war by paying off aggressors. The last thing Rome needs is another powerful, threatening enemy at this time."

Zenobia nodded to Verodes, paused in thought momentarily and then addressed the group, "Thank you for your wise counsel. We will render our decision in the morning."

✦

Later, at dusk, walking alone down the colonnade in the palace gardens, Zenobia discussed that day's revelations with Marcellinus. "Well, what would you do if you were me?"

He countered, "You ask a Roman to rebel against his own?"

"Isn't that what you did when you fought with us against Heraclianus?"

"That was different. We were stopping a tyrant and his stooge. Now we're talking about breaking the Empire up - an empire that has provided peace and stability to much of the world for hundreds of years."

She refuted, "Timagenes is a Roman. Our partnership with Rome has been quite profitable, and if I thought that it could continue unabated for even another fifty years, I wouldn't even consider any action."

It was obvious that Marcellinus was in a state of confusion. "My heart says "no, don't", but my head says, "it is time." This is very difficult for me. However, you have shown yourself to be consistently wise and also cautious in the past, when I have not. I don't know what to do, but I'll abide by whatever you decide."

"Well, I've decided to take Egypt. I'll send both Zabdas and Zabbai with Timagenes while I try to consolidate our position further north."

"I'm going with Zabdas. I still don't know if we can trust this Timagenes. Let Zabbai stay here in case he's needed." He paused, "With your approval, of course."

"Very well. But you will be sorely missed." She hesitated, then added, "Not only by me, but by the children as well."

Marcellinus' intentions were sincere – he really did not know if he could trust Timagenes - and Zabdas, although an extremely competent general, was ignorant of the myriad forms of Roman treachery.

He had another more selfish and intimate reason for leaving. Since Heraclianus's defeat over two years ago, Marcellinus had waited and waited for Zenobia to throw down her guard once again, like she had once done so very long ago – it seemed like centuries - but she had spurned each of his proffered advances when they were alone, responding, "not yet", "please be more patient", "the time is not yet right".

At times he became so frustrated, he would burst into a silent rage and need to leave her presence. His patience had worn thin. Knowing that he would be gone for several months, perhaps over a year, the separation might rekindle that spark upon his return and reignite the passions within her.

Both of these feelings passed through his thoughts, but, "Maybe we can achieve success within a few months. According to Timagenes, the conditions sound favorable," was the only consolation he had to offer. However, deep within him, he knew that even the most successful military campaigns lasted far longer than a few months.

That evening, although they were alone inside Verodes's official offices in the palace, Apsaeus cautiously spoke to his father in a low tone, "Do you think that she'll do it?"

"I'm certain of it. It's the right move to make. And it's the best move for Palmyra. Not even her Roman friend will be able to dissuade her."

His son countered, "But if she's successful, she'll become too powerful. We'll never gain control."

"Any successful move that she makes will only enhance our future position. This couldn't have worked out better! Now she can assume the risk of expanding Palmyra's borders and influence. If she fails, she alone suffers the consequences. Then we appeal to Rome and take control. If she's successful, we simply wait for the right time to eliminate her. However, we'll need to eliminate Marcellinus as well. He may be even more threatening to our designs than the queen. He may be much more difficult to eliminate, but no one is able to keep vigilant every moment of every day. We'll find a weak moment to strike."

Almost immediately, he added, "And I still can't help but feel that there's more than just friendship between the pair." He hesitated once again before he continued, "After their demise, her progeny may be eliminated with little difficulty."

Apsaeus did not share his father's optimism. "What if we don't get another opportunity like the one at Emesa?"

"People forget. They make mistakes. Another opportunity will present itself. In the meantime, the more territory and wealth she acquires, the greater our final reward."

"What if she decides not to defy Rome?"

"We'll just have to continue giving her a little prompting then, won't we?" Verodes affected a sinister smile that his son returned.

XI.

A NEW ROMAN EMPEROR

EARLY DECEMBER, 270 C.E.

Almost a year after Timagenes's proposal in the senate chamber, in the Great Hall of the palace, Zenobia, Vaballathus, Longinus, Verodes, and Apsaeus were discussing the success of Zenobia's diplomatic journey to Antioch as a page entered.

Without being prompted, the man spoke, "Marcellinus has arrived."

The entire group looked puzzled, but Zenobia finally spoke, "Let him enter."

As Marcellinus entered the hall, Zenobia's eyes ignited as they had often done in the past when seeing him after any of his extended absences, and this separation had been far longer than any other since they first met. "Marcellinus, you are most welcome, but is there bad news from Egypt?"

"No, the news is good. Probus arrived and attempted to retake Alexandria, but he is dead and Egypt is ours."

Her response was exuberant. "That's excellent! My

mission to Antioch has also borne fruit. Antioch and most of the cities in the area have decided to join us."

Marcellinus countered, "That's great news, but I have some even better. Claudius has died of the plague and Aurelian is now the Emperor of Rome!" After his announcement, Marcellinus looked at the others, expecting them to join in his elation, but they only looked back at him with blank expressions. Then, understanding his error... "Do you remember me telling you that there was one man that I thought could reunite the Roman Empire and restore order?"

The others remained silent affecting confused expressions.

He continued, "Well, that man is Aurelian. He's a military genius and he's as tenacious as a bull."

Awaiting some display of relief or, hopefully, even excitement, he was disappointed as their facial expressions continued to remain unaffected.

After an uncomfortable silence of several moments, Verodes broke the stillness in the hall. "Your news may have been welcome a year ago, but now we're committed to independence."

Marcellinus's smile quickly faded. "Independence? I thought we were committed to peace and stability. We believed that Rome was falling apart and that was the only reason we were doing this. Well, now there is a very good chance that it won't."

The scheming argapet quipped, "A chance? I'd like to think that the future of Palmyra has more than a chance for peace and stability."

"I'm not saying to return all of Palmyra's gains to Rome. I only suggest we hold off any further action until we see how he does."

The sage, Longinus then added, "Marcellinus has a point. It will cause Palmyra no harm to wait and see."

Marcellinus continued, "Meanwhile, I'll go to Aurelian and explain the reasons for our actions and tell him that we are waiting to see how he fares."

Verodes quickly and emphatically interjected, "No! That would not be a good idea."

The somewhat puzzled and frustrated Marcellinus retorted, "And why not?"

The sinister Verodes seemed to have a counter for every proposal the centurion offered. "What's the life expectancy of a Roman Emperor these days? Two years? Three? Five, if they're lucky? What *if* your friend is successful at reuniting the empire and then follows the usual course of emperors and is killed by his own men, some scheming politician, or dies of the plague like Claudius? Then what?"

He paused momentarily before continuing, "I'll tell you what will happen. One or more emperors are selected by the armies they lead; perhaps the Senate also puts up a candidate. Chaos ensues until one of them gains the upper hand. Or maybe … he is not quite successful and we have a divided empire like Rome has now in the West. We're back where we started."

"Face it! Your Roman Empire has seen its day. Let Palmyra take control of its own destiny and not rely on the *"chance"* that Rome suddenly sees a line of strong, wise rulers. We already have a line of strong, wise rulers right here in Palmyra."

Marcellinus's inner rage was becoming apparent. "Rome has served its Empire well for hundreds of years. A period of a few weak rulers doesn't mean that things will always continue that way."

The ever-inventive Verodes refuted, "Power is never possessed by one nation forever."

The clandestine villain's son and co-conspirator, Apsaeus, stepped forward and spoke scornfully, "Rome is old footwear. It's time to change sandals."

Marcellinus reached for the hilt of his sword. "This is

one old sandal that will assist you on your way to the **UNDERWORLD!**"

Vaballathus and Longinus stepped between the pair. Apsaeus had also reached for his sword, but it was obvious that he was grateful for the interlopers.

Although Zenobia had remained silent during the entire debate, she now forcefully interposed, "Enough! Everyone leave us! I wish to speak with Marcellinus privately."

Verodes, although speaking to Zenobia, was looking directly at Marcellinus. "Queen Mother, Zenobia, I am fearful for your safety."

She snapped, "Your fears are unjustified! Leave us!"

Everyone lingered, still stunned.

"**Now!**"

Verodes and Apsaeus walked off down the corridor leading to Verodes's offices muttering to each other. The others exited down various other corridors.

When they were alone, Zenobia spoke softly and tenderly to her companion, "I thought we wanted to make Palmyra safe and secure. I thought we might then relax and enjoy life. I thought that these were *our* common goals. Does one man, one new Roman Emperor, change all of this?"

He approached and began to embrace her, but then retreated slightly. "I love you with all my heart and soul. If only you were a merchant's daughter, there would be nothing that I wouldn't do for you. But I'm a Roman soldier in Rome's army and … Aurelian is my friend. I'm telling you that he's the one! I know it!"

She pleaded, "One man is like a grain of sand in the desert. Palmyra cannot pin all her hopes on just one man."

"All I'm asking is for you to cease any further action until I go speak with him."

"But we're almost there! The entire East is nearly under our control!"

Stepping back from her, he looked into her eyes and spoke somewhat curtly. "Almost there? Where is there? What do you want? Total domination? I thought that all that you wanted was to live quietly and be a good mother to your children, … but perhaps what you really want is to be the mother of the new Palmyrene Empire."

"That's not fair! I made a promise to Odenathus!"

"Your recent successes may be clouding your judgment."

She countered, "And your former friendship is clouding yours."

"Perhaps. I agree that I *am* a Roman and he *is* my friend. But I must warn you that Aurelian will stop at nothing to regain any Roman territory that has been lost. And he's as tenacious as a bull. *That* is why I must go and see him."

Zenobia began to shed tears. Then, in a whisper she asked, "And what am I to you? Nothing? I know that I've kept you waiting for a very long time, but I was just starting to think that our time had come."

"You are my life! You're *more* than life to me! But I must go to him to stop him from coming at you with all the might of Rome, not merely that small force led by that buffoon-of-a-general that Gallienus sent. I'm asking you to please think about what I've said and wait. Just wait!"

"Is there nothing I can say?" Zenobia now stepped further away from him and squelched her tears. "Then you will forgive me if I also do *my duty* on behalf of Palmyra?"

She didn't wait for a response. "Apama!"

Apama, a handmaid, promptly appeared.

Holding back her tears, "Marcellinus has a long journey ahead of him. Please provide him with provisions and an escort to the Orontes River."

Apama bowed her head. "Yes, Queen Mother."

As Apama began to walk away, Marcellinus stopped the servant. Uneasily, he told the queen, "An escort will not be necessary, but I would like to offer those Romans that came here with me an opportunity to return with me as well."

Zenobia, in a choked voice, but sarcastic tone, declared, "By all means…Take your fellow Romans with you."

Marcellinus bowed and followed Apama out of the hall. After they left Zenobia returned to her tears.

✦

The following morning in the palace stables, Marcellinus, ten Roman soldiers, and Zabbai saddled their horses.

Longinus entered and approached Marcellinus. "Take care of yourself, my friend."

He extended his hand and Marcellinus grasped it warmly, but added, "You're not rid of me yet! I'll be back after I straighten things out with Aurelian."

The sage countered, "Good luck then." He patted Marcellinus on the back as the latter mounted his horse.

Moments later, the twelve men in Marcellinus's party rode through Palmyra's main gate. Zabbai was with them. One of the Romans, originally Marcellinus's second-in-command, Gaius, spoke, "You're not angry with the others for staying, are you? They have wives and families here now. My wife is dead and the rest of the men with us are the only ones unattached, except for Crassus, here." He pointed to another rider who looked over and smiled. "He has three wives here. He believes himself now freed from the depths of the Hades." Both men laughed. Even the stone-faced Zabbai cracked a smile.

Marcellinus was somewhat apprehensive at his departure, but also hopeful. "I'm not angry, and I intend to return soon." Then turning to Zabbai, "How far will you ride with us?"

"For a while. Then I'll return to Palmyra and eagerly await your return."

"I welcome your company, my friend, and I promise that I _will_ return."

Zenobia watched Marcellinus and his group leave from the window opening of her bedchamber which overlooked the city. Once again, tears streamed down her face.

Just outside the doors of the palace, Verodes and Apsaeus stood and also watched the Romans leave the stables.

Verodes was beginning to feel that his efforts would be

frustrated once again. "She wants to stop any further action until Marcellinus returns. I can't convince her that giving Aurelian time to clean house is as good as giving everything back to Rome."

"What should we do?" his son and companion in perfidy inquired.

"Marcellinus must not meet with Aurelian," Verodes immediately responded.

"How do we stop him?" his son inquired.

Verodes abruptly smiled. Once again inspiration overcame him. "I want you to visit the Tanukhs for me."

Apsaeus was bewildered. "But they are Palmyra's enemies!"

"They're not *my* enemies. Go to the Hauran. Their chief is named Kifah. Show him this ring." Verodes smiled and handed a ring from his finger to his son. "I want Marcellinus and his men eliminated. Kifah can name his price." Apsaeus nodded in compliance, turned, and promptly departed.

✦

Several days later, traveling just east of Antioch, a soldier at the rear of Marcellinus's group called out, "We have company." He was looking behind them as he spoke.

They all turned to see about one hundred Tanukhs bearing down on them. When the intruders got closer, the Romans noticed that their pursuers' swords were drawn. Marcellinus pointed forward. 'Head for those rocks just ahead!"

But the Tanukhs had the momentum and were quickly upon them. The Romans were outnumbered ten to one. After some fierce fighting, it was all over. Only Marcellinus and Gaius remained alive. Held fast by many Tanukhs, they were stripped of their armor.

Two of the dead Romans were decapitated and the headless bodies were dressed in the armor of Marcellinus and Gaius. Both men's horses were led away. Meanwhile, other Tanukhs searched the dead bodies for valuables. The two survivors, now only dressed in white belted tunics, were bound by the wrists with ropes and began a long trek on foot.

Two weeks after Marcellinus and Gaius were kidnapped and their companions killed, Zenobia and Vaballathus were seated on their thrones in the great room of the palace. Longinus, Verodes, Zabdas, and Zabbai were all gathered around them. A herald entered.

"Majesties, a messenger from Antioch…"

Thinking the messenger may have some news of or from Marcellinus, Zenobia quickly responded, "Send him in." The herald bowed and exited. A moment later, an Antiochian approached and bowed. Four others followed, carrying a large wicker basket, which they promptly set down.

The leader spoke, "Most Noble King and Queen Mother, we have found the remains of a small Roman party just outside Antioch. It appears they were ambushed by Tanukhs." Zabdas walked over to the basket and peered inside it.

Stammering, Zabdas slowly declared, "My Queen…" He pulled some clothing and the armor known to belong to Marcellinus out of the container. The room was silent.

Zenobia was visibly shaken. Her voice stammering, she inquired, "Has the Roman, Marcellinus, visited your city in the last few months?"

"We've had no visitors from Palmyra since your departure, Your Excellency."

"Is there evidence anyone escaped this ambush, or perhaps were taken prisoner?"

"Any survivors would have fled to Antioch and there have

been no such refugees and the Tanukhs are not known for taking prisoners."

Zenobia collected her composure. "Thank you for reporting this to us." There was silence as the men of Antioch bowed, turned and exited the room.

The hush continued until Verodes broke the stillness. "It appears that our Roman connection has been severed at last. All hope of reconciliation with Aurelian is gone."

"It appears so," Zenobia spoke, appearing lost in her own thoughts and then, almost in a murmur, she repeated, "It appears so." She stood and rushed out of the room.

Zenobia entered her bedchamber and threw herself on the bed. After a few moments, Vaballathus entered. He walked to her bed, sat down next to his mother and put his hand on her shoulder.

Attempting to console her, "He will be missed by all of us. After father's and Herodes' death he made everything…" He stopped as he became overcome with emotion as well. Zenobia sat up and hugged him. They sat in silence.

XII.

AURELIAN IN CONTROL

That very day in Rome, Aurelian sat before a large group of Roman Senators who were accused of conspiracy.

As Rome's latest emperor, he asked the group, "What do you have to say for yourselves after hearing the evidence?"

One of the senators stepped forward and bowed before speaking, "Most August Aurelian, do not judge us based upon such meager evidence."

Aurelian was incredulous. "Meager evidence? Twelve witnesses, including some of your own servants and household members, is *meager evidence*?"

Cowering, the man pleaded, "My Supreme Lord, we are descended from the most distinguished families in Rome. Our forefathers helped Rome achieve its greatness. Please show mercy."

"Did you show mercy when you tampered with the currency and then started a riot to cover your crime – a riot killing thousands of poor citizens? I honor your ancestors, but you are a disgrace to their memory." Aurelian paused, "A man is not to be judged by the acts of his ancestors, but by his own deeds. My father was a simple Colonus of a senator whose name I bear, but I'd take his honest speech any day for the lying and deceitful barbs that have just been spoken by you senators of *distinguished lineages.*"

He looked to the captain of the guards. "Take them away for execution!"

Some senators walked to their fate stoically, but others cried out for mercy and were dragged from the room. Aurelian stood and walked to a table over which plans for a new city wall were sprawled. An architect stood by. He ran his index finger along one of the pieces of parchment and turned to the man. "When can you start on the new wall?"

"As soon as the funds are made available."

"You will have your funds. The invasion of the Juthungi terrified the people of Rome. They expected to see them at the gates and in their homes every day. The wealthy have the means to leave the city. The poor and the sick must remain behind to suffer the consequences. They will have a wall to protect them."

The architect obediently vowed, "I will not rest until it is completed."

His response pleased Aurelian. "Very well then."

A messenger approached Aurelian from behind. "Most August Emperor Aurelian…"

He turned to face the man. "I am almost afraid to ask. What is it?"

"The Goths have crossed the Danube again."

Aurelian sighed. Speaking more to himself… "Alas, I thought I now had the time to chastise our ambitious Eastern Queen and see what's become of my old friend." He gazed eastward. "Well, my rebellious Amazon, the gods have delayed the day of our meeting once again, but at least Moesia is in your direction." Then, to an aide beside him, "Tell my officers to assemble."

XIII.

THE SEARCH FOR MARCELLINUS

Several months after hearing of Marcellinus's presumed demise, Zabbai had just posted his horse at the entrance to Palmyra's open market and was sauntering through the market stalls when a Bedouin rode by on Marcellinus's horse. He knew it was his friend's horse because of the yellow streak - almost lightning shaped - just below the horse's mane. He was stunned momentarily, but quickly recovered and followed the man. The man dismounted and entered a foul-smelling tanning shop. Enduring the stench, Zabbai hid around the corner of the shop within just a meter of the man's waiting horse.

Evening shadows were beginning to appear before the man emerged from the shop. Before the Bedouin reached his horse, Zabbai vaulted from around the corner and grabbed the man's collar, dragging him back behind the building, his knife greeting the man's throat. "You have killed my friend, you desert scum!"

The panicking Bedouin squealed, "He is not dead! Your Roman friend is alive!"

"Alive? You lie, dog. I will slice your throat if you utter one more word." Zabbai paused, "I think I'll slice your throat anyway."

His captive pleaded, "It's true! Two Romans are captives of the Tanukhs. I have seen them! The Tanukhs sold me one of their horses. I am only a poor trader. Spare me! Please!"

Still in disbelief, but hoping the man's words were true, "Where? Where do they keep them?"

"South of Damascus…In the Hauran…"

Zabbai drew his knife even closer to the man's throat.

In fear and panic, the trader pleaded, "I'll tell you how to get there. You can trust me. PLEASE! Spare me!"

Zabbai took the man back to the front of the building. "You're coming with me. Get on your horse."

The Bedouin, still watching Zabbai's knife hand, mounted his horse. Zabbai grabbed the bridle and walked the horse and its passenger over toward his own horse at the entrance to the market.

Still trembling, the trader inquired, "Where are we going?"

"First to the palace and then to see your friends, the Tanukhs."

"They're not my friends! They'll kill me if I lead you to them!"

Zabbai was not to be dissuaded. "If the Romans are there, I'll release you." He reached his own horse, mounted and rode to the palace, leading Marcellinus's horse with its mounted hostage.

✦

Upon reaching the palace, Zabbai dismounted and spoke to one of the guards, "If he tries to escape, kill him." He entered the main doors of the palace.

Once inside, he walked briskly, his gait accelerating as his excitement swelled. Was the man telling the truth? Could his friend still be alive?

Suddenly a voice called out from behind him, "Zabbai! Zabbai!"

He turned to see Verodes approaching. "Where are you going in such haste?"

An excited Zabbai blurted out, "Marcellinus may still be alive! A Bedouin outside claims he saw two Romans held by the Tanukhs. I must tell the Queen!"

A startled Verodes quickly regained his composure. "Are you sure that they have him?"

"No, but the man has Marcellinus's horse. I intend to have him lead me to the Tanukh camp." He turned and resumed his animated pace while Verodes desperately racked his brain for a plan.

"Wait! Do you think that is wise?"

Zabbai stopped, turned around once again, confused. "What do you mean?"

The quick-thinking, ever-treacherous and resourceful villain explained, "What if it's not him? Remember how the Queen reacted when she was told he was killed? Don't put her through that again. And, if he's alive, there may be a conspiracy afoot. If so, we don't know who we can trust."

"We can certainly trust the Queen!"

"Of course, but who else?"

Zabbai was puzzled. "You have a better suggestion?"

The perfidious argapet explained, "Will the Bedouin lead you to their camp?"

"Yes."

"Have him do so - and take my son, Apsaeus with you. If Marcellinus is there, determine if you can rescue him yourselves. But, if there's too many of them, or for any other reason you determine that you may be risking Marcellinus's or your own lives in the attempt, return for assistance. You can tell the Queen then. But spare her any further disappointment until we know for certain that it is him that the Tanukhs hold."

Zabbai yielded. "Your counsel is wise as always, Verodes."

"I will speak with Apsaeus and tell him to meet you outside the city gates at dawn. The sun is already down and beginning a journey to the Hauran at this late hour would not be wise."

Verodes face bore a sigh of relief, but was quickly replaced by a sinister smile as Zabbai exited the palace.

After a long trek of many days, the Bedouin had led Zabbai and Apsaeus to within a few kilometers of the Tanukh camp. Apsaeus recognized the area and realized that he must act soon.

Zabbai grunted, "How much further? I am getting hungry!"

"We are near. It lies there," pointing in a southerly direction. "Perhaps you will let me go now?" The Bedouin had been growing increasingly apprehensive as they grew near the Tanukh camp. As he explained to Zabbai back in Palmyra, he feared the Tanukh's reaction when they discovered that he had led the two men to their camp.

"Not yet..." However, Zabbai's face had begun to display a softening smile. He had developed a liking for the trader. Nevertheless, he remained firm. "Keep moving!"

Suddenly, Apsaeus feigned horse trouble and dismounted, causing Zabbai to turn in his saddle. "It's only a loose strap. I'll catch up."

Zabbai nodded and continued on. His anxiety grew as he would soon be able to determine if his friend was still in the land of the living. However, just moments later, an arrow entered his back, traveling completely through his body with its arrowhead exiting his chest. Stunned, he turned to see a smiling Apsaeus, bow in hand, as he fell off his horse.

The Bedouin turned and, witnessing Zabbai's fate, instantly realized his life was in peril. He brought his horse *(not that of Marcellinus, which had been confiscated)* to a full gallop, but Apsaeus was already on his own horse, a much swifter animal, and soon he was beside the Bedouin. He raised his sword and sliced at the man's neck, severing the man's head from its owner.

✦

Not long after his treachery, Apsaeus approached the Tanukh camp.

Straining his eyes to see the approaching rider, Kifah, the Tanukh chieftain, recognized Apsaeus…

Speaking in a Tanukhid dialect, an early form of Arabic, he barked a command at an aide to his left, "Quick! Put the Romans inside." The man scurried off immediately to carry out the order as Apsaeus rode to within six meters of the leader.

Then in Syriac, "You wish our help once again, my friend?" Kifah smiled at his unexpected visitor.

"You hold a Roman prisoner from the group you attacked. His name is Marcellinus."

"We took no prisoners, as you requested."

Apsaeus rose in his saddle and glanced quickly around the camp. "Maybe you are hiding him."

Kifah looked aghast. "You don't trust me, my friend? A Tanukh's word is good. Search our camp if you like."

"I'm only one man. You could have hidden him in a hundred places." Apsaeus glanced around the camp once again. Resignedly he turned and started to ride away, but Kifah stopped him.

"It's not wise to travel in the desert alone. Aiza will ride with you until Damascus." Kifah motioned to a tall thin man, who mounted and rode toward Apsaeus.

"I thank you, but my father knows where I am and if I don't return he will send the whole Palmyrene army after me."

"Aiza is riding with you ..." but now looked at Aiza as if to cancel some previously implied instructions, "... to assure that no such calamity occurs. Goodbye, my friend."

When Apsaeus and Aiza were gone, Kifah walked over to a hut and, returning to his own tongue, yelled into the opening, "You can bring them out now." Marcellinus and Gaius, bearded and haggard-looking, were pushed through a doorway. Their hands and feet were bound. They were shuffled back to the holding pen that had contained them just before Apsaeus's appearance.

One of their guards approached Kifah. "Why do we continue to keep these two? We've had to feed them and guard them for over four months now."

The chieftain countered, "I thought holding them might be useful to us in the future. But now it seems that others may know we have them. It will be too much trouble and risk to keep them any longer. We must kill them soon. Perhaps tonight ... But right now, I have a thirst for some Lebanese wine."

✦

Very late that same evening, Kifah and his drinking companion exited the chieftain's dwelling and staggered over to the pen that held Marcellinus and Gaius. In the garbled speech of one with a belly full of wine, Kifah told the two guards at the gate, "Open it. We're going in."

One of the guards suggested, "Perhaps you should wait until morning?"

Kifah was outraged. "SILENCE! Open the gate! We will dispatch these two and free you of your burden!"

The guard, looking first at his companion, nodded and opened the gate.

Kifah stumbled across the open pen toward his sleeping prisoners, drew his sword and swayed to and fro over what he believed to be Marcellinus's slumbering body. However, Marcellinus, a light sleeper, had been already awakened by the sauntering moves of the drunken assassins. As Kifah raised his sword, his companion was in a similar manner swaying over Gaius. The guards stood at the gate, ten meters away, intending to watch the show.

Suddenly, Marcellinus's legs swung, knocking Kifah's feet out from under him. His hands and feet were tied, but he smashed Kifah across the head with both of his bound hands, knocking him out. Quickly, he grasped the chieftain's sword with both hands and put an end to his intended killer.

Unlike Marcellinus, Gaius had been asleep when the two intruders reached where they slept, but was awoken by the thud as Kifah's body fell heavily to the ground. Hearing the commotion, Kifah's drunken companion had momentarily looked over at his fallen chief, which was all the time Gaius needed to use the same maneuver on him that Marcellinus had used on Kifah, achieving the same effect. However, he wasn't as successful as his fellow Roman in knocking the man out with his bound hands. The pair wrestled on the ground as the two guards ran toward them.

Marcellinus quickly cut the ropes binding his hands and feet with Kifah's sword, stood up, and went to Gaius's aid. He drove the sword into the back of Kifah's companion and pulled downward. The man fell lifeless onto Gaius.

The two guards were now upon Marcellinus. Still holding Kifah's sword, he squared off with them. The guards began to circle him, smiling and enjoying the diversion. They jabbed at him with their swords, which he parried with his.

Gaius, who they assumed to be dead, stealthily grabbed the other dead Tanukh's sword and freed both his hands and his feet. He pushed off the dead man's body and stood to join Marcellinus. The smiles quickly faded from the guards' faces as they realized that the odds were now even. One looked at the other and they turned to run, but the desperate Romans were quickly upon them, stabbing, kicking and punching them until both men lay dead.

The pair looked around the camp and then at each other.

"Is it possible that we weren't heard?" Marcellinus whispered.

"The whole camp must be drunk," Gaius responded.

"We need some horses. Are you up for this?"

Gaius had fared the worst during their months of captivity. "The thought of escaping this cesspit has made me strong, but I don't know how long I will last. We must act quickly."

"The horses are over there." Marcellinus nodded his head to the right. Both men quietly moved toward the outbuilding where the Tanukhs kept their horses. There they found both guards sound asleep. They tethered two horses and then, very deliberately, slowly walked the horses out of the corral and then out of the camp.

But, just as their hopes appeared to be realized, Aiza appeared, walking his horse back into camp. He saw them, drew his bow and sent an arrow straight for Marcellinus.

Marcellinus, eyes lowered, was struggling in the darkness to follow the path before him and didn't see his assailant or the arrow heading toward him. But Gaius did and, summoning his remaining strength, hurled his body in front of his leader. The arrow penetrated his torso.

At once Marcellinus drew the sword taken from one of the dead guards and ran wildly at Aiza, who was now only five meters away. Aiza frantically tried to set another arrow in his bow, but before he could do so, Marcellinus arrived and slashed his sword diagonally across the Tanukh's torso, killing him instantly.

Then, returning to Gaius, he knelt and lifted his friend's head. "Thank you, my good and faithful friend." Gaius simply smiled before closing his eyes to embrace death.

Marcellinus returned to Aiza and stripped him of all his clothing, weapons, and light armor. He found a small bag of gold coins and looked upward for a moment, whispering thanks to the goddess Fortuna for his great luck. Then he mounted Aiza's horse and rode off into the darkness.

Two days later, in the semi-arid wasteland east of Damascus, the sun was intense. It was midday and no sign of life was in sight. An exhausted and sporadically dozing Marcellinus began to slide off his horse, but recovered his senses and straightened himself in the saddle. Moments later fatigue overcame him again and he fell to the ground.

As he fell, he was spotted from a distance by a merchant leading a group of camels loaded with goods. The trader strained his eyes to see and then turned to his servant. "Come, Babu. We are needed."

Babu hesitated, "Is it safe?"

Without wavering, the merchant urged his dromedary forward. "Nothing is safe or sure in this life. But we must behave as the teacher would, and how he taught us to, shouldn't we?"

They rode to where the unconscious Marcellinus lay. The merchant dismounted, grabbed his water vessel and raised Marcellinus by the shoulders. The Roman suddenly awoke and, fearing he was back in Tanukh hands, began a half-hearted struggle. "No! No! No!"

With little effort, the merchant pushed Marcellinus's hands down and raised the water vessel to his mouth. He spoke in Syriac, "Easy. You're among friends."

Marcellinus looked up at the merchant and resignedly drank.

✦

Two weeks later, Marcellinus sat on a dromedary beside

the merchant and his servant. Although he was not completely well-groomed and clean-shaven, he exhibited a much improved appearance. They were just south of Antioch.

While he could have returned to Palmyra several days earlier and, although his heart ached to see the woman he continued to love with all his being, Marcellinus did not intend to immediately return to his adopted home. He had heard that a Roman army was approaching from the north and it was being led by his old friend and comrade, Aurelian. He felt that it was imperative that he first meet with Aurelian to plead Palmyra's cause.

"Your Emperor is north of here with his army," the kind-hearted merchant explained. "My business lies to the east. This is where we must part."

Marcellinus warmly grasped the merchant's hand. "Thank you for everything, my friend. How can I ever repay your kindness and generosity? May the gods allow you to prosper."

"My _God_ provides me with all I need in this life. It is I that have benefited from our meeting. Go with God's grace and blessing."

Marcellinus hesitated briefly and then turned his camel north.

XIV.

REUNION WITH AURELIAN

ROMAN CAMP JUST OUTSIDE TYANA

(in a central area of modern day Turkey)

AUGUST 271 C.E

The Romans had just taken Tyana. Aurelian sat in his tent looking pensive.

An aide entered. "Emperor Aurelian, Centurion Marcellinus begs admission."

Aurelian's face lit up. "Show him in at once."

A now well-groomed Marcellinus appeared and the friends embraced. Aurelian slapped his friend on the back several times. "It is so good to see you." Then after a pause he continued, "But I should have you put in shackles! Why didn't you stop this Amazon Queen from rising in revolt against me? Or perhaps you put her up to it?" Although Aurelian's voice was stern, there was a twinkle in his eyes.

"She's not in revolt against you, Aurel..." Marcellinus caught himself and then continued, "... most August Emperor."

"Spare me, boy." Aurelian looked behind him to insure that no others were present. Noting that they were alone, he turned back to Marcellinus, "Come with me." Marcellinus followed Aurelian through another drawn curtain into a separate compartment of Aurelian's tent. After entering the enclosure, Aurelian poked his head back out again and said, "We're not to be disturbed." Then, pulling his head back inside, Aurelian sat down and said to his protégé, "Now please tell me what you've been up to for the last ten or so years."

"That story is long and involved."

Aurelian sat back. "That's OK. I've got time."

Marcellinus began, "Well, when I first returned to the East..."

But he wasn't even able to finish his sentence before they were both interrupted by a noise outside. Aurelian jumped up and went to the opening of the enclosure. A centurion addressed him. "The men want to know your will regarding the town."

A somewhat perturbed, Aurelian responded, "My will is that you wait PATIENTLY FOR MY ANSWER!"

The centurion cowered slightly, bowed and walked backwards, away from Aurelian.

As Aurelian ducked back inside the partitioned enclosure, Marcellinus inquired, "What's the problem?"

"I don't know if you've followed our progress since we crossed the Bosporus, but every town that we've approached until now has capitulated to us before we came within fifty kilometers of them. This town, Tyana, was the first town that dared to defy us and refused entry to us. I became angry when I discovered that they wouldn't open their gates and I vowed to the gods that I wouldn't leave even a dog left alive in the town when I was finished. Many heard my vow. Then, before we even began our attack, one of their own citizens betrayed them to us and we took the town without a struggle. Now the men – you know what a bloodthirsty lot they are – are clamoring for blood. They keep reminding me of my vow. You know emperors are not really the ones in charge anymore. It's their soldiers that dictate their actions. The men want blood and I am at a loss for what to do. My reason tells me that if I am lenient to the citizens of Tyana, other cities will more readily open their gates to us and my task will be that much the less. And there's another reason not to harm these people. I know that you'll say I'm going mad, but last night I had a dream. In that dream a man named Apollonius, a former citizen of this town, a holy man and a healer, a man long dead, visited me. He said, 'Aurelian, if you are wise, if you wish to reign long and prosperously, spare Tyana.'"

Marcellinus, always the skeptic, shot Aurelian with a quick grin.

"I know what you think, but this has never happened before to me. And this dream was so real!"

After thinking a moment, Marcellinus said, "The story about the vision of Apollonius is the one you should use in the official version - the one that's recorded in the accounts of this campaign. But the more prudent reason why you should spare this city is the one you mentioned earlier. If you show leniency to Tyana, other cities will more readily open their gates to you."

"But what about my oath?"

"What exactly did you say again?"

"I said that when I was finished, I wouldn't leave even a dog left alive in Tyana."

Marcellinus bowed his head in thought momentarily. Then, looking up slowly he said with a smile, "Well then, kill all the dogs."

Aurelian looked stunned for a second or two and then a smile began to fill his facial expression. "I really have missed you," he said to Marcellinus and then left the enclosure. Marcellinus followed him out into the main tent area. "I am ready with my decision regarding the citizens and town of Tyana. The waiting centurion and others huddled in to hear their emperor's pronouncement. "I did indeed say that I would not leave even a dog left alive in this town. Well then, kill all the dogs."

The centurion hesitated in momentary reflection and then smiled. "It will be done." He turned and left the tent.

Another centurion promptly appeared with a citizen from the town of Tyana named Heraclammon. This was the man that had showed Aurelian a weak spot in the town's walls and betrayed his own fellow citizens. He was of medium height, but severely overweight. It was also apparent from the curls in his hair and his manicured nails that he had never performed any heavy labor in his life. A broad smile rested on top of his rather unusually large set of double chins. The centurion spoke, "My Emperor, the merchant, Heraclammon is here to claim his reward for assisting us."

Aurelian realized that he had been presented with another means of placating the bloodlust of his men. "Yes, your reward, Heraclammon…" Aurelian shot a quick glance at Marcellinus and then continued, "I feel afraid for my own safety when you are near me, Heraclammon. For, if you would betray your own friends and fellow citizens, how could I, a man that came as an enemy to your city, possibly trust you?" Heraclammon's smile began to fade as Aurelian continued, "I would continually need to watch my back and would live in constant fear. This cannot be for a Roman Emperor. Therefore, I decree that you should be put to death at once. Take him away!"

By now, the previously smiling Heraclammon had completely changed into a whimpering, whining wreak of a human being. He shouted, "I'll pay you money... lots of money...please!"

"Your money is of no further use to you now. But be assured that we won't keep any of it. It will go to your heirs as it should. They won't suffer for your treachery!"

"Wait....Waitttttttt!!!!" Still pleading, the fat merchant was dragged from Aurelian's tent to meet his executioners.

So Aurelian's soldiers had their blood for the day: the life of the traitor, Heraclammon and every canine within five kilometers of the city. It was not necessarily pleasant for the four legged population of Tyana that evening, but its human population was saved. The yelping of dogs could be heard for hours into the night.

Later that evening Aurelian dined alone with Marcellinus in his tent. During dinner, they told old stories and then, just as dinner was completed, Aurelian prompted Marcellinus to tell him of the last ten years of his life. "I want to know every detail," Aurelian demanded as he sat back once again in his chair and wine was continuously served to both soldiers.

"There's a lot to tell and then again very little to say. I returned to the East ten years ago and met Odenathus and his wife Zenobia. Odenathus was a good man, a valiant warrior and a great leader. He reminded me a lot of you. You would have liked him. His wife, or should I say widow, Zenobia is one of the best woman battle strategists - no wait - one of the best battle strategists - man or woman - that I have ever met. She is also one of the most beautiful women I have ever seen. And she's just, loyal, gentle and her needs are few. There is no pretentiousness about her. She thinks always of her people. In short, she's what every ruler could ever want in a queen."

Aurelian began to sense that Marcellinus had more than a detached admiration for the Queen of Palmyra. He interrupted his friend, sensing an opportunity of teasing him, "Well perhaps I will divorce my wife and take her for a bride after we conquer Palmyra. Just think what we could accomplish together. And from what you say of her beauty, I might also enjoy making babies with her. How many children does she have right now, anyway?"

"Five." Marcellinus tried not to show that Aurelian's suggestion of marriage to Zenobia had affected him, but he had little success masking his feelings from a man who knew him so well. He continued his story:

"With Zenobia's battle tactics and Odenathus's political savvy, we were successful in every campaign against Sapor and his Persians. We were also able to deal successfully with every usurper or other enemy of the Roman Imperial authority that surfaced in the area. The Persians finally gave up trying to push further west, at least for the time being. Then, right after our last encounter with them, when everything seemed to point to peace and stability, Odenathus and his oldest son, Herodes, were treacherously murdered at Emesa.

His next oldest son, Vaballathus, was only twelve years old at the time so his mother, Zenobia was named regent until he reached the age of eighteen. He should now be about seventeen, I believe. And then Gallienus refused to pass to Vaballathus the Roman titles that had been bestowed upon his father Odenathus, after all that his father had faithfully done for Rome, without ever once trying to take power in the area for himself. I know that the titles that Rome had given Odenathus were not typically inherited titles, but for the sake of gratitude and peace, what was Gallienus thinking?

He and his father Valerian were unable to successfully defeat the Persians. His father died at their hands. So he avoids the entire area for years and then he suddenly decides to send a force against the one army that was successful against the Persians? How could he have expected to succeed in his attempt?

Zenobia repulsed the army sent by Gallienus into the territory to show her "who was really in charge". It did just what it was intended to do. For when Zenobia annihilated that force, all those in the area realized who the real authority was in the East. You must admit things haven't looked too good for Rome, especially from here. For the last ten years, Rome hasn't been able to defend its borders against the Persians. If not for Palmyra..."

He paused, glancing up at Aurelian, then continued:

"There were also other leading and influential figures in Palmyra that have been pushing her to move more aggressively against Rome's provinces. These others were beginning to convince even me that Rome's days as an Empire were over, especially after the assassination of Gallienus.

But even all this didn't prompt Zenobia to rebellion.

Then, Timagenes, the Roman centurion from our forces in Alexandria (Egypt) came to request Palmyra's aid, as the soldiers there were ready to revolt against Rome. He believed that Palmyra was the solution to their problem. He convinced the Queen that Palmyra's protection was what was needed to prevent other potential "strong men", that might not be as lenient and "hands off" as Rome has been, from seizing control. So, slowly, cautiously, she began to move against Rome. And, for a time, I assisted them. At first I went into Egypt with their forces. But I didn't just go there to help them in their conquest. I also went to size up the situation for myself – to see just how volatile things were – and I found that Timagenes was right. Therefore, I began to assist Palmyra in its conquest.

While we were in Egypt, Zenobia, now committed to action, went north and west on a diplomatic mission, successfully allying Palmyra with Antioch and other eastern cities.

Meanwhile, as the Palmyrene army began to invade Egypt, the Roman prefect of Egypt, Tenagio Probus, hearing of the invasion, returned from a punitive mission against some pirates. He proceeded to retake Alexandria and much of Egypt. The Palmyrenes and their allies counterattacked and regained everything except a small garrison town high in the mountains of the upper Nile where Probus made his final stand. Timagenes, being familiar with the terrain, found a way around Probus's position. Then Probus, realizing the hopelessness of his position, committed suicide with his sword. His men capitulated to the Palmyrenes and the dying man called for Timagenes, who he considered to be a traitor, and me, who he had been told was with the Palmyrene forces. It was there that I learned that you had become emperor. And I knew from that moment that the Empire was saved... I just knew it!"

Aurelian smiled as Marcellinus concluded his story.

"But after all that the Palmyrenes had seen happening in the west and after all their own successes, I was unable to talk them into returning to Rome's rule. I can't say that I blame them. I told Zenobia that you could put the Empire back together if anyone could and that I would talk to you. I left Palmyra to join you. That was now almost seven months ago. However, I was ambushed by some nomads in the desert and held captive by them until a short time ago. I escaped and came directly to see you. Since she hasn't heard from me in all this time, she must think that I was killed by the nomads or that I was unsuccessful in my attempts to dissuade you from your campaign in the East and that I have rejoined Rome's cause and abandoned them."

Marcellinus paused now, realizing the time. "I guess that my story was a bit longer than I thought it would be. Anyway, I don't know if I can still turn the Palmyrenes back from the course they're on. I believe that if it were up to only Zenobia, I would have a very good chance. But, as I've already told you, there are others now counseling her that are strongly against any reunion with Rome."

"Well we'll see what we can do. I'll announce that I'm restoring to Vaballathus all of his father's titles, but that's as far as I'm willing to go right now. For all their good intentions, they have rebelled against Rome. The next move is theirs."

"Let me go to her. I know that I can convince her. I just don't know about her advisors. But it will be worth a try."

Aurelian interposed, "That's exactly what I *don't* want you to do." He paused, and then, with a wry smile he continued, "You appear to be more taken with this woman than you're willing to admit, and I want you clear-headed and with me one hundred percent." After another pause he continued, "Promise me that you'll not try to contact her until this campaign is over."

"But…"

"I must have your word on this."

The centurion wearily obeyed, "You have it. But swear to me that whatever happens, you'll spare her and her children. They've done nothing that you or I wouldn't have done in the same circumstances."

"I so swear. Just remember that you're not to contact her - in any way."

Marcellinus resignedly consented, "You have my word." "Good. Don't forget they're in rebellion against Rome. Now, let's get some sleep."

Both men stood.

"Tomorrow we move on Antioch."

XV

BATTLE FOR ANTIOCH

NOVEMBER 271 C.E.

Antioch, *(a pre-Islamic era city near modern day Antakya, Turkey)* was originally founded at the beginning of the third century, B.C.E. by Seleucus I Nicator in his father's honor. It was renowned in the Roman world for its grandeur. Its planners attempted to emulate the layout of Alexandria, Aegyptus *(Egypt)* by having two sheltered colonnaded streets meeting and crossing each other somewhere in the middle of the original town plan. By the time it came under the jurisdiction of Rome in 64 B.C.E. it had four walled-in quarters, numerous fountains and parks and paved streets that were lighted at night.

Although Antioch had become part of the Roman Empire, it was granted the status of a free city. One of its suburbs, Daphne, with its beautiful groves of cypress trees and lovely gardens and villas, was known for its moral decadence. The sanctuary of Apollo was there and many perverse sexual practices and rights were performed in the name of religion.

Just to the east of the city, the Orontes River ends its journey northward and turns to flow in a southwesterly direction through the City of Antioch and then into the Mediterranean Sea. To the northeast of the bend in the Orontes lay the Lake of Antioch. On the western side of that lake, along the road to Alexandria (not Alexandria, Egypt, but another city with the same name on the Mediterranean Seacoast, about forty kilometers north of Antioch) Zabdas's forces, consisting of heavy cavalry and infantry units, lay in wait for Aurelian. He assumed that Aurelian would stay within close proximity of the Mediterranean Sea in order to more easily obtain supplies from his navy along the coast. The area along the Alexandria/Antioch Road was also better suited to the heavy cavalry which Palmyra now possessed.

The sun was about to set. Zenobia and Verodes stood on the wall of the city that was adjacent to the city's palace.

What do you think about Aurelian's offer?

Verodes scoffed. "The peace offer and the restoration of all Odenathus's titles to Vaballathus is a complete reversal of Gallienus's policy. It's a political ploy. Aurelian's trying to make it appear that our actions are unjustified. If we accept his terms, we'll be in chains as soon as he enters Antioch."

"But his offer may be genuine. Marcellinus said Aurelian was a good man." Zenobia was near tears.

"Aurelian was just a soldier when Marcellinus knew him. Becoming Emperor of Rome can drastically change a man. Do you want to gamble that his offers are genuine?"

He paused. "Besides, victory is near. Aurelian's in hostile territory. The odds are against him. Do you want to risk your family's lives – the lives of your children – on this man's dubious proposals? Do you?"

She sighed. "No, but if we're going through with this, I should be with our men. I've always been with them for such crucial battles. If we stop the Romans here, our success is assured."

"Zabdas has everything under control. He conquered Egypt without you."

"Yes, but Marcellinus was with him," she countered.

"You have always overestimated the talents of that Roman and *under*estimated the abilities of Zabdas."

"Zabdas is one of my most loyal and capable soldiers, I didn't mean…"

"Zabdas will be just fine. Besides, we can afford to lose a battle. We have more forces stationed to the south and east and Palmyra is impregnable. What we cannot afford to lose is Zenobia, the Warrior Queen of Palmyra."

He paused again, and then … "Zabdas sits with heavy cavalry on the only road between the Great Sea and the Lake of Antioch. Aurelian may just turn back once he sees Zabdas blocking his only path."

"From what Marcellinus told me of Aurelian, nothing will make him quit once he decides his course of action." She continued, "And the road you speak of is not his only option. He can go around to the east side of the lake, head south and attack us from there."

"If so, he must cross over some rough ground on the northern side of the lake. And then the lake would separate him from his supply ships on the coast of the Great Sea." Then the argapet, after a brief hesitation said thoughtfully, "No, he wouldn't do such a foolish thing."

"It is what I would do if I were him."

"If Aurelian does adopt your strategy, we'll meet his threat. Remember he's outnumbered."

As the sun was setting they observed a commotion at the northernmost bridge that spanned the eastern branch of the Orontes. A small party had crossed the bridge and was now entering the gate leading to the town's agora. A crowd was gathering.

Zenobia and Verodes watched the party round the southeastern corner of the palace and stop in front of the tetrapylon. Zabdas led the group and it appeared that they had a prisoner – a man wrapped in a purple robe. The growing crowd of Antiochians began pelting the prisoner with anything at hand. Zabdas, his men and the prisoner headed for the palace.

Zenobia quickly made her way down into the palace's great hall, commanding the guards to allow the party inside. As the palace doors flung open, Zabdas and his group surged inward. Part of the mob that had penetrated the doorway with them was quickly pushed back out into the courtyard.

Their lack of success did not dampen their spirits and once ousted, they broke into riotous laughter. With the object of their abuse removed, they slowly melted into various alleys and doorways.

Once Zabdas's group was safely inside, Zenobia looked at the man in purple. She turned to Zabdas, puzzled, but excited. "Who is this?"

One of my men pretending to be Aurelian. Then, to the imposter, "You can take the robe off now, Zimbas."

"*Supposed* to be Aurelian? What happened?"

"The news is not good and once the Antiochians find out that Aurelian got the upper hand today, their meager support will evaporate. We must leave at once."

She repeated, "But what happened?"

Zabdas glanced toward Apsaeus who was with the group and then at Verodes. Apsaeus lowered his eyes shamefacedly. The general then nodded his head toward a small room adjacent to the hall. "A word with you in private, My Queen?"

Zenobia nodded and the two entered the room off the main hall that Zabdas had just indicated.

Zabdas spoke softly in a low tone, "After seeing the strength of our forces before him, Aurelian went around the east side of the lake and I rushed my forces to meet the threat. But ..." He paused and took a long breath. "Remember how you tricked the Persians at Nisibis into following us into that marsh? Well, Aurelian did the same to us. The Romans began to charge us. I ordered the men to dismount and shoot volleys of arrows at them. After a few volleys the Romans turned and fled."

Zabdas took another protracted breath. "Then, before I could stop him, Apsaeus mounted his horse and ordered the men to charge after them. I tried to stop the men; I shouted and cursed, but they ignored me."

Zenobia was still puzzled. "Apsaeus? Why would the men listen to him?"

"Remember, Verodes requested you make him second-in-command after Zabbai vanished?"

"That position was supposed to be a sinecure! He wasn't given any real authority."

An exasperated Zabdas continued, "The men didn't know that! And they were all excited thinking they had a sure victory. I couldn't stop them so I followed them. The men were exhausted when we arrived at a marsh. That was when the Romans turned on them - their infantry also suddenly appeared."

He paused again, taking a much longer breath. "Apsaeus turned and fled as soon as he saw it was a trap. I wasn't in the marsh yet, but I realized what Aurelian was doing. I went in and got some of the men to work their way out of it and return to our starting point. I stayed to cover their retreat. At first I was successful, but soon I was surrounded by Romans. Then Marcellinus appeared and told the men around me to let me go."

Zenobia, initially alarmed, was now dumbfounded. "Marcellinus? Marcellinus is alive?"

"Very much alive - and I'm sure he also shared with Aurelian your strategy at Nisibis!"

Zenobia's eyes burned with joy, excitement, confusion and subdued anger. "Marcellinus? Why? I mean, how? I mean…"

"I have no idea. When he first appeared, I was stunned and froze. He kept shouting at me, "Go! Go!" I soon realized that he was excited because he wouldn't be able to control the men around me for too long." Again he paused, trying to gather his words. "I got out of the marsh. When I returned to our starting point, Apsaeus was already on his way to Antioch, supposedly to inform you. So I sent someone to stop him immediately. If this news got to Antioch sooner, you may have been killed."

Zenobia tried to clear her mind of Marcellinus. "So how bad was it?"

"Most of our heavy cavalry is gone, but the infantry is intact. They're going to Emesa with what's left of heavy cavalry. We have enough infantry and light cavalry there to meet any threat."

Zabdas continued, "I think Aurelian will stay close to his supply ships for as long as he can before he heads east. He'll probably follow the Orontes south to Emesa and then turn directly east. He continued, "Emesa is a good place to concentrate. Even if he decides to head southeast in a straight line toward Palmyra, we'll still be able to head him off from there."

Zenobia commended and consoled him. "That's good judgment, but I may make some changes. Let's return to the main hall."

The two exited the chamber and returned to where the others waited.

Once again, she exhibited her genius. "General Zabdas informs me that our forces concentrate at Emesa. But I see no need to engage Aurelian again in a frontal assault. Sooner or later he must leave his source of provisions and go east. Meanwhile, we'll harass him and whittle him down as he moves."

Zabdas was easily converted. "I agree, My Queen. What are my orders?"

"Evacuate all the farms along both sides of the Orontes. Send them all south toward Damascus. That's more than a four hundred ten kilometer trip, but they don't need to make it all the way there. They can take what supplies they have with them and they'll be able to obtain ample provisions as they go. The whole area south along the Orontes is fertile. Send enough men to hurry them along and assist them as best they can. You can put many of them on boats and barges – just make sure that they move south faster than the Romans do. Then, destroy everything in their wake. Burn their remaining crops and food stores and anything else Aurelian can use. I don't want him to find any provisions within ten kilometers on either side of Orontes from here to Emesa.

An anxious Verodes interjected, "But my queen…"

Zenobia held up her hand to stop Verodes and continued, directly addressing Zabdas, "Do we still have any men to the north of us?"

"A few hundred stragglers. We also have a small cavalry contingent just east of here."

"Have ten of the cavalrymen drive those stragglers to the heights above Daphne. From that position they can hurl stones and anything else handy down at Aurelian's army as it passes. If he does pass them they can leave the heights and attack his rear – hit and run raids - no full scale assaults."

"And our forces at Emesa?"

"Go there and organize the men so they're ready to attack and delay the Romans all the way to Palmyra, if necessary, but, again, only hit and run raids. Aurelian will attempt to transfer food and other supplies from his ships on the Great Sea[9] onto supply wagons, but also onto smaller boats and barges that can navigate the Orontes. Where the river narrows or turns, block it with trees and anything else on hand. Station small cavalry units at those locations to ambush those trying to clear the river – hit and run. Attack his supply wagons at certain strategic points – again, hit and run. But most important of all, as I just said, make sure that there isn't a morsel of food for him to find on either side of the river.

In about 2 weeks, if all goes well for him, he'll arrive at Emesa. Make sure that he's not able to obtain any provisions there either. Then, he'll need to head east toward Palmyra. There will be no river for him to follow once he leaves the Orontes and he's got an eight to ten day march before him. Destroy everything for ten kilometers on either side of the route he must take and continue to attack his supply wagons all along the route. I'm going to Palmyra to prepare its defenses. If things work out, as I expect they will, Aurelian will never get that far."

An exasperated Verodes seized a slight break in their conversation and spoke out, "But why do we prepare for a siege when we still outnumber Aurelian at least two-to-one? When has the Great Queen Zenobia ever had to retreat within the walls of Palmyra?"

Although Zenobia had had about enough of Verodes's military advice, she displayed no frustration before the crowd. "The strategy I have chosen will result in the least loss of life and I believe it to be the surest of success."

The Argapet objected, "Yes, but I have ..." Then he caught himself, "Many of our citizens own substantial property in the area surrounding the city. All would be destroyed if we allow Aurelian to reach Palmyra's walls. The wealth of Palmyra's citizens is what finances its military endeavors, My Queen."

"More importantly, the *blood* of its citizens sustains those endeavors. Property can be replaced, but not fathers, sons, and brothers," she countered.

Then, turning once again to Zabdas, "Promise me that you will do as I request and not directly attack the Romans."

Zabdas agreed. "Your plan is a sound one. Everything will be done as you wish, My Queen."

Zenobia turned to exit the hall. "Verodes, please come with me. I need your skills to prepare Palmyra."

Verodes turned, but then headed in another direction. "Certainly! I'll prepare for our departure." He motioned Apsaeus to follow him.

Zenobia whispered to Zabdas who walked beside her, "Try to contact Marcellinus. We may be able to settle this without further bloodshed."

"I'll send an embassy at once to the Romans," he readily agreed.

Verodes, followed by his son, walked rapidly down several corridors and entered a small chamber. Apsaeus closed the door behind them and listened as a frustrated Verodes sulked while racking his brain for plan to thwart Zenobia's efforts.

He spoke in a low, but agitated voice, "She stood against the Persians when no one else would and now she gets cold feet! We have them outnumbered two to one!" He paused momentarily. "Lives! What are the lives of a few poor uneducated scum that fill Palmyra's ranks compared with all that we may achieve for Palmyra if we are successful; compared with all we have built and saved?"

Apsaeus attempted to console him, "Maybe she's right. The Romans may quit before they ever reach Palmyra."

"You don't understand. I took advantage of Palmyra's recent military and political successes and have invested throughout this entire region. We - you and I - own property all along the Orontes and from Emesa all the way to Palmyra. She's going to cost us a fortune if Zabdas destroys everything."

Apsaeus was dumbfounded. "But what do we do?"

Verodes was now resolved. "We take control. We attack the Romans and stop them before they come any further and push us into financial ruin." He then turned and looked directly into his son's eyes. "How could we possibly have lost to them today?"

Apsaeus stammered. "I...I...I think Zabdas just got out of control."

A glow now appeared in Verodes eyes. The ever treacherous, but quick-witted villain countered. "We'll have to take care of him then, won't we?"

"How?"

Verodes removed a small clay flask from under his tunic. "As you know I secured your place as second-in-command of the Palmyrene forces – second only to Zabdas. If anything happens to him, it is you that will lead our forces in battle." He handed the container to Apsaeus. "This is a very potent poison. It is colorless, odorless and two drops of it in a man's drink will kill him within fifteen minutes. Wait until two days after Zenobia and I have departed. I don't want to give her enough time to return and lead the men. Then, while dining, put this into the drinks of both Siboy and Zabdas. After they're gone, declare your leadership and that there's been a change in plans. Then lead our troops into battle against the Romans at once. If you wait too long, word will get to Zenobia and she will return to stop you."

"But I don't have the experience…" Apsaeus recalled his recent encounter with the Romans.

"You've always said that you could do a better job than Zabdas. You outnumber them. Just stay on level ground and there's really nothing they can do. But stop them before they ruin us. Stop them and you - not Zabdas - will be Palmyra's hero of the hour."

Those final words transported Apsaeus into a hypnotic, dreamlike state. He mumbled, half to himself, "Hero of the Roman War… Palmyra's redeemer."

"Then we can dispose of Zenobia and her brats!"

Apsaeus now spoke with renewed confidence and resolve, "I will not fail, Father."

XVI.

THE ROMAN MARCH TO EMESA

JANUARY – FEBRUARY 272 C.E.

Aurelian lingered far too long in the Antioch area. The majority of his time was spent restoring the mint and reestablishing Roman authority. When they finally did begin their journey south, they were first harassed by Palmyrene soldiers positioned on the heights of Daphne, just as Zenobia had instructed. From their lofty positions, the Palmyrenes hurled large boulders and shot arrows and other projectiles down upon invaders, killing and injuring many.

Aurelian sent men up to clear the troublemakers, but when they finally scaled the heights, the position was empty – the Palmyrenes had evaporated into the landscape, later to join their compatriots to continue tormenting the intruders as they headed toward their intended ultimate goal: Palmyra.

The bulk of the Roman force followed the Orontes River toward Emesa. The valley surrounding the river was fertile and the river presented a means to transport much of their supplies, at least until Emesa, where they were to turn almost directly east toward Palmyra.

The supply wagons, boats and barges were extremely important to Aurelian because he was now separated from his supply ships on the Great Sea[10] and only devastation existed all along the two hundred fifty kilometer journey to Emesa. Crops and homes were burnt and many wells were poisoned. Cattle were nonexistent, as all had been driven off south toward Damascus or to supply Palmyra for a potential siege.

In addition, the supplies the Romans had transferred to boats and barges on the Orontes were slowed and ambushed at every turn and/or tapering of the river. And those supplies not traveling by water, but in supply wagons, were also repeatedly subject to quick hit-and-run raids by the Palmyrene cavalry.

All along their route, the Palmyrenes persistently attacked the perimeter of the Roman forces as well. At times, the leading ranks of a Roman column would tumble into concealed pits dug by the Palmyrenes. Those falling into the pit would be impaled by spikes driven into the floor.

Occasionally, Roman soldiers foraging for food would find a farmhouse that had not been burned. But when the delighted soldiers entered the structure, the Romans still remaining outside the house would be riddled with arrows. Those trying to exit the shelter would meet a similar fate. The remainder inside, intending to barricade themselves within and shoot arrows at their assailants from the window openings met a more gruesome ending. Palmyrenes would rush and surround the house, close the window shutters, block the door and set fire to the house, incinerating its occupants. The tactic was macabre, but this was war after all.

The Romans were hungry and tired. Not only the men, but horses and other essential animals were withering away from lack of nourishment. Zenobia's strategy appeared to be working. Her plan to make the Romans' march to Palmyra a living hell was bearing fruit.

✦

Two weeks after the Romans' march had begun, Apsaeus, Zabdas, and four other commanders attended an evening meal in the main tent of the Palmyrene army. The army was camped approximately thirty kilometers north of Emesa, but well off the main road to the city.

The mood was jovial for the first time in weeks. Zenobia's strategy and been working even better than the commanders had anticipated.

Lokay, the wine steward and the steward's assistant, carried a jug of wine to the commanders.

Zabdas greeted the steward warmly, "Ah, Lokay, you

anticipate us well."

Lokay bowed toward the general. "It is my privilege to serve, to the best of my ability, those that offer such great service to Palmyra."

Wine was poured for all.

Of all those present, Zabdas felt not only pleased, but vindicated after the disaster that had befallen him just two weeks earlier on the east side of the Lake of Antioch. Although it wasn't his fault, he was the leading commander and responsible for any outcome, whether successful or not.

Prior to the current campaign, he had pulled Apsaeus aside and, in a threatening tone told him, "Remember, you are second-in-command in NAME ONLY! You are NOT in any way to give any orders to the men – not any!" The sullen Apsaeus bowed his head and acquiesced, but gritted his teeth.

A short period of time after Lokay had delivered the most recent jug of wine to the commanders, Apsaeus left the table, apparently to attend to an overactive bladder. He took his wine goblet with him, drinking from it as he exited the tent. After relieving himself at a nearby bush, he emptied his goblet and retrieved from his clothing the small clay flask containing the poison that he received from his father. He had waited far too long to act, but he now realized that if he didn't act soon it would be too late. His hand shook as he poured the poison slowly into the goblet. After throwing away the empty container, he did not reenter the main tent, but the tent of the steward and his assistants that were responsible for the preparation of the meal. This smaller tent lay to the left of the main tent. He stepped inside, pretending to have just taken a gulp of some wine in his goblet by wiping his mouth with the back of his free hand. He saw the large earthen jug that held what he assumed to be, the next supply of wine for the commanders. At that time there were only two men in the tent besides Apsaeus: the steward, Lokay, and one of his assistants. Apsaeus nodded to the steward and walked over to the cask. "Is this the next jug of wine we will drink?"

The steward merely nodded.

"Where is it from?" Apsaeus asked.

"A vineyard just south of Emesa… It is quite good, no?"

"Yes, it is very good. May I taste a small sample?"

Somewhat irked at the commander's impatience, but not wanting to risk a reprimand from a superior officer, he said, "We are just about to bring this one inside, but if you must have some this moment…" The steward lifted the somewhat weighty jug and poured wine from it into Apsaeus's goblet, not noticing that it was already a third full. Before the steward was finished pouring, Apsaeus stopped the man by lifting up his goblet against the mouth of the jug and pushing it upward, thereby halting the flow of wine. The steward, looking puzzled, returned the jug to its full upright position.

Apsaeus responded to the steward's look of bewilderment. "You're right. I should be more patient and wait for my comrades to share this drink with me." As Apsaeus said this, he lifted his cup up to the mouth of the jug, turned it over and poured its contents back into the giant container. The poison accompanied the wine from his goblet back into the container. He then set down his goblet on a nearby table and placed his hands on either side of the jug that was still held by the steward. He shook it vigorously saying, "Nectar of the gods! You are my only comfort!"

Being satisfied that he had shaken its contents sufficiently to allow the poison to penetrate throughout the liquor, he released his grasp, turned, and exited the tent.

The steward looked at his assistant standing close by, "Strange man…"

The other man nodded in agreement as the steward passed the jug to him to be carried into the main tent.

Inside the main tent, Apsaeus had just reseated himself when the steward, with his servant carrying the jug of wine, entered the tent and brought it to the commanders.

Zabdas greeted the steward with gusto once again, "Ah, Lokay, your timely appearance is always welcome."

Lokay smiled wryly, bowed toward his slightly intoxicated patrons and repeated what must have been by now his standard obsequious response, "I always try to please those that offer such great service to Palmyra."

As the wine was poured into all the goblets, including that of Apsaeus, Zabdas spoke, "Well our fair queen's plans appear to be working. I think that Aurelian will be headed for home before the week is out. His men are hungry and tired. He knows that if he doesn't turn back soon, they'll start planning to murder him."

"Yes, but in another week there won't be any crops remaining within 50 kilometers of the Orontes. We're going to have a long hard winter to face after this campaign is over," Apsaeus countered.

"Perhaps, but we'll face it as free men." As Zabdas said these final words, he took a drink of the fatal wine. Siboy and another commander closest to him also took a drink. Two other commanders continued a while longer in conversation after Zabdas's comment and so momentarily delayed taking any drink. Apsaeus, now feigning a fit of coughing, rose once again, goblet in hand, and went to the two commanders still engaged in discussion, intending to distract them still longer and prevent them from swallowing the lethal mixture until the poison had had its effect on the other three. He realized that he mustn't kill *all* of the Palmyrene commanders. When he reached them he asked several questions regarding the disposition of their troops, fully engaging their attention until it was obvious that Zabdas, Siboy, and the other commander were beginning to feel the effects of the poison. The first to show symptoms was Siboy. He placed his palms on his waist as he felt the stomach cramps that signified his doom. Quickly Zabdas and the other commander followed suit and before long all three were doubled up on the floor. They writhed in agony for a few minutes and then all three expired.

The steward and his servant knelt before the dead leaders having tried to offer some assistance. Still in bewilderment, they rose. As they did, Apsaeus sniffed his goblet and then shouted his accusation at the two men, "Poison! Traitors! Roman agents! You're trying to kill us!" He threw his goblet away, drew his sword and rapidly approached the two unfortunate men. He knew that he must silence the steward and his assistant first before they implicated him in the affair. He quickly dispatched Lokay before he was able to utter a word. His servant held up his hands and pleaded his innocence, but soon met the same fate as his master.

Apsaeus then knelt over the corpse of Zabdas with his hands on the dead man's torso. After a moment he rose. "Noble Palmyrenes, these treacherous Roman dogs must pay!" The two remaining commanders were dumbfounded. They looked to Apsaeus for guidance.

"Call our forces back from the north. Call all of our forces from everywhere within twenty-five kilometers of Emesa. We're going to teach these perfidious Romans a lesson they'll never forget right here at Emesa!"

The two commanders, now both quite agitated, shouted in unison, "We will, at once, Commander!"

XVII.

PALMYRA

LATE SPRING 272 C.E.

Once again, Zenobia stood on a city's walls, but this time they were the walls of her own city, Palmyra.

Palmyra's walls were roughly in the shape of the letter "D" lying mostly on its side, with the flat portion of the letter following the course of a small stream running mainly to the west[11]. There were several gates to the city, but three primary ones: the northern, or Dura gate, situated just to the right at the top of the hump portion of the "D", opened upon a road leading toward the town of Dura on the Euphrates River, almost directly east of Palmyra; the western gate allowed access to a road ultimately leading north toward the towns of Soura and Carrhae; and the Damascus gate, located at the far western end of the relatively flat portion of the "D", lay just south of the western gate. The road exiting that gate turned in a southwesterly direction, crossed the stream before it and then divided: the southern branch of the road heading toward Damascus and the western branch leading to Emesa. Two other smaller gates: the theatre gate, led to the theatre and the agora *(the meeting place of the Palmyrene*

Senate or Assembly); and the gate that exited the Temple of Bel, whose southwestern wall formed part of the city's defenses. Zenobia stood just to the east of the Damascus gate, looking down the road to Emesa.

Her aide, Abba approached. "Everything is ready, My Queen."

"How much food is stored?"

"Four months' supply…and all animals are now inside. Only the outlying villagers remain."

The uneasy Queen Mother added, "I want another two months' worth. Do whatever you must to acquire and store them."

Abba assented, "Yes, My Queen."

"Do we have any news from Zabdas?"

"None yet … I sent a rider this morning …" Then, glancing up at the horizon, "Wait! Look! A rider on the Emesa road!"

They descended the wall and raced toward the southern gate.

Passing through the entrance, Apsaeus immediately fell off his horse. Zenobia was quickly at his side. Fearful of the response she now felt she was about to receive, she inquired, "What happened?"

"We had them outnumbered. We were forcing them back, but…Aurelian just came on and on… The men broke and ran…they were slaughtered."

Zenobia was incensed. "Why did you disobey me and attack the Romans head on?"

Apsaeus feigned innocence, "After the Romans poisoned Zabdas and Siboy, there was no holding the men back."

"Zabdas was poisoned?" She paused and swallowed hard, but continued, "How do we know the Romans were responsible?"

"Who else could it be, but the Romans?"

"They entered your camp to apply the poison?" she sarcastically inquired.

"Lokay the steward was in the Romans' pay."

"How do we know this? Where is Lokay?"

"He's dead. I killed the traitor."

"How could you be so foolish?"

Verodes arrived, intending to stop the interrogation, but she turned and walked away, leaving Apsaeus with his father.

The following day, Zenobia ascended the wall to her usual position, just to the west of the southern gate. Since she had received the most recent news of the defeat near Emesa, she continually muttered to herself, "Marcellinus, why don't you contact *me*? Don't you care for me - for us - anymore?" She paused momentarily. "Why are we failing so miserably? Are the gods against us?"

She took a long heavy breath. Longinus and Vaballathus appeared behind her, but sensing her despair, they said nothing. They waited a few moments and then, stepping on either side of her, Vaballathus placed his right arm around her shoulders and Longinus grasped her right hand with both of his. All three stared out at the road to Emesa.

The road appeared to stretch for several kilometers in either direction. And, just as along the Orontes, the Roman's route east toward Palmyra had been laid waste of all food and other supplies. However, two full weeks after their battle at Emesa, their primary goal, Palmyra, was now within a half day's march. Marcellinus rode beside

Aurelian near the front center of the column. Although the pair were on horseback, they were surrounded by infantry. As scouts approached, the Romans halted.

They rode directly into the column to where Aurelian was positioned, the foot soldiers parting to admit them. "Well?" he inquired.

Somewhat short of breath, the first scout reported, "They're all inside the city's walls and definitely ready for a fight."

"Do the walls look as impregnable as Marcellinus has said?"

The second scout responded, "Worse. They're at least eight meters high and look to be two to three meters thick."

Aurelian turned back to an aide. "How far back is our siege equipment?"

The aide promptly responded, "A day."

Then, turning to the scouts again, "How much farther?"

"No more than eight kilometers."

"Good, then we'll arrive this evening."

Two servants held a pole between them on which a small dead pig was fastened. One of them removed one hand from the pole in order to scratch his ear and wipe the sweat off his forehead. Suddenly, his end of the pole slipped out of his other hand and the back end of the pig hit the ground.

An excited Aurelian bellowed, "Be careful! That's the only meat left within twenty-five kilometers and it's my dinner!" The frightened servant quickly picked up his end of the pole and both men stood nervously, but stiffly with pole and pig between them.

From her familiar position on the wall west of the southern gate, Zenobia spotted the Roman forces. Longinus and Vaballathus were with her. They watched as the Romans began to encircle the city's walls.

She quickly emerged from her reverie and suddenly announced, "I think it's time to stir things up a bit."

A curious Longinus inquired, "What do you have in mind?"

"Just a little something to give them a bloody nose and a small taste of what they've got to look forward to. I still don't see Marcellinus, but Aurelian left for the northern gate about thirty minutes ago. It will take him ten minutes to get back to this side."

She turned to Vaballathus. "Just watch me. You can lead the next group."

He protested, "Why not this one?"

Her response was rapid and succinct. "Both of us should not put ourselves in danger at the same time. We've got to take turns. You can lead the next group."

He hesitated, undecided at first how to respond. "Very well…"

She smiled at her son and then turned to give a few commands. "Get my horse. Tell Job's men to be ready for a sortie." The aids nodded and hastened off.

Soon, Palmyra's Damascus gate opened and a force of a hundred light cavalry, led by Zenobia galloped through it. Some rode to a bridge crossing the stream[12] that ran approximately thirty meters from the southern wall of the city and attacked the few Romans left to guard it. Others crossed the stream on their horses.

Soon, their entire force rode furiously toward the supply train with Zenobia in the vanguard. The startled orderlies cowered as they saw the enemy suddenly upon them.

Aurelian and Marcellinus had stopped near the city's northern gate. Aurelian was issuing instructions for the disposition of the Roman forces when suddenly a rider feverishly advanced toward them and pulled up within two meters of both men.

The rider's eyes were wide; his expression rushed. He shouted, "She's attacking our supplies! ... At the southern gate!"

Aurelian and Marcellinus exchanged glances and then began a furious ride around to the Damascus gate.

Zenobia's group had thrown ropes around the Roman provisions and began to drag them toward the bridge and back toward the Damascus gate. Zenobia then noticed the pig intended for Aurelian's dinner that was still fastened to a pole and supported by two upright beams. The porters of Aurelian's dinner must have decided to take a break in their master's absence. She threw a rope over the pole and rode away, jerking it off the beams and dragging it across the bridge. The remaining Palmyrene force closed in behind her. In seconds they crossed the bridge and headed for the gate.

Aurelian and Marcellinus turned on the western edge of the southern wall just in time to see Zenobia and her force entering the Damascus gate. Realizing they were too late, they halted.

Aurelian pointed at Zenobia and her trophy as she entered the gate. "That's my dinner!"

Marcellinus smiled as the gates closed behind the Palmyrenes. "Emperor Aurelian, may I present Septimia Zenobia, Queen of the East."

A resigned smile of admiration appeared on Aurelian's face. Looking downward, he shook his head.

XVIII.

THE SEIGE OF PALMYRA

LATE SUMMER 272 C.E.

The siege lasted for months. Many attempts were made to breach the city's walls with little success. Scaling ladders, when used, proved fatal for all those that attempted to clamber up its sides. Those arriving at the top first became impaled by spears, decapitated or cut in two by sword-swinging Palmyrenes. Those Romans on lower rungs of the ladder fared little better, breaking limbs or backs when colliding with the ground as defenders at the parapets pushed the ladders backwards and off the ramparts after disposing of the first Romans reaching the top.

Sometimes, their scaling efforts were supplemented with other modes of attack to improve those efforts, or as a diversion. Fifty Romans pushed a mobile siege tower similar to a latter-day Mal Voisin[13] up to Palmyra's walls. The Romans at the top of the tower, looking down upon the wall's defenders sent arrows down upon them. While volleys of arrows were also sent upwards at the overlooking Romans, accelerants were promptly applied to the support beams and set alight. Initially, flames began to overcome the lofty attackers who attempted to climb down the structure. However, the entire structure collapsed before its occupants were able to complete their descent.

At one point, Aurelian was looking at a map with one of his officers when they heard a commotion about two hundred meters away. They looked up and saw a group of men that had been operating a catapult being attacked by a party of Palmyrenes led by Vaballathus. After the Roman crew had been killed or disbursed, the king and five other Palmyrenes threw ropes over the machine. Two other men broke containers of a flammable substance over the contraption and a third, carrying a torch, touched it to the catapult and watched as it burst into flames. Then, all the raiders, including Vaballathus and the five others towing the burning apparatus, rode toward the smaller theatre gate. The device began to disintegrate as they rode. At the base of Palmyra's walls, before re-entering Palmyra, they abandoned the remains of the catapult, now a charred stump. Being too far away to offer any assistance, Aurelian and his fellow officer helplessly watched the entire ordeal.

Another siege tower was urged against the walls, but just as it reached its destination, Zenobia led a sortie of sixty cavalry that killed or disbursed most of the Romans pushing it and set fire to the structure. At the top of the burning device, twenty Romans were about to jump onto the city's walls, but King Vaballathus and others with long poles pushed it away from the wall. The fiery tower fell backwards and crashed to the ground.

Shielded from projectiles above by a movable roof-like structure, men operating a battering ram pounded at Palmyra's western gate. Aurelian lent his muscle to the battering ram at the very back of the device. Above the gate, Zenobia, Vaballathus, and many others tipped a large container holding hundreds of gallons of a flammable fluid onto the makeshift roof below. Two archers then shot flaming arrows at the shelter, setting it ablaze. The flames engulfed not only the roof, but penetrated through to the men and battering ram below. Since Aurelian was at the rear of the device, he jumped back and escaped the flames. Frustrated once again, he drew his sword and waved it menacingly at the Palmyrenes above. Zenobia, seeing an easy target, shot an arrow at him. The arrow penetrated his shoulder and he fell to the ground. Other Romans around him rushed to his aid.

Marcellinus sat inside Aurelian's tent, eating a date as Aurelian was helped in by several men. He was indeed, wounded. He rose to his feet. "What happened?"

"An arrow…I think that it was your Amazon Queen. What did you ever see in that woman?" Although wincing in pain as two physicians dressed his wound, with begrudging admiration, Aurelian forced a smile, which was returned by Marcellinus.

"Were you able to get us any provisions?"

"Some. I convinced most of them of our eventual success, so they let me buy enough food to last us another month or so. I also journeyed a bit to meet the Armenians that are coming to her aid and persuaded them, I think, to switch sides. I offered them a few concessions, of course. We'll know within a few days whether I've been successful or not."

That information significantly improved Aurelian's spirits. "Great! Your knowledge of the area and its tribes has proven to be invaluable."

"You just don't trust me to fight against my former comrades – especially after I let General Zabdas go."

Aurelian smiled, then winced as the physicians touched a sensitive area.

Marcellinus appealed, "Now will you let me talk to her?"

"Not now! Not ever! At least not till this campaign is over. I've told you why."

"Fine! But this siege may be your undoing."

"If I am to die here, so be it! But I'm not giving up –

especially not to *this* woman.!'"

In deadly earnest, Marcellinus looked directly into Aurelian's eyes. "I want you to promise me that until this campaign is over you will never take the fact that you are dealing with a woman into consideration in your plans against the Palmyrenes. Because if you do, it will certainly be our undoing. I have fought with Zenobia for over ten years and I assure you that she is no ordinary woman."

"I so promise. Now is there anything else?"

"Yes, I can't figure out why she or her son haven't tried to contact me. They may have thought that I was killed by that ambush when I first left Palmyra, but Zabdas saw me at Antioch. Even if they're angry with me they still would consider using me as a mediator with you."

"Perhaps because you're a Roman and they intend to remove our presence from the East."

"No, Zenobia wouldn't do that…she's…I…"

"You love her? Is that what you're trying to say?"

A flustered Marcellinus paused and attempted to collect himself.

"Since you returned to us, every time her name is

mentioned it's been written all over your face. And I have a confession to make. They *have* tried to contact you and I've turned them away."

"What? But why? Do you realize that if I can talk to them we can possibly stop all this without any further waste of manpower and provisions?"

"Marcellinus, I made you agree not to contact them for two reasons. The first reason I've already told you about before Antioch; your feelings for both her and her family. I want our campaign to be conducted with no emotion – with clear heads. But there is another, more significant reason that has developed since you first joined us at Tyana. It's a gut feeling that I have. I can't tell you what it is specifically, but there is another force here at work of which neither Zenobia, her son, you, nor I are aware. There is some other group or individual working against Palmyra's cause. I can't tell you what or who, but it's there. Part of my feeling relates to how the campaign's been conducted thus far. I'm in agreement with you that the attack at Emesa was not originally in Palmyra's plans. A lot of what you've just said tends to support my gut feeling. This force or person may also be responsible for the murder of Odenathus and his son, Herodes. So what I'm telling you is that whether we are successful or not against Palmyra, I think that Zenobia and her family are in danger anyway. I can feel it in my bones. Any attempt to come to an understanding with the Palmyrenes at this juncture will not help Rome, Zenobia or her family. We must move forward!"

"There's got to be a way to end this without taking Palmyra." Then Marcellinus, in a low tone, appearing to be speaking solely to himself, "There must be another way."

"At this juncture there's not. I want you to trust me and keep your word not to contact them. Do I still have your word?" Aurelian's voice grew louder in order to regain Marcellinus's attention, whose thoughts appeared to have drifted inward. He spoke louder and directly at his comrade and friend. "Marcellinus! Marcellinus!" Marcellinus suddenly returned from his temporary trance and looked at his emperor, commander and friend. "Marcellinus, do I have your word not to contact any Palmyrenes until this campaign is over?"

Marcellinus lowered his head. "Yes."

✦

Zenobia and Vaballathus entered the throne room where Verodes, Apsaeus, and other city leaders were waiting. When the rulers took their seats, Verodes spoke, "Your Excellencies, we have a proposal."

Vaballathus spoke, "You have our attention, Verodes."

"Most Noble King and Queen Mother, I am an

administrator, not a soldier. So far, we have done well against the Romans, but our provisions will not hold out forever and we know that Aurelian is as tenacious as a…"

"How your tune has changed, Verodes!" Zenobia interrupted. "Would that you had adopted this attitude *before* you drove Marcellinus away!"

Although, affecting penitence, Verodes's tone remained extremely assertive. "Most Noble Queen, I do not mean to downplay our recent successes. Your strategies have been of great value. Aurelian's army is tired and hungry. So just think what the appearance of an allied army of 50,000 to 100,000 men would do to Roman morale."

Both the King and the Queen Mother were puzzled, but Vallabathus spoke first. "What allied army? We are about to be reinforced by several other armies. The Armenians, for one, are headed this way."

"They have arrived, but have already defected to the Romans. Our men on the city walls by the north gate watched them go over to the Romans soon after they arrived." The perfidious argapet continued, "Your fortress on the Euphrates is just north of the town of Dura-Europus which, as you know, was destroyed by the Persians some sixteen years ago. But your fortress remains. That passage can be made in two or three days on dromedaries, maybe less. You can take the ferry across the river. Sapor is near death. For years you have put off his offer of marriage to his son, Hormizd. Perhaps it is time you accepted. The arrival of a Persian army at our gates would compel Aurelian to withdraw."

Zenobia was incensed. "Even if we have lost the assistance of the Armenians, we still do not need the Persians! And Aurelian might be tenacious, but even he has his limit. Surrounded by desert and hostile tribes, he is as much besieged as we are. He won't last another ten days. Besides, I think that I wounded him with one of my arrows."

"He is not surrounded by as many hostile tribes as he once was. Many of them are now supplying him with food and provisions." The villain hesitated. "But perhaps Aurelian will not last. Maybe he will reach his limit and leave. But Romans do not like to relinquish what they own. They are quite possessive that way."

He took in a long deep breath. "They will be back, next year or the year after, and with a much larger force. So why not join forces with the only other power in the East that has been successful against them?"

The king interjected, "My mother is not going to marry that dim-witted Persian oaf. Do we want to subject ourselves to a Persian's yoke? I, for one, would much prefer a Roman ruler to a Persian one. We *must* continue our current course and control our own fate."

Verodes seemed to have an answer to counter every remark presented by the King or Queen Mother. "The fact that Hormizd *is* dim-witted will prevent us from ever wearing a Persian yoke. Hormizd will be putty in your mother's hands. It will be she that will rule the combined Persian and Palmyrene Empires."

Then the argapet proffered the one comment that he knew would compel Zenobia to yield to his plan: "A queen must think of her people."

Vaballathus was enraged, "Now see here!!!"

Zenobia raised her hand to stop her son. He sat down, fuming. She lowered her head to conceal the inner turmoil that was written all over her face.

Vaballathus whispered, "You've done your duty for Palmyra your whole life. I do not wish for you to spend your final days with a man not of your choosing."

After a pause, Zenobia looked up and smiled. She touched his cheek with the palm of her hand. "I will go to the Euphrates and see Sapor."

Vaballathus was insistent. "There's no need for you to go."

"There is every reason for your mother to go, and you as well. Your mother's persuasive powers and her physical beauty will convince Sapor and his son of our earnest intentions," Verodes argued.

"I will go, but not Vaballathus. We will not risk the loss of both of Palmyra's leaders."

"But…"

"There is no argument you can make to justify the risk of losing the King on this mission." She breathed intently. "Now, how do we get through the Roman lines?"

Verodes continued, "Do you remember the system of tunnels that Odenathus's grandfather dug? The entrances lie beneath the Temple of Bel."

Zenobia nodded.

"One of them exits behind a thicket on a bluff well beyond the Roman perimeter by the north gate. I have already sent a messenger through it to Adar. He will meet your party with ten dromedaries at the Ookla Oasis." He paused. "It is two kilometers to the Oasis after you exit the tunnel. You can take seven Royal Guards; my son Apsaeus, Lord Timolaus and you, my Queen, for a total of ten."

Zenobia was puzzled. "Timolaus? Why am I to take Timolaus?"

"Merely as a precaution, Highness. Should anything happen to King Vaballathus, Lord Timolaus would be next in line for the throne. In Ctesiphon, he would be safe."

"And also a hostage of the Persians," she added.

"If you are not comfortable leaving him there, I understand. But you must admit keeping one of the heirs in another, hopefully safer, location is the wise thing to do. You only need leave him with the Persians until you and the Persian army finish chasing away the Romans."

"Very well..." she answered hesitatingly. "Your counsel is sound."

The treacherous servant feigned, "Your family's welfare is my chief concern."

Verodes turned and exited quickly, followed by Apsaeus.

A few hours later, Septimius Haddudan, the chief priest of Bel, Verodes, Apsaeus, Vaballathus, seven of the Royal Guard, and Zenobia waited in the cavern beneath the temple of Bel at the entrance to one of the tunnels. Just then, the reason for their delay, Timolaus, appeared in full battle attire. Zenobia fought to suppress her laughter.

She spoke like the mother that she was, "Timmy, why are you dressed like that?"

"My name is Timolaus, Prince Timolaus." He straightened himself and continued. We may need to do some fighting along the way, so I came prepared."

Zenobia looked to Longinus who had accompanied the boy. "Are you responsible for this?"

"I'm responsible because I did not try to stop him. But would you not prefer he wear protective gear?" the sage responded.

Still trying to maintain a somber look, "Alright, but not the spear … The tunnel is too narrow. Leave it here … the helmet too."

"Alright … Mother." The group all laughed and Timolaus blushed slightly.

"When are we leaving?" the prince inquired.

"Right this minute."

She turned to address the whole group. "Let's get started, shall we?" Getting down on their hands and knees, they began to enter the tunnel.

Verodes turned to Vaballathus. "You had better get some food and rest, My King. You have not had much sleep lately. I will have some food sent to your chambers."

The king readily responded, "I think I will take your advice most willingly, Verodes, but only for a few hours. Please wake me an hour before dawn."

"Most certainly, My King."

✦

A soldier entered Aurelian's tent just as the emperor was being attended to by the same physicians that originally dressed his wound. The tent was within a few hundred meters of Palmyra's walls.

The man bowed. "My Emperor, a Palmyrene wishes to see you."

Aurelian readily and anxiously responded, "Does he carry another message from the Queen?"

"I don't think that she knows he is here.

Aurelian stood immediately. "Show him in."

The soldier bowed and left the tent. Aurelian waved away the physicians and, as they exited the tent, put his tunic back on. Verodes entered with a Roman guard on either side.

"You wish to speak with me?"

Verodes bowed low. "Emperor Aurelian, true ruler of the East..."

Aurelian became annoyed. "Enough flattery. Why are you here?"

"I am Verodes, Argapet of Palmyra." He paused. "Most Palmyrenes have been content under Rome's enlightened leadership. If you grant us certain concessions we will surrender King Vaballathus *and* Queen Zenobia to you."

"You have them in your power? Where?"

"The King has been drugged and now sleeps in the palace. I also have information that will allow you to seize Queen Zenobia and end this siege, but first, the concessions."

Aurelian was skeptical, but cautiously proceeded, "I am listening."

"First, if you spare Palmyra we will pay reparations for you and your soldiers, but leave the city unmolested. Second, we would like things to be as they were with Rome before the revolt. If you must leave soldiers here, make it a small force and allow us to rule ourselves as we have in the past."

He handed Aurelian a piece of parchment. "Third, this is a list of those that convinced Queen Zenobia to rebel against Rome. They must be executed. And most important, my final term: promise that I will be allowed to remain Argapet of Palmyra and that no harm will befall me or my son, Apsaeus."

Aurelian began to read from the list, "Cassius Longinus, Nicostratus of Treizond, Callinicius the Sophist, Nicomachus..." He paused. "There are many distinguished names on this list. They all conspired against Rome?"

"They are all of Greek, Egyptian and Syrian descent. Those nationalities all bear great animosity for Rome. They should be executed."

Aurelian put the parchment down. "You're a traitor to your people. If your fellow citizens can't trust you, how can I?"

"I am no traitor! I am ridding us of a power-hungry woman that led us into a war to satisfy her own selfish ambitions!"

After pausing in thought momentarily the emperor conceded, "Your terms are granted. Now the information..."

"How do I know that *you* will keep *your* word?"

"You don't, but *you do have* my word and, if that does not mean anything to you, it does to me. Now, the information..."

"Queen Zenobia is headed for her fortress on the Euphrates. She intends to cross the river there."

"Ah, the Persians! When did she leave?"

"Less than two hours ago."

"How many are with her?"

"Ten in all, including my son Apsaeus – and remember your promise."

"I remember." Then Aurelian spoke to one of the guards that entered with Verodes. "Bring Marcellinus here, now."

Verodes startled. "Marcellinus? You are not sending him after the Queen? They are friends and perhaps much more. We may not be able to trust him."

"I trust Marcellinus with my life. We can trust him. You can count on that."

Soon Marcellinus entered the tent, and was surprised to see the argapet. "Verodes? What are you doing here?"

Aurelian interrupted, "Never mind that. Queen Zenobia is headed for her fortress near Dura-Europus. She left an hour ago with ten in her party. Go and get her."

"If they're on dromedaries we've got to move quickly.

Does she know she'll be followed?"

Verodes answered swiftly, "No."

"Good. If they were going at full speed, we'd never catch them. But they may not ride with as much haste if they don't know they're being followed. I'll take the few dromedaries we have. The rest can follow on horseback." Marcellinus turned to leave, but glanced back at Verodes with a blend of contempt and confusion.

Before the centurion left the tent, Verodes stammered, but in haste reminded Aurelian, "Emperor Aurelian, my son…"

"Yes…" Aurelian recalled and looked to Marcellinus. "No harm is to come to Queen Zenobia or to Lord Verodes's son. Is that understood?"

Marcellinus looked again at Verodes and then Aurelian and said, "I understand," as he exited the tent.

The fog coming from the west was getting quite thick. As Zenobia's party began boarding a ferry just south of her fortress to take them across the Euphrates, they saw Marcellinus and his men riding furiously out of the fog, not seventy meters from them.

Zenobia and Timolaus were on the boat but the others were not. She cried anxiously, "Leave the dromedaries! Get in quickly!"

Apsaeus pushed his way past the other men trying to board and jumped on himself. Four soldiers, realizing there was not enough time for them all to get on, drew their swords and faced the Romans. Seeing this, the three soldiers on board jumped off to join their comrades. Only Apsaeus, Zenobia, Timolaus, and three boatmen remained on the ferry.

"Spare any you can! But keep them busy!" Marcellinus cried.

The Romans encircled the Palmyrenes while Marcellinus headed for the ferry pilot, who was unfastening the last few lines that held the boat to the dock.

Zenobia was frantic. "Hurry!'

Marcellinus grabbed the last rope the pilot had just untied and tried to hold on, but the rope was slipping out of his hands. He turned to his companions, "I need help!"

Soon three others also pulled on the rope with him. The pilot struggled unsuccessfully to free the rope, but Marcellinus, now able to let go of it, drew his sword, leaned across the narrow divide of water, and placed the blade's tip threateningly under the man's chin. The man lost all interest in the struggle and raised his hands.

"Tell them to stop rowing."

The pilot nodded to the oarsmen and they ceased their efforts.

The centurion continued, "Have them fasten the boat back to the pier."

The pilot nodded again and the oarsmen knew what to do. As the boat was tied to the wharf, Zenobia, Apsaeus, and Timolaus all drew their swords. Four of the Palmyrene soldiers were now dead and three others had been subdued. Marcellinus jumped on board the ferry and shouted to his men.

"They're not to be harmed!"

Zenobia stepped between Marcellinus and Timolaus, drawing her sword.

Timolaus, trying to step around his mother, raised his own sword. "Leave my mother alone, Marcellinus!"

Apsaeus advanced behind the boy and ran him through with his sword. As he withdrew the blade, Timolaus fell to the ground. Zenobia, at first bewildered and then horrified, dropped to her knees. She cradled her dying son in her arms.

"Timolaus! My Timolaus. My dear, dear Timmy."

Timolaus, coughing up blood, apologized, "I'm sorry mother. I tried…"

"Shhh, no, no, no. You were very brave. Your father would have been proud of you." She smiled through her tears and kissed his forehead as he expired. Crying softly, she tenderly began to rock the boy's lifeless body.

Marcellinus, in a mix of remorse and rage, moved past Zenobia in order to have Apsaeus in range.

"I k…k…killed him for you!" The panicked Apsaeus saw Marcellinus raise his sword. "I am not to be harmed! I am not to be harmed!"

Shaking with rage, Marcellinus lowered his sword. Trying desperately to control his fury, he turned to his men.

"Bind him!" Now glaring at Apsaeus he added, "Make the bonds tight!"

His men took Apsaeus and Marcellinus dropped to his knees beside Zenobia, but she pushed him away. "Don't touch us! Get away from us!"

As he rose to his feet, Zenobia began to hum a Syrian lullaby, still gently rocking her son's lifeless form. Intermittently she muttered, "My dear Timmy. Dear

Timmy…"

Marcellinus compassionately looked at the pair and left the ferry. He approached Apsaeus, whose hands were tied behind his back, and placed his face within two centimeters of his. "I am going to kill you. It may not be now, but I <u>am</u> going to kill you."

He punched Apsaeus in the abdomen and Apsaeus doubled over. As Marcellinus walked away, he looked back over his shoulder. "I promised not to harm you. Did that hurt?" Apsaeus glared at Marcellinus as he walked away.

✦

Marcellinus and two aides, with swords drawn, strained their eyes to see through the fog. They heard horses, but the fog was too thick to reveal the source of the clamor. As the sun rose, the fog thinned and he breathed a sigh of relief as he saw the first of his remaining command.

"We'll ride the horses back. I don't want to spend another minute on those dromedaries."

One aide smiled, nodded and left. Marcellinus turned to another. "Marcus, get two men and follow me."

He boarded the ferry where Zenobia still knelt on deck, gently rocking Timolaus's lifeless body. Marcus and two soldiers arrived moments later. Marcellinus motioned for them to separate Timolaus from Zenobia. As the soldiers took the boy, Marcellinus took both of Zenobia's arms and pulled upward, raising her to a standing position. She resisted when his soldiers took Timolaus and again when he made her stand, but her efforts were meager. She looked at him. "How…could…you?"

Marcellinus, his voice failing, mumbled, "I…"

But she fainted before he could compose himself. He gathered her into his arms and carried her off the boat. The boy's body was wrapped and placed on a dromedary. Walking to a waiting attendant who held his horse steady, he passed Zenobia to the man, who held her until he had mounted and then passed her up to him.

The sun, now completely up, had burned off any remaining fog. Looking westward, he spoke to the officer near him, "Surely the gods sent the fog last night to protect us." Then, after a pause, "The sooner we arrive in Palmyra, the sooner this siege will end. Let's go!"

The group rode westward, away from the rising sun.

Aurelian sat with an arm in a sling as a soldier entered his tent. There were several other soldiers inside the tent. The soldier bowed. "My Emperor, Centurion Marcellinus has returned."

Aurelian, excited, stood up. "Show him in."

The man nodded, exited and returned with Marcellinus.

"Emperor Aurelian, I present Queen Zenobia."

Zenobia entered with two guards.

Aurelian approached her. "So, this is my most worthy adversary. Well, my Amazon Queen, you're the toughest opponent I've faced for quite some time!"

Zenobia didn't flinch, but her eyes were downcast. Aurelian stepped directly in front of her and, placing two fingers under her chin, gently forced her head upward. Then, in a barely audible whisper he muttered, "Ah, Marcellinus did not do you justice."

Zenobia turned her head to the left, attempting to avert his gaze.

He spoke to a guard at the entrance, "Bring in the King."

Zenobia quickly turned to see a groggy Vaballathus enter the tent. He was supported by two soldiers, being barely able to stand. A sigh of relief that *this* son yet lived briefly lightened her grief. She attempted to move toward her son, but stopped suddenly as the emperor continued, "… and tell Lord Verodes that I wish to see him."

Hearing Verodes's name, she glanced at Marcellinus with a puzzled expression.

Marcellinus spoke haltingly, "Verodes is the one who betrayed you."

Initially Zenobia expressed disbelief, but soon her countenance transformed to one of fury.

"Verodes's son, Apsaeus, the one we were not supposed to harm, killed Prince Timolaus. He stabbed the boy in the back."

Marcellinus's news startled Aurelian. He paused momentarily, "I am truly sorry for the loss of your son, Queen Zenobia." Then, after hesitating, "But I gave my word to Verodes that his son would not be harmed."

Initially she shook with anger, but when she heard of Aurelian's promise, she burst into tears. Instinctively she buried her face in Marcellinus's chest, but when he put his arms around her, she recovered and pushed him away. Covering her face with her hands, she wept bitterly.

Then suddenly she stopped and, through her tears, screamed, "WHERE IS VERODES?" With an extreme force of will she lunged toward the tent opening.

Aurelian raised his hand, "Stop her!" She was immediately subdued by two more soldiers at the tent's entrance. Then, to the two soldiers supporting King Vaballathus, "Queen Zenobia and her son will return to Rome with me. Their fate will be decided later. Marcus, take King Vaballathus and Queen Zenobia to their assigned quarters."

Zenobia and Vaballathus were led away. There was silence for a long moment. "Go to her. Explain things. We move out in the morning."

Marcellinus wanted to speak, hesitated, but eventually turned and left the tent.

After Marcellinus left, another aide approached Aurelian and whispered somewhat guardedly, "My Emperor, the men are hungry for blood. This city has been under siege for months and a hard siege it has been. They have all shed blood, endured pain and lost comrades in this siege. The amnesty policy that you've adopted since we crossed the straits has prevented them from sacking a single city. And because of your agreement with Verodes, they have been forbidden to loot and plunder Palmyra. Your leniency has deprived the men of any revenge they harbor as well as their main source of income when on campaign."

After a pause he continued, "And remember her arrogant response to your letter?"

Aurelian smiled. "I remember. I was quite incensed when I read it. But I realize now that it was just the written sparring of two adversaries in war. I've read it again several times and it doesn't really sound to me as bad as it did when I originally read it."

"But the men are still angry over its contents. Remember that you had me read it aloud to the entire army when you first received it."

"I remember. I thought that the letter would inspire them to fight harder during this siege. But it had little effect on the outcome. If not for the treachery of that man, Verodes, I doubt if we would have ever succeeded in our efforts."

Aurelian put his arm around the man and said softly, "I realize that you're just providing me with advice, Lucius. And sound counsel it is. The city of Palmyra will pay us reparations of which the men will share. And we're going to leave for Emesa tomorrow morning. I intend to put the instigators of this rebellion on trial there – unfortunately not the real instigators, but the ones the men will accept as the real ones. They will get their blood."

Zenobia sat on a bed in the tent that had been assigned for her confinement. Two guards stood just inside her tent flap. Marcellinus entered. "Leave us. Stay just outside. I must speak with Queen Zenobia privately."

The guards looked at each other, shrugged, and left. Zenobia looked listlessly into space as Marcellinus approached.

"Can you forgive me?" he pleaded.

Zenobia slowly turned her head toward him. Her face was expressionless at first, but then turned to scorn.

"Where are the rest of my children?"

"I don't know, but I've ordered them to be brought here in the morning."

"What happened? Why didn't you contact us?"

"We were ambushed by Tanukhs after we left. When I finally escaped from them I heard that Aurelian was already in the area so I went straight to him to see if I could stop things before they got out of hand."

"Well, did you succeed at stopping things?" she asked sarcastically.

After a pause she expressed her frustration. "If you only would have tried to contact me …"

"Aurelian insisted that my feelings for you were clouding my judgment. He made me promise not to communicate with you."

Although Zenobia appeared to be listening to him, she

suddenly turned away from him and covered her eyes.

"I want my Timolaus… I want my family back!"

He sat beside her, and tried to embrace her, but she pushed him away.

"Get away from me! Leave me alone!"

Marcellinus froze, not knowing what to do next.

"Leave me alone! Get out!"

Marcellinus rose, stood motionless for a moment, and then exited the tent.

After he left, Zenobia returned to her tears.

The following morning, a seated Aurelian looked up as Marcellinus arrived and stood hesitantly at the entrance to his tent.

"Come in, my friend." Aurelian appeared uneasy and paused momentarily. "I am Emperor of Rome and may do as I please, but because of your loyalty and friendship, I feel I must explain myself. Sit."

Marcellinus sat down on a chest opposite Aurelian as he

continued. "If I were to marry Zenobia and adopt her son, I would secure both ends of the empire."

"But…" Aurelian raised his hand to silence Marcellinus.

"I'd secure the East by marrying one of its leading rulers. I could adopt Vaballathus and, who knows? Together we might produce a son of our own, further uniting the Empire."

"But you're already married!" Marcellinus interjected.

Ignoring Marcellinus's interruption, "I've led a soldier's life. My returns home have been few. My only child, a daughter, barely knows me. My wife knows me even less. A divorce would mean nothing to them."

He continued hesitantly, "I know how much Zenobia means to you and as a friend I would never do anything to ruin our friendship, but we are servants of Rome and must do what's best for her."

Marcellinus swallowed hard. "What do you want me to do?"

"You will be prefect of Mesopotamia. Choose any location as your base. We cannot trust Verodes and his son and soon I may send Vaballathus to replace them."

He paused and then, "They will have to do for now, but watch them carefully."

As Aurelian stood, Marcellinus also rose to his feet.

Aurelian placed his hand on Marcellinus' right shoulder. "So, my friend? Will you be all right?"

"The only woman I ever loved was once the spouse of one of the two men that I respected most in this world, and now I will see her become the spouse of the other…"

Marcellinus attempted a smile. "Does she know of your plans?"

"No, and I don't want her to know yet. Things may change."

He placed his other hand on Marcellinus's left shoulder and stared him directly in the face. "Thanks for everything, my friend." Aurelian repeated himself once again as Marcellinus bowed his head and turned to exit the tent. "My decision is not final."

Marcellinus braved another smile as both men quit the tent.

Aurelian and Marcellinus emerged from the tent to see the Romans preparing to break camp. Zenobia and Vaballathus stood before her tent with the remaining three children. Zenobia hugged them all for what she knew might be the last time. Marcellinus approached her.

She was still cold and detached, but as she fought back her tears she spoke softly to him. "It's a comfort knowing they will be with you."

"It does not have to end like this. There is always hope," he pathetically offered.

She returned to a cold, bitter, sarcastic tone. "You were expecting a happy ending? Like that of a child's tale?"

Marcellinus was unable to respond. Zenobia and Vaballathus's guards indicated it was time to leave. The two mounted their horses and moved inside the Roman column. The children all wept as their mother and older brother advanced with the column.

Not long after the column with Zenobia and Vaballathus had marched out of sight, a soldier fell to the ground. Then another fell. The column halted and a third man fell. A physician was summoned and, upon his arrival he examined one of the men, then the second and then the third. Aurelian appeared.

Apprehensively the physician spoke, "My Emperor, it appears to be the plague."

After he spoke, all those near him backed way. The physician continued, "Fortunately, they are all in the same company. This group should stay here."

Aurelian hastily backed his horse away as well. "Leave them! Have Marcellinus make provisions for them. We must get these columns marching again … Quickly!"

XIX.

THE TRIAL AND THE SACRIFICE

SEPTEMBER 272 C.E.

Two weeks later, Aurelian's army arrived at the outskirts of Emesa and established a camp there. A trial of Palmyra's conspirators was to be held the following day. That evening, Aurelian had called the academic, Cassius Longinus to his tent and soon the sage appeared at the entrance, escorted by two armed guards. Another guard, stationed outside the tent, peered inside and announced Longinus's arrival.

Aurelian replied tersely to the guard's announcement, "Have him enter." Longinus entered, but remained silent. The emperor handed him a letter and waited as he read it.[14]

The philosopher looked up when he finished. "You believe that Queen Zenobia sent this letter to you?"

This is what I received from her in response to my letter offering her and her city clemency if she surrendered.

"This letter could not possibly have been from her. Her Greek is not as good as that of the one who wrote this letter."

"That is why I think that she may have been assisted, or coached by another whose learning is far greater."

"So you believe that I wrote this letter?"

"You, Nicostratus of Treizond, Callinicius the sophist, or one of your other associates."

"So you indict all those learned that provided her counsel and not those that actually fought against you?"

"Yes, and I do so for two reasons: First, Verodes provided me with a list containing all of your names when he betrayed the city. When he presented me with that list we were overheard by others and all the men are now aware of its existence. And second; my men have fought hard and bled much in this campaign. They've lost many friends in the effort. They want blood. According to my agreement with Verodes, I have spared the city and its citizens. For that reason and the list that traitor provided to me - now known by all - I am certain the men will want the lives of Zenobia AND her counselors as recompense. And you know what they will do to her before they kill her. But I can offer them those that counseled her and possibly spare her life."

Longinus still held the letter in his hands. "What if I told you that I had a very strong feeling that her betrayer,

Verodes, is the most likely author of this letter?"

"I would say that you are probably right. But there is nothing that I can do about Verodes, at least for the present. However, based upon my past experience with those that deal in perfidy, they eventually receive justice. For one thing, Vaballathus will not appear at the trial. I intend to replace Verodes with him as soon as it becomes feasible."

After a pause Aurelian continued, "In any case, all of your lives are certainly forfeit. But I may be able to spare Zenobia with some help from you and your fellow scholars and also from Fortuna"[15]

"Are you not the Emperor of Rome? Do you not have ultimate authority over your men?"

"As emperor I am extremely powerful and extremely vulnerable. I am sure you do not need for me to tell you how many emperors with supposed supreme power have been killed by their men, in many cases, by their own bodyguards. However, I have no fear of death. What I do fear is that, if I am killed, as you must realize, there will be civil war once again in the empire."

Before Longinus could interject, Aurelian commenced a long diatribe on the virtues of Rome. "I, myself, am Illyrian by birth. However, I am now a Roman citizen. Rome has united the peoples of many nations. It has provided a safe environment for trade and husbandry throughout its territories. Before I was raised to the throne the empire had splintered into many pieces. I have brought most of those fragments back into Rome's jurisdiction. And I intend to bring the remainder of those yet mutinous factions back into the fold before I die."

After a brief hesitation, 'What I *am* saying is that I truly believe that I am the one that can unite the peoples around the Great Sea[16] once again and so, I must live, at least for a while, in order to complete my task. The empire has provided security to those within its borders and I am committed to restoring that empire. So I must remain alive for the greater good, even if some of those that are innocent must be sacrificed in the morning – for the greater good."

A solemn Longinus now looked directly into Aurelian's eyes. "So you are saying that we, Zenobia's counselors are to be that sacrifice?"

"You AND she, but think of her fate if she is to be sacrificed."

After a brief moment in thought, Longinus stoically replied, "I will speak with the others." He turned to leave.

Thinking that he would commiserate with the scholar, Aurelian commented, "I have no doubt that I will soon join you in your fate, but, hopefully, not before my task is complete."

To the guards that originally escorted Longinus, Aurelian ordered, "Take him back to the others."

✦

The trial began mid-morning of the following day in the open air. Warm, gentle breezes fanned the enormous throng that had gathered before a table where Aurelian sat, accompanied on each side by two of his aides. The table had been placed on a small oval-shaped mound in order to allow as many as possible of the assembled soldiery to witness its proceedings. Zenobia was seated to the left of the table appearing apprehensive, but also somewhat puzzled as to the purpose of the meeting.

One of the aides to the right of Aurelian stood and called out, "Bring forward the conspirators!" A single file of the learned counsel that Zenobia had gathered about herself for the last several years, nine men led by Longinus, filed before the table and turned to face Aurelian.

The same aide then went out from behind the table, stood just to Longinus' left and, looking down the line of philosophers, raised a tablet before him and read aloud the names of the academics, "Cassius Longinus, Nicostratus of Treizond, Callinicius the sophist, Nicomachus ...." until all the names of Zenobia's learned counselors were declared.

After a pause, the aide continued. "While Palmyra was still under siege, after our most August Emperor, Lucius Domitius Aurelianus, graciously offered to pardon your queen and the citizens of Palmyra for their infidelity, you counseled your queen to transmit to him the following letter:

"From Zenobia, Queen of the East, to Aurelian Augustus. None save yourself has ever demanded what you now demand. Whatever must be accomplished in matters of war must be done by valour alone. You demand my surrender as though you were not aware that Cleopatra preferred to die a Queen rather than remain alive, however high her rank. We shall not lack reinforcements from Persia, which we are even now expecting. On our side are the Saracens, on our side, too, the Armenians. The brigands of Syria have defeated your army, Aurelian. What more need be said? If those forces, then, which we are expecting from every side, shall arrive, you will, of a surety, lay aside that arrogance with which you now command my surrender, as though victorious on every side."[17]

A voice from the crowd cried out, "The Queen must die! Zenobia must die!" A murmuring in the throng then followed the outburst and began to increase in volume, the entire mob, now shouting in unison, "Zenobia must die! Zenobia must die! Zenobia must die!" until the clamor was deafening.

Aurelian stood, and raised his hands to calm the men.

Longinus turned quickly to face his accusers. "I, and I alone, wrote that letter. I wrote that letter without the knowledge of Queen Zenobia or my fellow advisers. It is I, and I only, that should be executed."

Zenobia, initially confused, had fallen into an almost surreal state until she was awakened from her dreamlike trance after hearing Longinus's false confession. She bolted upright from her chair and placed herself directly across the table in front of Aurelian. "What are you doing? Why are you doing this?"

After Aurelian remained stone-faced and expressionless for several moments, she quickly propelled herself before Longinus and threw herself at his feet. Now in tears and looking up into his face, the only word that she was able to mutter was, "Why?" Then, swallowing hard she stood and hugged her trusted counselor and dearest friend tightly about the waste, burying her head in his chest. "I never knew my father. And, since meeting you, I have always considered you as mine. Please do not do this – please!"

The soldiers again began to grumble, louder and louder.

Aurelian raised his arms to silence the men. "Give them a few minutes!" he commanded.

Longinus smiled at his "adopted" daughter and stroked

her head until she looked once again into his eyes. He whispered to her, "We are all dead men anyway. What I have told the crowd was to spare your life. It was Aurelian's idea. Remember that we are old and you, even though you do not realize it yet, have much more life to live. What you have just told me has made my journey to the next life much more pleasing to bear." He hesitated. "Do not despair. We will meet again soon – in fact, in the twinkling of an eye." They both tightened their squeeze of each other for a few more brief moments and then he gently nudged her to the side and turned back to face Aurelian once more.

He bowed his head. Aurelian displayed a somewhat subdued smile in admiration of the sage and returned the gesture.

The aide then continued, "Turn about to face the men that you have counseled your queen to oppose, injure maim and destroy!"

The philosophers all turned to face the men. The aide now addressed the men. "What say you should be the fate of these traitors to the emperor?"

Virtually in unison, the men cried out, "Death! Death to them all! And death to their queen!" With the exception of one elder, whose knees buckled somewhat, all of the others stood upright and expressionless before the crowd.

Aurelian forcefully shouted over his men, "No! Not the

Queen! She is innocent of these charges. I am taking her to Rome."

After the emperor had spoken, the aide pronounced, "Take them away to receive their just punishment!"

At the cry of "Death to them all!" Zenobia fell to her knees and wept bitterly as her counselors were led away.

Turning to an aide on his left, Aurelian ordered. "Prepare a feast for the men after the executions, but make sure that they are ready to leave at dawn."

XX.

A SECOND REVOLT

EARLY SPRING 273 C.E.

Seven months after Aurelian, Zenobia, Vaballathus and most of the Roman army had departed, Verodes sat at the desk in his office in the palace.

Apsaeus entered. "Great news! Aurelian has been fighting the Carpi since he crossed the straits. He'll never be able to return this year."

A jubilant Verodes stood. "That is great news! I have raised an army of 150,000. We will be half a million strong by June. No need to delay any longer."

"What about Marcellinus?"

"His force is so small we can keep him a virtual prisoner in the Summer Palace. But we must get Antiochus from him. We will rule in his name. Have this sent to Marcellinus." He handed Apsaeus a sealed document. "It says the Senate demands the boy's presence."

Apsaeus puzzled at his comment. "You have not even

met with the Senate yet."

"Merely a formality. We meet in an hour."

"After I send this message, I will join you."

"No! You must terminate Sandario and the rest of the Roman garrison right after you send the messenger."

"I am to kill them all before the Senate approves our actions?"

"Once again, the Senate's approval is merely a formality. The Romans dine in an hour. Take them by surprise. I want no survivors."

"The Persian mercenaries will do for this job." In their current positions, Apsaeus had progressed even further under his treacherous father's tutelage.

"Good. Now let's proceed." The former argapet, who was now nominally the supreme ruler of Palmyra, beamed as he left his office.

A little more than an hour later, in the senate chamber, Septimius Haddudan, the chief priest of Bel, staunchly opposed Verodes's proposal. "What you suggest is sheer lunacy. Why start another rebellion and recall Aurelian to

Palmyra once more?"

As Haddudan finished, Apsaeus entered the chamber with two Persian mercenaries and approached his father. He whispered in Verodes's ear, "It is done."

Verodes then turned toward Haddudan and the other senators. "Sandario and his soldiers have been eliminated. We are now, once again, free of the Romans." A loud uproar arose and all of the senators stood in protest.

A stunned, but infuriated Haddudan demanded, "Who authorized this act?"

Looking extremely pleased with himself, a smug Verodes responded, "I did."

"Have you now made yourself King of Palmyra?" the priest sarcastically inquired.

Verodes responded with a brief and pre-rehearsed rejoinder, "I am regent for Antiochus, son of Odenathus. That is sufficient."

"Why did you even bother consulting us? You were going to kill them all anyway. You really have no need of us, do you?" Haddudan rhetorically inquired.

Verodes replied curtly, "You are right. I do not. You may all leave."

A second uproar ensued. Apsaeus signaled a Persian guard in the room. He walked to the entrance and shouted something in Persian and twenty-five more Persian mercenaries entered. The senators were literally herded out of the room.

Later that day, now in the throne room of the palace, Verodes paced the floor as Apsaeus entered. "Well?"

"Marcellinus is stalling. He says he wants to check with Aurelian first."

"That will take months. We must have the boy now. Surround the Summer Palace immediately. Do not let anyone in or out."

At the summer palace, fifty kilometers to the east of Palmyra, Marcellinus walked into the main hall as his aide, Marcus, entered. "A messenger from Haddudan has arrived."

"Certainly. Show him in at once."

Haddudan's servant, Offa, entered. "Greetings, Offa. You have news for us?" Marcellinus inquired.

"They have killed Sandario and all his men."

"Damn! I should have seen this coming," Marcellinus reproved himself.

Speaking in his leader's defense, Marcus commented, "How could anyone know just how treacherous that pair really is?"

Marcellinus did not even acknowledge Marcus's intended justification of his inaction thus far. He knew that, based upon the duo's previous treachery, there was really no limit to the possible trouble they might instigate. His mind was already working feverishly to develop a plan of action. Turning to Marcus, "I want our two best men to take messages to Aurelian by separate routes. In fact, wait a minute…" He moved toward the entrance to the main hall and called out, "Verus, I want Crassus and Otho."

Within seconds, Verus entered. "Sir, the compound is being surrounded. I believe it is Lord Apsaeus and his men."

Still pondering his options, Marcellinus, now Prefect, inquired, "How many of them are there?"

"A hundred or so."

He turned to Marcus. "We must create a diversion to get Crassus and Otho out. Let's move before they complete their encirclement."

✦

At the Roman camp in Dacia[18] Aurelian was dining with Zenobia when one of the guards at the entrance to his tent announced that a messenger with a dispatch from Marcellinus had arrived. Standing, Aurelian bid the guard to let the soldier enter. He had not noticed that Zenobia was also standing.

The message bearer entered. "My Emperor, a dispatch from Marcellinus."

Aurelian held out his hand. He took the message and read it quickly. As he did so, Zenobia looked apprehensively at him. "Call my commanders at once." He stepped outside his tent, not noticing that he was followed by Zenobia.

Within minutes his commanders arrived and stood before him. Upon their arrival he immediately announced "We knew that Lord Verodes and his son were not to be trusted, but we didn't realize how quickly they would turn on us. We'll leave a skeletal force here now to keep the Carpi at bay, but the bulk of our forces are returning to Palmyra."

"Lucius, you will remain here with three cohorts and contain the Carpi until our return – and YOU MUST CONTAIN THEM AT ALL COSTS. DO YOU UNDERSTAND?"

"Yes, My Emperor."

Aurelian turned to reenter his tent and was startled to find Zenobia standing right behind him. "What has happened? Are the children safe?"

"They are still with Marcellinus, but Verodes and Apsaeus want him to surrender Antiochus to them. They started another revolt and intend to act as the boy's regents to bolster their authority. They must believe that, since no one will be working treacherously behind the scenes as they did with you, their prospects for success are much better. As you know, the siege of your city was extremely difficult and without the workings of that devious pair, may even have proved to be impossible."

"Then I should go with you. I can be of great help to you. I know of ways into the city and can work from the inside against them as they did with me."

Aurelian turned to look at her. Her eyes pleaded her cause. "Do you swear by the gods that you will not try to escape and that you will return with me when the revolt is suppressed?"

"I so swear. What about Vaballathus?"

"He stays here. I can't risk both of you."

"You can keep him safely guarded with you. But once

I'm inside, his knowledge of the city may prove to be very useful to you."

Aurelian reconsidered. "Perhaps you're right."

✦

Sitting in the main hall, Verodes coughed as Apsaeus approached.

"Father, you do not look well."

Verodes looked listlessly into the distance. "I am cursed! For every Persian that arrives to bolster our forces, two die of the plague."

He coughed once again and turned to Apsaeus. "What news do you have?"

"We have tried to take the boy several times, but Marcellinus always beats us back. I think that damned Haddudan informs him of all our actions. But we can use him to flush Marcellinus out of his hole. He doesn't know we seized the messenger he sent to Aurelian." Apsaeus was unaware that Marcellinus had sent two messengers to Aurelian and one had already reached the Roman Emperor.

He paused in thought momentarily and then continued. "I will make sure that it comes to Haddudan's ears that

Aurelian is at Antioch. Marcellinus will want to go to Aurelian since he's so close. When he leaves we will storm the palace again with a larger force."

His father protested, "But others will hear the rumor as well."

"So? It cannot make things any worse!"

Verodes coughed and then nodded in assent. "Very well then. Good luck, son."

✦

In the summer palace that evening Marcus watched Marcellinus fasten his sword. "Are you sure that you can hold them off until I return?" the latter inquired.

"Certainly! There are only about a hundred of them and they are mostly Persian mercenaries. And I think that half of them are sick. Maybe they have succumbed to the plague." Then, after a brief pause, "How many men are you taking with you?"

"Just two or three."

"Even with that few, how will you get out?"

"By the same way Offa brought the information from Haddudan to us – through the tunnel."

Still somewhat concerned, Marcus cautioned, "But you'll need horses. The tunnel isn't large enough for horses."

"Offa will have horses waiting for us. I have already instructed him to do so." Marcellinus hesitated momentarily. "We'll move quickly, going on a direct angle for Antioch and not through Emesa. We should be back in a week at the latest. Are you certain that you can hold out 'til then?"

"Without a doubt. They shouldn't be a problem. They've proved themselves to be quite sedentary since their last attempt."

"Good! I'm responsible for those children. I don't want to leave them in any potential jeopardy while I'm gone. But the sooner we leave, the sooner we'll be back! So we'd better get started."

Later that evening, after Marcellinus's departure, Apsaeus returned to the summer palace with another five hundred Persian mercenaries. Just before dawn, they scaled its walls. A sleepy sentry stirred, heard the attackers and woke the entire garrison. The element of surprise gone, the Persians shouted as they continued to scale the walls. Although they had been alerted, the Romans on guard duty were quickly killed and their bodies tossed over the walls. There were simply too many of the invaders. Those soon inside quickly opened the gates and the remainder of their force stormed inside the courtyard.

Awaking from sleep, Roman soldiers quickly exited their barracks, hastily put on their fighting gear and grabbed their weapons as they ran to support the other defenders. But their noble efforts were in vain. They were overwhelmed by the sheer number of the intruders. The assailants swiftly ran throughout the compound, striking down the half-dressed, half-armed Romans. Within moments, all form of resistance had been eliminated.

In the children's quarters, Marcus quickly gathered up the children.

With his sword drawn he whispered to them all, "Follow me." He headed toward the tunnel, but was intercepted by Apsaeus and about ten Persians.

Apsaeus called out, "Surrender the children and you will live!"

Marcus snorted, "Somehow I don't quite believe you."

Apsaeus nodded and all ten Persians attacked him at once. He fought bravely and ferociously, but was eventually overcome.

"I'll kill him if you come any closer."

Apsaeus looked up and saw Faustula holding a knife to Antiochus' throat. He held up his hand to stop the others and slowly walked toward her.

"Go ahead, kill him. I will take him dead or alive. It doesn't matter to me." He continued walking toward her.

Livia was crying behind Faustula, holding onto Faustula's night clothing.

"I mean it! I'll really do it!"

Apsaeus grinned. "Go ahead. I want to see you do it."

Her bluff called, she released Antiochus and rushed at Apsaeus with the knife. "Traitor!" She screamed.

He sidestepped her assault, but her knife tore across his upper left arm. He screamed in pain. He grasped her knife hand and held her momentarily, looking into her eyes.

Then, with a lustful smile, "You're a lot like your mother and quite beautiful - maybe even more beautiful."

He passed her to a one of his Persian accomplices. "They all are not to be molested." We are taking them all back to Palmyra." Emerging from the entrance to the palace into the courtyard, he moved quickly toward three Persian mercenaries standing beside the bodies of two dead Romans.

"Are they <u>all</u> dead?" he asked.

"I think so, we have…"

As the man spoke, a Roman within thirty meters of them jumped onto a horse and quickly rode through the open gate. "You idiots!" Apsaeus cried. For the moment they glanced at one another as if looking to divert the blame to the other. "Well…go get him!" He bellowed.

Ten Persians mounted their horses to chase the runaway.

The Roman fugitive rode at breakneck speed, pursued desperately by the ten Persians. There was about two hundred meters distance between the pursued and his pursuers. However, the Roman proved to be a good horseman and was gradually pulling away from them.

Two of the Persians coughed. One, then the other, fell from his horse. The Roman soon had a considerable lead on the remainder of the mob. He abruptly stopped his horse and dropped to the ground, grabbing his bow and quiver. Balancing on one knee he took aim and released an arrow. A Persian fell to the ground. He released another arrow and another Persian fell. The Roman was obviously one of those that had originally arrived with Marcellinus many years ago and had picked up the Palmyrene's proficiency with the bow.

He quickly jumped back on his horse. During his archery attack, the Persians had closed the gap to within a hundred meters of him, but he soon widened the gap once again and now only six men followed him. Once he had recouped a sufficient lead, he stopped, dropped to the ground and quickly felled another Persian. The remaining five pulled up, hesitating.

As they sat on their horses and debated their next move, the Roman released another arrow and eliminated another of their lot. The remaining four looked at each other, turned and rode toward the Euphrates River.

The Roman then replaced his bow and quiver, mounted his horse and rode steadily and directly northwest toward Antioch. His pace was not as rapid as it was during the chase, but still he advanced at more than just a leisurely trot.

On the second day of their journey, as Marcellinus and his group rode on their projected direct path toward Antioch, they saw the survivor of the attack on the summer palace approaching from their rear. Although they were moving at a brisk pace, after seeing the group, the survivor had further increased his already rapid tempo to a full gallop, riding at a speed that might soon prove fatal to his horse. Marcellinus signaled his companions to pause and before long the man halted before them.

"They took the palace! Everyone was killed!"

In a fearful state, Marcellinus cried out, "They killed the children?"

"I don't know. I didn't see them."

"Marcus…" Marcellinus hesitated. "I should not have left them." He bowed his head in silence, then looked up. "They wouldn't kill the children. That's their only claim to legitimacy. I will have to assume that. I <u>must</u> assume that."

In a somber mode, he spoke slowly, "Well, since we're so close to Aurelian at this point, we will continue on and meet him. Then we can return, hopefully, for the children." Turning to the messenger of the dismal news, "Stay here and get some rest. There is a water hole not far back. We'll return for you." The messenger was provided with some food provisions and then, to the others, "Let's go quickly!"

They galloped off toward Antioch and Aurelian's army.

Aurelian had also elected to travel on a direct angle for Palmyra and they had traveled at an amazing speed for an army of its size. Marcellinus's group rendezvoused with them by noon of the following day. The Roman army had paused for a brief respite from the heat that was unusually severe for the season. He was taken immediately to the emperor and was surprised, but pleased, to see Zenobia riding with him.

Upon seeing him, Aurelian grew anxious. Marcellinus's arrival could not possibly bear good tidings. "Why have you come? Do you have some further news?"

"When I heard you were close, I left to meet you. I have just received word that Apsaeus took the palace soon after I left."

Zenobia spoke out, "The children?"

"I don't know, but Verodes wanted Antiochus so that he could act as his regent. So there's a good chance they weren't killed."

"A good chance?" There was fear in her voice, but also a touch of sarcasm.

He put his head down in shame. "I should never have left them, but at the time I started out to meet you we had beaten them back several times and it appeared that they had resolved to just keep us penned in. Apsaeus must have brought a lot more men."

He turned to Aurelian. "With your permission, I'd like to return to Palmyra immediately and try to free the children."

Aurelian paused in thought and then, "A smaller force will definitely move much quicker. Do you think you can do it?"

"I can try."

"Take one unit of light cavalry with you."

Marcellinus countered, "I'll be better off with less – ten or twenty at most."

As he turned his horse to leave…

"Wait! I can get us inside the city to free the children and then work from the inside to open the gates to your army when you arrive. And I can do that all without being noticed." Zenobia looked pleadingly at Aurelian and then Marcellinus.

After a long hesitation, Aurelian reluctantly agreed, "All right. Go! But be careful." He hesitated again. "I must be getting soft in my old age."

Marcellinus and Zenobia rode off toward one of the cavalry units as Aurelian watched them momentarily. Then he shouted to his men, "All right! Move out!"

Back at the summer palace, Marcellinus carried Marcus's

body to a funeral pyre. He gently laid it down and stepped back. Turning to the others, he asked, "Do we have everyone?"

"Yes, Sir," the soldier nearest to him replied.

"Light it."

Marcellinus and the others watched as the flames rose.

Turning to Zenobia he asked, "So how do we get into the city?"

"We can get inside the same way I got out. There's a tunnel that originates in the Temple of Bel. Verodes thinks that everyone who went through the tunnel with me is either dead or far away, so he won't have blocked it."

"All right – if we do get in and rescue the children, we can barricade ourselves in the Temple and hold off Apsaeus's men until Aurelian arrives. Or perhaps I can leave you and the children in the Temple and create some mischief inside of the walls to help Aurelian gain access from the outside."

Zenobia, Marcellinus, and the others watched the flames slowly burn. He held out his hand and gently took hers. At first she startled and then slowly pulled her hand away, but not in a defiant manner. After the passage of several months since her capture, her passions, at least those toward her former lover, had cooled. But they were not completely spent and she was yet uncertain as to how to feel. She was still anxious about her children and was impatient to leave for Palmyra as soon as possible.

Verodes sat smugly on the throne as Apsaeus entered. The latter appeared quite agitated.

"Do you have the boy, Antiochus?"

"Yes, and the rest of her brats. But …"

Verodes cut off his son, "He is all we need. We can rule in his name. The others you can dispose of as you wish."

"But Father, Aurelian has returned. He's only a few kilometers from us and we're not ready! We have less than 100,000 healthy troops!"

The news stunned Verodes. "How could he possibly have made it back here so quickly?" However, the quick witted villain swiftly recovered. "You still have as many men as he does and he must scale our eight meter high walls. He will not be able to lure us out like we did to Zenobia." He smiled, quite pleased with himself. "Indeed! All we need do for now is hold this city until the main Persian force arrives."

Verodes stood and walked toward the main entrance. "I am going to check on our siege supplies. You cannot be too careful!"

An initially muted smile suddenly expanded across Apsaeus's face. He whispered softly to himself, "But first, I think I will check on the princess." In a few moments he entered the corridor leading to Faustula's chamber.

✦

Just an hour earlier, one by one, Zenobia, Marcellinus, and the members of their group emerged into the Temple of Bel through its entrance to the cavern below. There were, in all, twelve in their group. As they entered, a startled Haddudan turned toward them.

In a whisper, Marcellinus greeted the priest. "Haddudan, it is good to see you!"

Haddudan, seeing Zenobia as well, was somewhat puzzled, but replied slowly and cautiously, "And even better to see you!"

Zenobia spoke first, "Aurelian's army will be here shortly. We are here to try and rescue the children before he attacks. Do you think the children are still in the palace?" Bel's high priest responded guardedly, "Most likely. How may I assist you?" He understood Zenobia's desire to free her children, but was still perplexed as to why she was being allowed to accompany the group.

Marcellinus spoke before Zenobia had time to respond. "If we are successful, we may soon need to place some young guests in your keeping. Is there somewhere that they may be kept safely hidden?"

"Certainly," the priest replied. "But do not return by way of the tunnel. It will be too risky."

There began a pounding on the main door to the temple. "Open up! Open up in the name of Lord Verodes!"

Marcellinus commented to Zenobia, "Verodes must have remembered the tunnel."

Haddudan pointed to a rear door. Then in a hushed voice he whispered, "Use that door! You must leave immediately! Use that door for your return as well."

Marcellinus and Zenobia looked at one another.

The pounding increased in intensity. The priest's concern heightened, "GO NOW! QUICKLY!"

"Be ready for our return," Marcellinus whispered and turned to Zenobia. "Lead on My Queen."

Zenobia turned and looked quizzically at him, but then, stealthily, she, Marcellinus, and the rest of their group went through a rear door of the temple that entered the street leading to the monumental arch.

Just as they exited, a voice from outside the main door screamed, "Open up or we'll knock it down!"

"Patience! Patience, please! I'm coming!" Haddudan went to the door, opened it and a swarm of twelve Persian soldiers surged into the room. He quickly stepped aside to avoid being trampled.

In a hurried voice, a Persian officer bellowed in heavily accented Syriac, "The tunnel…where is it?"

"This way." Relieved by the timing of their arrival, Haddudan led the entire group through the entrance to the tunnel below. Naturally, due to their tardy appearance, there was nothing or anyone to be found.

Marcellinus, Zenobia, and their fellow interlopers soundlessly maneuvered from their exit to a building across the road from the entrance to the palace. They peered at the four Persian soldiers guarding the entrance to the palace. After a few moments, the group split up into three units of four. Marcellinus and Zenobia, remaining in the shadows, led two of the units stealthily across the street - each group to either side of the entrance.

When they were in place, Marcellinus nodded to the four remaining men across the street. The men began their rowdy walk toward the palace entrance. At first the guards were cautious, but, since the approaching men appeared to be drunk, they relaxed their vigilance.

One guard shouted at them, "Go away! You're not coming near this place, especially in your condition! Now go away!" The guards stepped out a few paces into the street to halt the drunken party's progress.

Moments later, all four guards lay on the ground pierced by several stab wounds. Quickly, the bodies were removed to a dark corner and the entire group entered the palace.

They stalked through the deserted main hall and entered the corridor leading to Zenobia's chamber. The bedchamber was empty.

Zenobia pointed down one corridor. "This one leads to the boys' room," … then pointing to another, "The other leads to the girls' room." Zenobia had momentarily failed to remember that only one of her sons remained in Palmyra. She had forgotten, or forced out of her memory, the fact that Timolaus was no more.

She immediately headed down the corridor leading to Antiochus's room. Marcellinus motioned for four of his men to follow her. He and the remaining men proceeded down the other hallway.

After a few moments, Zenobia entered the room of the sleeping Antiochus from the rear. She walked over to him, trying to quietly wake him, but he was surprised to see his mother…

"Mother! You're back!" He shouted with glee.

She tried to silence him, but it was too late. Four Persian guards charged in, but they were quickly overcome. However, one of the Romans with Zenobia was also slain in the scuffle.

Meanwhile, Marcellinus sent three of his men to Livia's room and then approached Faustula's room with the remaining three men. As he approached, he heard sounds of a struggle. He swiftly entered the room.

Apsaeus, having knocked Faustula unconscious onto the bed, was beginning to take off his belt. However, during the process, he saw Marcellinus enter.

Marcellinus goaded him, "Go on…keep going."

The villain drew his sword from his loosened scabbard. He lifted the unconscious Faustula up until she was upright, facing Marcellinus. She regained consciousness just as the blade of Apsaeus's sword was placed against her neck.

"Keep away unless you want to see her pretty throat cut."

Apsaeus backed up toward the foyer entrance. He shouted over his shoulder to the Persian guards standing in the foyer.

"Guards! Intruders!"

Six Persian guards, swords drawn, burst through the doors, stopping right at the entrance to the bedroom. Apsaeus continued to back up with Faustula, his blade still pressed against her throat. He forced himself backwards through the Persians until they were between Marcellinus and himself. "Get them!"

The Persians moved quickly into the chamber to attack the somewhat smaller band of Romans. Apsaeus lowered his sword, dropped Faustula and fled.

Although they were slightly outnumbered, Marcellinus's men slew all the Persians within minutes, but lost another of his number in the *mêlée.* He then quickly went to the foyer, knelt, and picked up the semi-conscious Faustula.

Lifting her up by the shoulders, "Are you hurt?"

She was a bit dazed, but responded surprisingly fast, "I'll be fine."

He helped her stand. The three guards Marcellinus had sent to Livia's room, now entered Faustula's bedchamber with the seven year old. They all then headed toward the main hall.

Zenobia and the others were already in the hall with Antiochus when Faustula, Livia, Marcellinus, and his group arrived.

"Did Apsaeus come through this way?"

"I don't know. We just got here." Then, after a brief hesitation, she anxiously asked, "Was Apsaeus in Faustula's room?"

"Not long enough," Marcellinus assured her. "Let's go."

After abandoning the princess, Apsaeus rushed down the corridor into the main hall and then escaped through the main entrance. As he did, he heard a distant clamor further down the colonnade at the Damascus gate. It was Aurelian's forces beginning their assault. The emperor, more warrior than emperor, had decided to put all of his force at the Damascus gate, assuming that, by concentrating, they would apply maximum pressure at one key point.

Apsaeus immediately realized that his fate now hung in the balance, so, as terrified as he was, it had become a case of fight or perish. Thus necessity enabled him to overcome his fears and gave him sufficient determination to run toward that gate. Soon he was in the thick of things and the fury of battle allowed him to forget all else but preventing Aurelian's forces from breaching the gate.

As Marcellinus, Zenobia and their entire group emerged from the palace they also became aware of the commotion at the somewhat distant Damascus gate.

"Aurelian's here! The attack has begun!" Marcellinus turned to two of his fellow Romans. "Take the children to the Temple of Bel. Enter through the same door we came out. Leave them with Haddudan and then," pointing down the Grand Colonnade, "meet us at that gate."

The children and their two guards left in the direction of the temple.

"There may be some Palmyrenes left that can help us. Apsaeus and his Persians couldn't have killed them all." Zenobia looked to Marcellinus for a response. He returned her glance, but appeared dubious.

"There must be some left alive! I must try!" she pleaded.

"Take three men. Gather what men you can and meet us at the Damascus gate." He pointed to three Romans. "You three! Go with the Queen."

Looking at Zenobia, he began to say something, but stopped himself. Then after a pause... "Good luck." Zenobia and her trio of Romans headed down one of

Palmyra's streets.

Then to his remaining Romans compatriots, "This way. Let's go!" They hastened toward the Damascus gate.

✦

Aurelian directed the assault on the gate. Some attacked the gate with a large battering ram and others attempted to mount the nearby walls with scaling ladders. Boulders launched by catapults smash at Palmyra's walls overhead.

Vaballathus approached, guarded by two Roman soldiers. "Why is this man here?" Aurelian questioned the pair. "I left orders that he was to remain back at the camp."

But before either man was able to reply, Vaballathus spoke, "That is my city. My family is in there. I must help!"

Aurelian sighed. "All right. But you're staying right by my side. Is that clear?"

"Of course."

Aurelian looked at him wryly. But Aurelian, always more at home on the battlefield, was a hands-on-type emperor. Soon he, Vaballathus and the pair originally assigned to guard the king, joined in the group using the battering ram.

✦

Marcellinus and his group stopped fifty meters before the gate. At its top they saw Apsaeus and his Persians, feverishly fighting off the Romans that were attempting to scale Palmyra's walls and throwing large rocks down upon those operating the battering ram against the gate.

They rushed the gate, fighting through the few Persians that were reinforcing it and applying force to counter the battering ram's blows. The surprised Persians turned on their assailants and fought desperately while still trying to hold the gate shut against the Romans on the outside.

Marcellinus's group was initially successful. They cleared their side of the gate of Persians and slowly began to lift from its fasteners the heavy wooden bolt that kept both gate doors shut. However, the Romans on the outside operating the battering ram unknowingly increased their difficulty by pushing inward against the gate.

Soon Persians high up on the wall noticed Marcellinus's successful efforts and some began dropping down to the ground to remove the menace that threatened their efforts to keep the gate closed. Marcellinus and his men now had to abandon their attempts to open the gate in order to fight off the new arrivals.

As Marcellinus swung his sword wildly at two Persians before him he heard a voice from above. "Hey Roman, do you want to kill me?"

He looked up and saw Apsaeus directly over him, but he continued attacking the two Persians before him.

"Hey Roman! How was your visit with the Tanukhs?"

Marcellinus still focused on his two immediate assailants and continued to ignore Apsaeus's taunts.

But Apsaeus persisted in goading him. "My father had Odenathus and Herodes killed." He paused. "But I took care of both Zabdas and Zabbai myself!"

He was now screaming at the top of his lungs to ensure that he would be heard over the din of battle.

Apsaeus's last words were more than Marcellinus could bear. The villain pushed some of his Persians in Marcellinus's way as the latter attempted to climb the stairs, but Marcellinus fought and hacked his way through them as Apsaeus waited at the top.

When he reached Apsaeus, his fury was so great that he forced Apsaeus backward with continual violent, maniacal, downward slashes of his sword. Apsaeus was barely able to deflect the blows. His parries grew weaker and weaker. He was finally forced to his knees as Marcellinus knocked the sword from his hand. The villain cowered as Marcellinus raised his sword.

"My only regret is that I cannot kill you more than once." Just as he was about to slash downward for the coup de grace, a boulder from a Roman catapult smashed away a piece of upper wall, knocking part of the wall and Marcellinus all the way to the ground. His sword flew out of his hand.

Almost instantly, another boulder smashed into the upper wall not far from where the first one hit. A broken section of the wall fell to the ground and rolled over onto Marcellinus's legs. Realizing his peril, he desperately tried to remove the broken segment that was pinning him, but his efforts were of no use. He looked for the three men that had accompanied him to the gate, but they all lay dead before the entrance that had remained closed. He reached desperately for his sword, but it was just beyond his grasp.

✦

After several thrusts at the gate, Aurelian and Vaballathus stopped to watch a Roman at the top of a scaling ladder being pushed off to his death by a defending Persian.

Suddenly, Vaballathus bolted to the dead man, took his sword and scurried up the now empty scaling ladder.

Aurelian's eyes followed the boy for a moment on the ladder. "Well, your fate is now out of my hands, boy." Aurelian turned and resumed his place at the battering ram.

✦

Apsaeus stood and looked down at the fallen Marcellinus below. He couldn't believe his luck. "The gods are truly with me!"

He raced down what remained of the stairs to the point at the wall where Marcellinus lay and stepped on Marcellinus's arm that was still reaching for the fallen sword. He picked the weapon up himself.

"Kill me many times? You can't even do it once!" He laughed. "I will kill you with your own sword, Roman, and once will be enough for me."

But as he started to slash downward, an arrow pierced his neck. He dropped the sword, grasping his throat. Blood gushed out the opening made by the arrow.

In astonishment, Marcellinus turned to see Zenobia, six meters away, bow in hand. With her were about a hundred Palmyrenes and the three Romans that had accompanied her in her search. With hand motions, she directed them to assist in opening the gate. Then she drew her sword and, with slow, deliberate steps, she approached Apsaeus to finish him.

Suddenly, Verodes emerged from the shadows of a building directly across from the gate. He picked up a mace from a dead soldier and rushed at Zenobia from behind. As he advanced he squealed, "No! Noooooo! My son!" She didn't see him in enough time to react.

Moments earlier, Vaballathus, climbing the scaling ladder, had reached the top of the wall and, with two swipes of his sword, killed an approaching Persian defender. He looked down and saw Verodes approaching his mother from behind. He raised his sword overhead, squared himself toward his target and, with both hands, threw the sword end over end at Verodes.

The sword penetrated Verodes's abdomen and protruded through his lower back. The force of the blow knocked Verodes backward, but he recovered and staggered forward. He reached his dying son, who was still wavering on his feet. The father fell forward against his son and both looked into one another's eyes. Incredibly, they both remained standing, one leaning body supporting the other.

Zenobia reached the pair and raised her sword to finish them, but held it poised in midair as they both turned their eyes to meet hers. Then she stepped back, raised her foot and pushed both bodies over with it. Still joined, they fell to the ground.

To two Palmyrene soldiers near her, she pointed at the broken section of wall that was pinning Marcellinus. "Help me move these!"

All three, with some help from Marcellinus, pushed the giant piece of wall off his legs.

"Can you walk?" she asked.

"I think so." He struggled to raise himself.

They helped Marcellinus to his feet. When the task was complete he looked into her eyes. "I owe you one."

"You owe me more than one, but then who's counting?" she quipped.

Displaying a broad smile, he leaned on Zenobia and began to walk, but after a few paces he recovered much of his strength. Now unassisted, he limped toward the gate. Vaballathus dropped to the ground beside them.

Zenobia was the first to speak, "Now let's finish this!"

Marcellinus, Vaballathus, and Zenobia joined the remaining Palmyrene forces and the Romans that had arrived with Zenobia and were at that time already at the gate. With a super-human effort they succeeded in removing the great beam holding the gate closed. The door sprung open, and the Romans rushed in, but initially they began to attack the Palmyrenes.

"Wait! Wait! They helped us open the gate!" Marcellinus pointed to the Persians fleeing into the city. "Get them!"

The Romans promptly left Marcellinus, Vaballathus, Zenobia and the Palmyrenes behind and began a hot pursuit of the Persians fleeing back into the center of the city. This time the city would not be spared from being sacked and burnt, but Aurelian had issued a decree that the Palmyrene citizens were not to be molested *(killed, tortured or raped)*. They would be homeless when the conquest was complete, but physically unharmed. The men were to limit their destruction to the Persians. And because the Persians, since their arrival in the city, had rendered their own devastation upon the Palmyrenes, there would be little left to molest or damage anyway.

Marcellinus placed his arm around Zenobia's waist once again as the rush of Romans passed by them. He looked through the opening in the gate just as Aurelian walked through. Seeing his commander and emperor, he awkwardly removed his arm from her waist, but Aurelian was either oblivious to his action or had chosen to ignore it.

The man that was more soldier than emperor smiled. "It would have taken me quite a while to break down this gate."

He paused. "Senator Marcellinus… Yes, that has a nice ring to it. Or perhaps even Consul Marcellinus. I like that even better."

XXI

THE ROMAN SUBURB OF TIBUR

(Modern Day Tivoli)

SPRING 275 C.E.

Aurelian returned to Rome, but soon thereafter, he deposited his captives, Queen Zenobia and her son, in the Eternal City and immediately departed for Gaul to bring the last rebellious faction back into the Roman Empire. Tetricus, the leader of this group, was soon subdued. And so finally, in the late fall of 274 C.E., he marched his conquered hosts, including Tetricus, Queen Zenobia and her son, Vaballathus, in his triumphal procession as Rome celebrated the reuniting of the entire Roman Empire once again. Zenobia was paraded bearing golden manacles and chains. But thereafter, she subsisted in a form of home arrest. And, although her quarters were far from uncomfortable by any standards, the days of mindless tedium dragged on and on. Day after day she waited, but for what?

It was a beautiful spring morning in 275 C.E. Aurelian, Zenobia, and Vaballathus all rode in a carpentum[19], but this ancient Roman carriage was even more open than those conventionally seen on the roads. There were many windows in the vehicle, allowing unobstructed views of the Roman countryside by the vehicle's occupants.

They had been on the ride for over an hour and silence had reigned throughout most of the journey. Their ultimate destination was known only to the emperor. And, even though the morning was beautiful, Zenobia was sullen. But then, she had often been quite somber since their arrival at Rome. All of her thoughts still dwelt on the children she had not seen for so long *(and dare she think of Marcellinus as well?)*.

At the crest of a hill they gazed at a quaint little hamlet. Aurelian suddenly spoke, "This is Tibur. As you see, it's not far from Rome. Many of our wealthy citizens have estates here. The Emperor Hadrian built a palace here." He then directly addressed Zenobia, "Why so gloomy, my Amazon Queen?"

Zenobia feebly shrugged her shoulders, but said nothing.

"Ah! Still missing your children. It is no good to dwell on things that are beyond our control. It has been over two years now." However, his ill-suited attempt to lighten her spirits fell upon deaf ears.

It was true that Zenobia ached for her children – and Marcellinus, but she was also continually haunted by the vision of her beloved Palmyra burning to the ground as the Romans completed their devastation of the city two years earlier.

She puzzled, "But why…"

"Why are we here? … I leave for the East once again. There is trouble in the Balkans…but then, there is always trouble in the Balkans. I also plan to go further east and put an end once and for all to the Persian problem."

Turning to Vaballathus, "You, my lad, will go with me. With your knowledge of the East, I have an administrative position in mind for you. Perhaps as Prefect of Mesopotamia."

Then to Zenobia, "But for you, My Queen, I have different plans."

He hesitated momentarily. "We could have done great things together, you and I, but I am more of a soldier than an emperor - and I like my work. You, on the other hand, fight brilliantly and valiantly, but only out of necessity."

He dithered once again, "So I have decided to keep you here in Tibur."

They stopped in front of the entrance to a beautiful quad-shaped compound, a villa rustica. Not much was visible of the buildings that enveloped the open-squared space within, but what could be seen from the opening was extremely promising.

Stepping out of the carriage he offered his hand to Zenobia. She forced a smile and both she and Vaballathus descended from the contrivance.

"Consider yourself under house arrest." He took her hand and led her through the entrance. Their eyes were suddenly assaulted by a riot of color. Flowers from every part of the empire covered most of the open space, with marble benches cleverly situated throughout. Aurelian continued, "Come meet your jailor - the man assigned to keep an eye on you while you are here. Consider yourself honored by my selection. He is a senator and my co-consul this year."

Zenobia looked upward hopefully as Marcellinus appeared.

"Go on! Go to him! That's an imperial decree."

Aurelian and Vaballathus both beamed as Zenobia ran to Marcellinus and embraced him. As she did so, Faustula (now 19), Antiochus (now 10), and Livia (now almost 9) ran to the pair and collectively grasped them in an enormous hug. Vaballathus walked quickly toward the group and gently joined the fray. Zenobia, with tears in her eyes, looked back at Aurelian.

"Your life here will not be as exciting as it was leading the victorious forces of Palmyra in battle, but as the wife of a consul and senator you will have a certain social status that will be envied by many."

Zenobia continued to look gratefully at Aurelian as he nodded his goodbye, turned, and departed. Vaballathus knelt with his arms around his younger brother, Antiochus, and Marcellinus embraced Zenobia with both Livia and Faustula surrounding the pair, their arms locked around both of them in a second embrace.

Marcellinus looked into Zenobia's eyes. "Yes, I was expecting a happy ending. Like that of a child's tale."

"...they say that thereafter she lived with her children in the manner of a Roman matron on an estate that had been presented to her at Tibur, which even to this day is still called Zenobia, not far from the palace of Hadrian..."

Trebellius Polio

Of her children, they "married into noble families, and her race was not yet extinct in the fifth century."

Edward Gibbon

Based on a true story.

(The End)

NOTES REGARDING THE HISTORICAL ZENOBIA

Until the last two or three centuries, most writers/historians may be more appropriately classified as "chroniclers." Since there was no public market for "bestsellers," these chroniclers wrote for the benefit of their sponsor (the one paying them to record the event). The sponsor was often a political leader such as a king or emperor and therefore events, although actually having occurred, were generally colored to favor that individual or group of individuals. Therefore, any information to be gleaned from their writings should be taken with a "grain of salt."

Zenobia – According to various chroniclers, Zenobia was the queen of Palmyra. She ruled that city with her husband, King Odenathus, during the period circa 250 – 266 C.E. (C.E. refers to "Common Era," but formerly the term "A.D." – Anno Domini – Medieval Latin for "In the year of our lord" was used). Her spouse, King Odenathus was assassinated at Emesa circa 266 C.E.

Zenobia later led a revolt against the Roman Empire and, for a time, took control of the eastern portion of the Roman Empire, from Antioch to Egypt. The latter, at the time, was considered the breadbasket of the Roman Empire. The Roman Emperor Aurelian invaded the East and conquered Palmyra and its famous Queen Zenobia. Then, according to Zosimus *Historia Nova, The Decline of Rome, Book I,* written between 410 and 468 C.E., Aurelian headed toward Rome, stopping at Emesa where Zenobia, in order to free herself from blame, implicated many of her counselors as having led her - being a woman - astray. Many of those counselors, including the philosopher, Longinus, were then put to death. According to that history, during the transit to Rome, Zenobia died either "contracting illness or abstaining from food." Zosimus then relates that, with the exception of Zenobia's son, all others in her group drowned in the strait between Chalcedon and Byzantium (the straits of Bosporus).

However, Trebellius Pollio *Scriptores Historiea Augustae Vol. III,* which was written circa 303 C.E., over one hundred years earlier than the history of Zosimus and within thirty to forty years of the actual events states that:

"... his [Odenathus's] wife ... in the opinion of many was held to be more brave than her husband, being indeed, the noblest of all the women of the East and, as Cornelius Capitolinus declares, the most beautiful. As declared at the introduction to this story, Pollio stated "Her face was dark with a swarthy hue, her eyes were black and powerful beyond the usual wont, her spirit divinely great, and her beauty incredible... frequently she walked with her foot soldiers for three or four miles... She herself was not wholly conversant with the Latin tongue, but nevertheless, mastering her timidity she would speak it. Egyptian, on the other hand she spoke very well… Roman history, however, she read in Greek."

According to Pollio, Zenobia did not die during the transit to Rome. On the contrary, Zenobia was led in Aurelian's triumph through the streets of Rome adorned with gems "so huge that she labored under the weight." She was bound with golden shackles on her feet and fetters on her hands and a chain on her neck the "weight of which was borne by a Persian Buffoon." Aurelian let her live and "thereafter she lived with her children in the manner of a Roman matron on an estate that had been presented to her at Tibur."

Flavius Vopiscus, succeeding writer to Trebellius Pollio, in the *Scriptores Historiea Augustae Vol. III,* (It is estimated that his writing was completed circa 303 – 304, C.E.), does not state that Zenobia implicated her advisors to save herself after her capture by Aurelian. However, Aurelian is said to have slain the philosopher, Longinus, because he was told that the latter had dictated Zenobia's arrogant response to Aurelian's letter offering the queen terms of peace while Palmyra was still under siege, although, in fact, the letter was composed in the Syrian tongue.

Was Zenobia a black woman? This fact has been long-debated. In Syriac, her name Bat-Zabbai means, "Daughter of Zabbai." At the time of her birth, there was one male in the household of Odenathus's father named Zabbai (not to be confused with Zabbai, the general in this novel). However, she may have received this name to legitimize her birth in the eyes of the nobility of Palmyra. In the centuries that followed the conquest of Palmyra, the queen has been generally portrayed as Caucasian, or a woman with a slightly darkened complexion. However, this may have occurred due to the generally-held belief at the time that people of color, especially black women, were incapable of achieving the success ascribed to Zenobia. Agnes Carr Vaughan, *Zenobia of Palmyra, January 1967* wrote, "… she is believed to be of Arabic descent. We don't know who her parents were. Palmyra seems to have regarded Zenobia as a peregrina, a foreigner."

However, the chapter on Zenobia's origins is a complete fabrication by the author.

A FINAL NOTE REGARDING AURELIAN

Unfortunately, Aurelian never reached Persia. He was murdered in September 275, C.E., in Caenophrurium, Thrace while waiting to cross into Asia Minor. High-ranking officers of the Praetorian Guard, fearing a certain punishment from the emperor, murdered him.

BIBLIOGRAPHY

Clarke, John R, *The Houses of Roman Italy, 100 B.C. – A.D. 250*, Copyright 1991 by the Regents of the University of California

McKay, Alexander G., *Houses, Villas and Palaces in the Roman World*, Copyright 1975 Thames and Hudson, London

Gibbon, Edward, *The History of the Decline and Fall of the Roman Empire,* Volume the First 1776, Chapters 10 & 11, Penguin Books Ltd., 27 Wrights Lane, London W

Scriptores Historiae Augustae, from the Loeb Classical Library,
   a three volume series translated into English by David Magie, Ph.D.
Harvard University Press, Cambridge Massachusetts and William Heinemann Ltd., London
The authors within whose writings have been utilized are contained in Volume III. Those authors are:
Trebellius Pollio (circa 303, C.E.) and
Flavius Vopiscus of Syracuse (circa 303 - 304 CE)

Stoneman, Richard, *Palmyra and its Empire*, The University of Michigan Press, Copyright 1992, Ann Arbor, Michigan

Scarre, Chris, The Penguin Historical Atlas of Ancient Rome, Copyright 1995

Vaughan, Agnes Carr, *Zenobia of Palmyra*, Copyright 1967 by the author

Watson, Alaric, *Aurelian and the Third Century,* Routledge, Copyright 1999, London & New York

Webster, Graham, *The Roman Imperial Army*, 3rd Edition 1985 *(First published in 1969)*, Copyright 1985, 1969, 1979 Graham Webster

Zosimus, *Historia Nova*, The Decline of Rome, Book I (Circa 410 - 468 CE.)

An additional note from the author:

The first two paragraphs of chapter 15 (XV) were not originally composed by the author. However, at the completion of this book the author was unable to determine their source after an exhaustive search. Therefore, it may only be assumed that the information was obtained from Wikipedia. That excellent information service continually updates, corrects and changes its descriptions for many of its entries. And so, at the time of completion, the article in Wikipedia on the ancient city of Antioch may have been updated and/ or changed by that organization and did not match the information presented in the first two paragraphs of the aforementioned chapter.

END NOTES

[1] Koine was also known as the "Alexandrian dialect".

[2] Ctesiphon was the Persian capital.

[3] Although the metric system was not developed until more than a millennium and a half in the future, it will be used to define all distances in this narrative. Roman soldiers, when marching, actually used a measure of distance which has been referred to a Roman mile, but that term will not be used in our story.

[4] An Agora was similar to a Roman Forum. In Palmyra, the Agora was just beside the Senate chamber, but I assume that the Palmyrene Assembly generally met in the open air Agora.

[5] City business manager

[6] A dromedary is a type of camel with only one hump. They are very swift and more durable than the two humped Bactrian camel variety.

[7] Numida was located in the northeastern portion of modern day Algeria.

[8] In Roman times, Egypt was called "Aegyptus". However,

the current title in English will be used throughout the remainder of this story.

[9] The Great Sea – the Romans called the Mediterranean Sea the "Mare Nostrum" – "Our Sea"

[10] Ibid

[11] "There is little doubt that ... [Palmyra and its territories were] more fertile in classical times ... There is little evidence of irrigation, but there was a greater amount of water in the whole territory. Pliny described Palmyra as "a city noble in its situation, in the richness of its soil and the pleasantness of its waters ..." " Palmyra and its Empire; Zenobia's Revolt against Rome", Richard Stoneman, The University of Michigan Press, © 1992
In later times the stream lying before Palmyra's southern wall(s) was more appropriately classified as a "wadi" – a dry riverbed that only held water after experiencing heavy rains.

[12] Ibid

[13] A "Mal Voisin", literally in French, a "bad neighbor", was a siege engine developed in the latter Middle Ages.

[14] It was common practice in those times to read all documents and letters aloud. The practice of reading silently to oneself was not common. (The library in Alexandria, Egypt must have been an extremely loud place.) However, to eliminate any potential need for

further explanation in the context of this writing, Longinus is presented as remaining silent while reading the letter purportedly to have been written by Zenobia.

[15] Fortuna was the Latin/Roman goddess of luck and good fortune. (Her Greek equivalent was "Tyche".)

[16] See note 10.

[17] The foregoing is taken from "The Deified Aurelian, by Flavius Vopiscus of Syracuse (written circa 305 or 306 C.E.) and included in "The Scriptores Historiae Augustae". This translation of the foregoing was taken from Volume III, which was translated by David Magie, PhD. and published by Harvard University Press (Cambridge Massachusetts) and William Heinemann Ltd (London).

[18] The boundaries of ancient Dacia have moved over the centuries. At times it was bordered on the east by the Black Sea and the north by the Danube River. It lay principally within present day Romania and Moldova.

[19] A carpentum was the limousine of Roman times. It had a wooden roof and was much more comfortable than other cars. It also had a decorated interior.

Printed in Great Britain
by Amazon